CROSSING THE POND

A Transatlantic WLW Romance

Sienna Waters

Copyright © 2022 Sienna Waters

All rights reserved

The characters and events portrayed in this book are fictitious. Any similarity to real persons, living or dead, is coincidental and not intended by the author.

No part of this book may be reproduced, or stored in a retrieval system, or transmitted in any form or by any means, electronic, mechanical, photocopying, recording, or otherwise, without express written permission of the publisher.

Find out more at www.siennawaters.com. And stay up to date with the latest news from Sienna Waters by signing up for my newsletter!

SIENNA WATERS

To N.–
My one and only
xxx

CHAPTER ONE

"Try to see this as an opportunity."

Ted Scanlon attempted what could be called a smile and Piper kind of wanted to punch him. Not that she would, but she wanted to.

Fifteen years of devoting her life to this stupid, lousy job and getting fired was supposed to be an opportunity?

An opportunity to do what exactly?

"Maybe I'll raise trick goldfish for the carnival," she muttered, not quite as under her breath as she'd thought, since Scanlon raised his eyebrows in surprise.

"Well, uh, that's certainly one possibility," he said. He cleared his throat. "You'll get all the normal benefits, of course." He slid a piece of paper across his desk to her. "A generous severance package, health insurance until the end of the year, glowing references." That half-assed attempt at a smile again.

Piper wondered if she'd ever actually seen him really smile. Maybe not, now that she thought of it. He'd only be around for a half year or so though, not enough time to really fit into the Foster and Davis family.

"Please understand, Ms. Garland, this isn't personal."

How could having her job snatched away not be personal? Piper's jaw ached as she tried to keep her mouth shut.

"The publishing business has been going through a hard time, there are a lot of lay-offs here, it's just unfortunate that you're one of them. We at Foster and Davis really do appreciate all you've done for the company."

Which was about as much as she could take.

She slid the paper off the table, crumpled it and shoved it into a pocket, and stood up to leave.

And because she'd worked professionally for fifteen years, and because she knew she needed the severance settlement and health insurance, and because she was a grown damned adult and not an impulsive child, she smiled. "Thank you," she said, before she walked out.

Even though she still really, really wanted to punch him.

She could have gone back to her desk. She could have collected all her things, the manuscripts and desk ornaments and awards and everything else. Instead, she patted her pockets to make sure she had her wallet and walked right out the door.

Because despite being professional and an adult and all the rest, and despite it only being three o'clock in the afternoon, she really, really needed a drink. A big one. With umbrellas and at least three different colors and enough chunks of fruit around the rim of the glass that it was almost impossible to drink.

"THINK OF IT as an opportunity?"

"Uh-huh," Piper said, sucking up her second cocktail through a chunky straw.

"What an asshole." The bartender smiled sweetly at her and grabbed the cocktail shaker. "Here, let me make you another, this one's on me."

Piper, who had been planning to leave after two, shrugged. Why the hell not? It wasn't like she had work tomorrow.

The bartender flashed her a pretty smile. Actually, all of her was pretty, not just the smile. Pretty and young, she couldn't be more than twenty or so. Piper sighed and tucked a lock of blonde hair back behind her ear.

Young enough that she had her whole life ahead of her. The thought made Piper feel vaguely nauseous.

"Actually, thanks for the offer, but I'd better be going." Before she made a fool of herself.

"Oh," the bartender flushed. "Oh, sure, no problem." She bent and scribbled something on a napkin. "Uh, here you go."

"What's that?" Piper asked, taking the napkin.

"My number."

Piper chuckled. "That's sweet, but I'm fine, really. I've only had two drinks, I'm perfectly safe to get home, but you're lovely to be concerned." She put a ten dollar bill on the bar next to the napkin as a tip and slipped off her bar stool. "You have a good evening."

She was more than half way home before she realized that perhaps the sweet young bartender hadn't been concerned about her getting home. More concerned with getting her home. Then she groaned and put her sunglasses on.

Could this day get any worse?

"THINK OF IT as a fucking opportunity?" Joey shrieked down the phone. "Seriously?"

"I know, I know," said Piper, opening the fridge door and surveying the contents.

"An opportunity to do what?"

"Travel the world with money I don't have? Get out of the city? Become a stripper or a mechanic? The possibilities are endless." She selected a yogurt that was only two days past the date stamped on the lid.

There was the sound of a sigh rattling down the phone line. "Pipes, you want me to come over?"

"No, I'm fine." An adult, a professional, very able to take care of myself, Piper's brain said. Despite the fact that she kind of wanted to sit on the bathroom floor and cry. "Besides, I have plans. Sitting on the bathroom floor and crying is at the top of the list of my priorities right now."

"Yeah, I kind of feel like I should come."

Piper peeled the foil off the top of the yogurt then sat on the floor to eat. She hadn't had time to buy a sofa. Now she didn't have money to buy a sofa, so it was probably just as well that she hadn't had time.

"No, really," she said, dipping her spoon into the yogurt. "I'm two big drinks down, I'm eating yogurt on the floor of my still unfurnished apartment, I'm not exactly at my best."

"I'm your best friend, I'm not sure that stuff matters."

"You're my only friend, currently," Piper pointed out, stirring the yogurt.

"That can't possibly be true."

"It is. I lost most of the others in the break-up. Then the rest will go with the job I've just lost. Which leaves you."

Joey snorted. "Bullshit. Okay, maybe the work stuff is true. But as for everyone else, well, they just feel kind of awkward, I guess. Like most people do after a big break up. They don't know what to say. Reach out to them, they'll be fine."

"I don't think I've got the energy." She put a spoon of yogurt in her mouth and promptly spit it back out into the pot. "Eugh."

"What?"

"Yogurt's gone bad."

"How can you tell? Isn't yogurt just bad milk or something?"

"Your culinary knowledge is extraordinary," Piper said, putting the yogurt down and leaning back against the kitchen cabinets. "I don't want to reach out. I kind of don't want to be reminded of Lex, if I'm being honest."

"Understandable. Breaking up after a decade isn't easy."

"No, more because I still sort of want to slap her. I mean, cheating on me with a student, how clichéd can you get?"

"Lucky she's a college professor and not a middle school teacher," Joey said.

"Bad taste, Joe."

"Right, sorry." There was a pause. "Sure you don't want me to come over?"

Piper sighed. "I think I'm just going to go to bed."

"It's quarter to seven."

"So? I'm thirty six years old, my partner has left me, I've lost my job, and the only thing to eat in my refrigerator is out-of-date yogurt, which doesn't matter since I don't have any furniture to sit on to eat anyway. An early night sounds like it might be a good idea, under the circumstances."

"No need to get snappy," Joey said. "But, yeah, I get your point. Listen, how about I pick you up tomorrow and we get drinks? My treat?"

Piper softened. She did want to see Joey, there was a reason they were best friends, after all. Joey's smile was contagious and right now that seemed like the only way Piper was going to get a smile, by catching it off someone else.

"Yeah, okay. I'll call you in the afternoon, okay?"

She hung up, putting her mobile into her pocket, standing up and looking over the kitchen. She really might just as well go to bed. There was no TV, no food, and her laptop was in the bedroom where at least there was a bed.

She'd soothe herself with old episodes of The Golden Girls until she fell asleep.

She was about to go when she caught sight of the mail on the counter where she'd left it. Probably bills and junk, but she might as well get it over with. It wasn't like her day could get any worse.

Three offers for super fast internet, one ad for a Chinese restaurant, and one electricity bill later, she was left with only one envelope to open.

Scowling down at it she wondered if this was really for her. The envelope was heavy, not because it was too full, but because the paper was thick and good quality. The stamp in the upper corner was unfamiliar, larger than she was used to. She flipped the letter over and saw the return address.

Huh.

The United Kingdom.

She flipped it back, double-checking that it really was her name on the front.

Yep, no doubt there. Her name alright. And her old address scratched out, the new one written in a cramped hand that she knew wasn't Lex's. Maybe it was that student of hers. Piper's stomach hurt at the very idea.

She grabbed a knife from the sink, wiped it off on her pants and slid it under the flap. This envelope was too nice to open with her fingernails, too nice to be ripped. She up-ended it and a thick letter fell out.

Weirdly, her fingers trembled as she opened it. She read the address one more time.

"Where the fuck is Sutton's Walk?" she murmured.

Then she frowned as she read down the rest of the letter.

CHAPTER TWO

Cam's spade hit something hard and she grunted, wriggling the blade until it got under the stone and she could heave it up.

Sweat was collecting in the small of her back and she was dying for a drink. But she'd promised herself that she'd dig over the whole flower bed first, and she always kept her promises.

'There's nothing worse than a broken heart except a broken promise,' her father always said. So her mouth was going to stay dry until she was done.

"What you doing out there, girl?"

Cam groaned inwardly, then stood up, stretching out her back. "Digging up the flower beds, Arthur," she called back.

Arthur Slater peered over the fence and sniffed. "No point in doing that now, is there? Not now that Her Highness has popped her clogs. Ain't no one to pay you."

Which was all too true, not that Cam cared to think too much about it. Lucy Cromwell had upped and died two months ago, done her shopping in the morning, come home for lunch, and was dead by tea-time. Not that it should be that surprising, what, with her being all of ninety-eight. Still, she'd been a sprightly ninety-eight.

Which shouldn't excuse the fact that Cam had, technically, signed a contract with a woman on death's doorstep, but still. Lucy Cromwell had been a village institution in Sutton's Walk, it had been hard to imagine the place without her until she was gone.

"Got to keep the place looking nice," she said now. "There'll be a new owner soon enough."

"One of them city types, I reckon," Arthur said. "Or a tourist. Someone with a wad of cash to spend, anyways." His eyes narrowed. "Which is why you're doing what you're doing, I suppose."

Cam's face prickled with heat. "What's that supposed to mean then?"

"That you're putting in the extra work in the hopes that you get noticed and the new owners take you on," he said.

Which again, was all too true, but Cam really didn't feel like confirming it. Not when Arthur was the village gossip and not altogether charitable at the best of times. She picked up her spade again.

"It'll do you no good. They'll hire one of the big companies, not a slip of a girl like you," Arthur pushed.

"Then let's say I'm doing this for the good of the village," Cam said. "Keeping things looking nice for all of us."

"Huh." Arthur sniffed again and Cam sighed, putting the spade down.

"You doing okay there, Art?"

"Don't call me Art. And I'm fine, just think I might be coming down with something, that's all."

"Want me to get the doctor out for you?"

"No, no, I don't want any fuss. It's probably just a summer cold."

Cam looked at the flower bed she'd been turning over, then the four others that still needed doing. Arthur was right, of course, she was hoping to impress whoever the new owners would be. She needed the work.

Being a female contractor wasn't exactly easy. But more of a problem was the fact that Sutton's Walk was a small village and there just wasn't all that much to do.

In the two months since Lucy Cromwell had died, taking with

her the promise of a hefty renovation contract, Cam had had exactly five call outs. And three of those were for Mrs. Carter's kitchen tap which dripped incessantly. Mostly because her five year old twins used it as a handhold to climb up to the biscuit tin on the shelf above the sink.

Then she looked over again at Arthur, who was no spring chicken himself. "What can I get for you, Arthur?"

"Well, I was just about to go to the shops and get a nice tin of soup for lunch."

She nodded. "Give me ten minutes to finish this bed and then I'll go get it for you."

He beamed a smile that was missing more than one tooth. "Don't forget the bread. And an extra pint of milk wouldn't go amiss either. Oh, and some of that chewy licorice if they've got some in again."

Cam took a deep breath, then nodded and smiled. "Alright, I'll finish up and then go."

"Don't forget to take Billy with you, he could use the walk," Arthur said as he tottered away from the fence and back to his kitchen.

Cam bit her tongue. The rest of the flower beds would have to wait. She wasn't getting paid for them anyway. She leaned back down over her spade. But she did really, really want to re-claim this renovation project. She'd been so close, and the opportunity had just slipped through her fingers.

She sighed and got back to work.

"YOU LOOK JUST about done in," Beth said, banging a cup of tea onto the counter.

It was dark enough to stain the cup, real builder's tea, and it made Cam grin. Beth was just about the most supportive person she knew. Cam was a contractor, so she got builder's tea, just the same as any of the workmen would have gotten.

"I've had better days," she said, picking up the mug gratefully.

"Oh yeah? I thought I saw you over at the Cromwell place?

Didn't know you were a gardener too," said Beth, picking up a tea towel and starting to dry some cups.

"Ha ha, I was just keeping my hand in." She took a sip of tea and it was far too hot. "Not like I had anything else to do today."

Beth pulled a face. "That bad, eh?"

"Kind of," admitted Cam. "And then to top things off I ended up at Arthur's, making him lunch and then looking at his war scrapbooks again."

Beth rolled her eyes and leaned on the counter. "You've got to learn to say no, Cam, seriously. I mean, being nice to an old man is one thing, but just how many times has he dragged you through those scrapbooks?"

"About seven," groaned Cam.

Beth laughed. "You're a glutton for punishment." She reached under the cafe counter. "Here you go, this just came in today."

Cam took the book and then squealed in delight. "Is it gory?"

"Look at the cover, you eejit. There's more blood on there than the shower scene from Carrie, I think it'll fulfill your prurient desires."

Cam clasped the horror book to her chest. "You've made my day."

"Doesn't take much," said Beth.

"It's escapism is all. And after today I could use a little escape. Actually, after the last two months I could use an escape."

Beth pushed over a plate of ginger biscuits. "Go on, take one," she said.

Cam grinned again. Beth was not only the owner and sole staff member of Sutton Walk's only cafe stroke bookshop, she was also the village's unofficial therapist and Cam's best friend. Which meant she knew all about her weakness for ginger biscuits.

"Been thinking about other opportunities?" Beth asked, pulling the plate out of reach after Cam had selected a biscuit, knowing that if she didn't the entire plate would disappear.

Cam shook her head. "I can't do anything else. Building and contracting is what I'm good at. The only other choice would be to move away and I really don't want that."

"None of us want that," Beth said. "But you've got to do something, my love. You can't go around half-unemployed."

"I'm lucky really," said Cam. "I mean, I've got my family, I've got enough to eat and friends and a lovely village."

Beth stood up and put her hands on her hips. "Camilla Fabbri, you live in a van."

Cam took a breath then let it go. "I do."

"You do."

"It's a nice van," Cam said.

"It's a van parked in your parent's farmyard," said Beth. "You're thirty two years old."

"And hardly a success story," groaned Cam, going back to her tea.

Beth leaned on the counter again. "You've got to start putting yourself first, Cam. You're always doing things for other people, always putting your plans on hold, and then you end up losing out. I love that you're generous and giving, but at some point, *you* need to be your priority."

"It's not like I haven't tried."

The Cromwell contract was supposed to be the turning point. A long term job that she could use to prove her worth. The job she'd needed for years, something that would let her really show off her skills, and that would lead to more work down the line.

And the promised cash would come in more than handy. Lucy Cromwell had been sweet, slightly eccentric, and very lovable. She'd also been generous and Cam had had to rein her in when it came to payment, replacing Lucy's unbelievable offer with something a little more reasonable.

Reasonable, but still enough to put down a deposit on a cottage when added to the savings Cam already had.

Now that chance was gone. Unless she could persuade whoever was taking over the house to honor the contract.

"I know you've tried," Beth said, patting her hand. "Your day will come, Cam. I'm just worried that you'll be too busy shopping for Arthur or babysitting your brother's kids or helping me unload boxes of books to realize that it's your day, that's all."

Cam frowned but said nothing. There was no point. Beth was right. She did have a hard time putting herself first. And she didn't think that was a bad thing. She thought, she hoped, it made her a good person, and that was all she really wanted to be.

"Hey, you know it's half past five, don't you?" Beth said looking up at the big clock above the shop door.

"Jesus," said Cam, practically dropping her cup of tea as she scrambled off her stool. "My mum'll kill me."

Dinner was on the big farmhouse table at six sharp and Cam still hadn't showered or even brushed her hair that day now that she came to think about it.

"Run," Beth said, collecting Cam's cup. "You'll make it. Just."

Cam shouted her thanks over her shoulder as she ran out the door. Everything else in her life would just have to wait. No one was late to Mama Fabbri's dinner table. At least not if you wanted to eat.

CHAPTER THREE

The taxi careened around a corner and Piper yelped, clinging on to the back of the driver's seat.

"You okay there?" Joey asked over the phone.

"Yes, fine," Piper said as the car settled down onto a straight part of road.

"I can't believe you're doing this."

"So you've said," said Piper. "Which is why I'm calling you, as instructed, to let you know that I landed safe and sound and that so far I've not been kidnapped."

"I still can't believe it," said Joey. "I mean, you're actually following through with this. You get a letter telling you some crazy old stranger left you a house and you're just crossing the globe to go check it out. I've heard true crime podcasts that start this way, you know?"

"She wasn't a stranger," Piper said. "She was my great aunt."

"Who you'd never met."

Fair point. She'd vaguely known that she had a great aunt at some point, in the same way that she vaguely remembered her English grandmother. Her grandmother had died when she was four, and her lasting memory was of the woman giving her cookies that tasted nothing like Oreos and then being upset when she didn't like them.

"I'm the last surviving member of the family line," said Piper.

"You make that sound so much grander than it probably is."

"You don't know that. I could be drawing up in front of Downton Abbey any second."

"If you do then it's definitely a scam," said Joey.

Piper shook her head. "I've told you, this isn't a scam. I've seen lawyers, signed paperwork, it's all above board, Joe."

Joey grunted. "I suppose it's a good excuse to get you out of the city for a while. It'll be good for you to be in a new environment." Her voice brightened. "Hey, you might even meet Ms. Right. An English wife, how about that?"

"I like eating too much to marry an Englishwoman," Piper said darkly.

"Oy!" The taxi driver turned around as the car veered to the edge of the road.

"Sorry, sorry!" Piper said immediately. "Just kidding."

The driver scowled but at least he turned back to the road.

"I needed a break," Piper said to Joey. "Getting out of town is a good thing. Getting away from things is a good thing. It'll give me time to think about what I'm going to do next, about where my life is going."

"Agreed, agreed, and agreed," Joey said. "I just wish you didn't have to go half the world away is all. I'm going to miss you."

"I'm not staying forever, I'll be home in a month. Two tops."

"That sounds like forever. Plus, you'll be gone a whole lot longer if this is a scam and you do get kidnapped."

"Who would want to kidnap me?" Piper said.

"I've heard there's a big market in some middle Eastern countries for middle-aged blonde women who complain too much and are unemployable."

"Joey, bad taste," Piper said automatically.

The taxi was slowing now as it entered a village. Piper stared out of the windows as quaint cottages passed by, and then a half-timbered pub, before they pulled out into a real village green, complete with a duck pond in the middle.

"Jesus," said Piper. "You should see this place. It looks like something out of Midsommer Murders."

"They filmed a couple of episodes down here," the cab driver said over his shoulder.

"Is this Sutton's Walk?" Piper asked.

"The one and only."

"Listen, Joe, I'm here, I've got to go. I'll text you later, okay?"

"Fine. You be careful out there, Pipes. I mean it. I get that you need time away from everything, but don't forget that you have me to come home to. Don't forget that you have a whole life back here, right?"

"Right," Piper said, even though her stomach shivered at the thought. What kind of life did she have back home? No relationship, no job, a barely furnished apartment. Still, it was her life, she supposed.

"This'll be it then," said the cab driver, pulling up in front of a house.

Piper's mouth dropped open. They'd stopped in front of a house so sweet she couldn't believe it was real, like something off an old fashioned chocolate box. The windows had diamond panes, the roof was thatched, and tiny windows peeked out from the eaves.

"Are you sure?" she asked.

"'course I'm sure, I'm a cab driver, aren't I?" He clicked at the meter. "That'll be thirty pounds even, love."

Quickly, Piper found her wallet and pulled out some of the ridiculously big and ridiculously colored pound notes she'd got from the airport. "Here you go," she said, handing some over.

The cabbie's face shone and then very, very reluctantly he handed one of the notes back. "You, uh, tipped too much," he said. "Most Americans do. Just a pound or two is lovely."

"You sure?" Piper asked doubtfully.

"I am now, but if you don't get out in a hurry I might change my mind," he said with a grin. Then he climbed out and began unloading her luggage.

Piper took her time opening the door and getting out. She breathed in deeply, tasting the fresh air, feeling the coolness of the breeze, smelling cut grass and old wood fires and sweet flowers.

"Want these by the door, do you?" asked the cab driver, a case and backpack in his hands.

"Please," Piper said, still taking in the house.

Could this really be hers? All hers?

She couldn't believe her luck. After the worst year of her life suddenly getting that letter had changed everything. She couldn't help but hope that this was turning a corner, that things were going to get better from here. She couldn't help but feel a pulsing of excitement in her stomach.

"Nice place you've got," the cab driver said, having deposited her bags by the front door.

It felt strange that this all belonged to her. She still kept expecting someone to say that it was a mistake, that she had to give the keys back. Yet the keys hung heavy in her pocket. "Thanks."

"I'll be off then, give me a ring if you need me, I left a card on your case up there. I'm not far away and there aren't too many cabs around here."

She smiled at him but still couldn't quite tear her eyes away from the house. She heard a car door slam and then an engine pulling away.

"Alrighty then," she said, steeling herself to step onto the garden path. Onto her garden path.

"What you doing out there then?" said a voice.

"What? Who..." She turned around, first one way, then another, before she saw a man standing half hidden by a hedge at the edge of the garden. "Who the hell are you?"

He cocked his head and then pushed through the hedge. "You the new owner then?"

She took a step back. He was an old man, but that didn't necessarily mean that he was harmless. "Um, yes," She cleared her throat and remembered that she was in a village. A small village. And that she was probably not making the best first impression. "Piper Garland," she said, holding out her hand.

"An American?" he said, taking her hand and shaking it, his skin dry and papery.

"Yes."

"Don't mind Yanks, me," he said. "Met enough of them during the war. They were always friendly. Stole all the girls, mind, but they were polite about it at least. And they had chocolate. Always the best chocolate."

"Oh," Piper said, not sure what else to say.

"Where are my manners? I'm Arthur. Arthur Slater." He smiled and there were definitely missing teeth. "I live right next door. Just you knock on the door if you need something, I'm always around."

She was being unfair, she got that. She needed to switch her mindset out of cynical city-liver and into being a part of a community. So she smiled. "That's very kind," she said. "I'm sure I'll need some advice sooner or later."

"Just arrived, did you?"

"Fresh off the plane." She looked down at her wrinkled pants. "And jet-lagged as all get out."

Arthur grinned. "I'll let you get inside then." He paused, then asked: "You a relative of Luce's then, are you?"

Piper nodded. "She was my great aunt."

"Just, I don't remember you visiting or anything."

"I never met her," Piper said honestly. "In fact, I haven't heard a word about her since my grandmother died thirty years ago. This all came as quite a surprise."

"I'll bet it did," Arthur said with a laugh. "Oh, hold up a minute, there'll be someone you'll be wanting to meet." He whistled between his teeth, a sharp, high sound, and the hedge rustled until something appeared.

Piper took a huge step back. Then another, just to be sure. "What the hell is that?" she said, looking at the ginormous black beast.

"Oh, this here is Billy."

"What is he? Some kind of pony or..." She trailed off. She wasn't great at geography or zoology, but she was fairly sure that England didn't have any weird animals. Not as weird as this anyway. The animal stepped forward on long, thin legs.

19

"No, Billy's a Great Dane is what he is," Arthur explained. He fumbled in his pocket and pulled out a frayed looking leash, holding it out.

Piper frowned at it.

"Take it," Arthur said. "You'll be needing it."

"Why on Earth…"

Arthur laughed again. "Billy's yours, girl. Well, he was Luce's. I've just been looking after him since she'd been gone. He'll be glad to get back home again, won't you, boy?" He patted the enormous head, then tapped a huge flank so that the dog approached Piper.

"But…"

The dog's tongue was almost as big as a dishtowel as it lolled out and licked all the way up Piper's arm.

"See," Arthur said. "He likes you."

Piper could only watch as Billy strolled over to what was very clearly the front door to his home. Their home, she thought. She could still hear Arthur laughing as she followed the beast into the house.

CHAPTER FOUR

Cam poured honey into the porridge, added a pinch of salt and picked up her spoon. Just in time for someone to swoop in and steal the bowl from in front of her.

"Perfect, Cam," said Carmel, the oldest of her brothers. "Just the way I like it."

"Ma," complained Cam.

"*Falla finita*! Carmel, don't be bothering your sister," said Isabella Fabbri, bustling around the table and laying more plates.

"You sure she's our sister?" teased Christophoro, pouring himself some juice.

"Yeah, I mean, the other six of us are boys, what are the chances that you got unlucky with a girl that one time?" put in Carlos. "Probably you're adopted, Cam, just face it."

"Your sister is not adopted," said Isabella. "And even if she were, she would be a child I chose, instead of one I ended up with, so what would that make you, huh?"

Carlos wiped the grin off his face and Cam stuck her tongue out at him.

Honestly, they were all out of school, and Carmel was over forty, but put them around the table and suddenly they all descended to the level of primary school all over again.

"Ma, he stole my porridge," Cam said.

"Then get more," said Isabella. "There's plenty, plenty." Which was pretty much the word to describe Isabella Fabbri's food.

There was always plenty.

"Why didn't you bring the *bambini*?" Isabella said to Carmel.

"Because it's a school day and Jen's getting them ready to go. Also because any time I bring them up here, you and dad over-excite them and they want to come live with you instead of at home," said Carmel, helping himself to toast.

"They would be welcome," said Lorenzo Fabbri, coming to take his place at the head of the table.

Which just about summed her dad up. Lorenzo had an open door policy, not just for grandchildren, but for anyone in the neighborhood, plus any stray or unwanted animals that were around. Cam grinned at him as her mum clucked around the kitchen.

"More children to raise, like I didn't do enough already," Isabella said, putting a vast plate in front of her husband.

Cam watched as her father began to chip away at the enormous breakfast her mother had served him. Sixty something years old and wiry as a pipe-cleaner, she had no idea where her dad put the massive amounts of food her mother fed him.

But working the farm at all hours had to burn energy, she guessed. Even with six sons to help. Well, five sons to help.

Carmel was the oldest, followed by Cosmo who was attending to the milking, then Christophoro. Cam herself came next, firmly in the middle. Followed by Carlos, Casmiro, and finally...

"Ah, you're awake, *finalmente*," Isabella said, smiling fondly at her youngest son.

Donte lingered in the doorway for a second, yawning, then came to join the rest of the family.

"If you sleep so long, you won't know when you're dead," Lorenzo said, swallowing a big mouthful of bacon.

"Ignore him," said Cam. "A good night's sleep is important." She'd always had a soft spot for her youngest brother. Donte wasn't like the rest. He didn't have a C name, which always set him apart. And he was skinny, wiry like his dad, rather than bulky and well-muscled like the rest of his brothers. He was also barely nineteen and just out of school.

"You get a good night's sleep after a hard day's work," grumbled her father.

Cam rolled her eyes at Donte, who gave her a slow smile in return and started to help himself to breakfast.

"So, no babies from you," Isabella said to Carmel. "What about you?" She turned to Christophoro, who grinned.

"Jeannie will bring Lucas over this afternoon, if that's alright, mum? She's got a class tonight and doesn't want to interrupt his nap time, so if he can stay for dinner and everything, that'd be great."

"Of course, of course," Lorenza answered for his wife. "He can stay the night, whatever you need."

Ignoring the fact that he wouldn't be the one doing the extra work, it'd be her mother, thought Cam. But Isabella looked pleased anyway. Her three grandchildren were adored and Carmel and Christophoro were the only two who no longer had to suffer through Lorenzo's 'when you have children of your own' speeches.

"The boiler is making those strange sounds again," said her mother.

Cam nodded. "I'll take a look at it." It wasn't like she had so much else to do.

"And leave the keys for your van if you go out," said her father. "We're moving stock around today and I may need to move the hulk." Which was what he called the van.

"Sure."

"Oh, and before I forget, I talked to Mary and she says that they have the chocolate I ordered in, so you can pick that up too, *tesoro*?" added her mother.

Cam sighed. "Yes, fine."

"And don't forget about the cat vaccines," said her father.

Cam put down her spoon. "Can't someone else handle that?" She looked around the table. "Casmiro, maybe?"

"Oh, but the *gatti* love you so much," Isabella said. "Come, come, have some toast, I made the peach preserve you like."

"Fine, fine." Anything to avoid a fight.

"You could avoid all this by moving out," hissed Carmel from beside her.

"Oh, like you did?" she said. "You turn up here every morning like a bad penny."

"I work here."

She growled at him and he grinned in return as she wiped off her hands. "I'll take a look at the boiler, ma."

Isabella shook her head in mock despair. "Whatever did I do to have a *figlia* that fixes boilers and builds with bricks instead of one who marries and gives me grandchildren?" she said sorrowfully.

But Cam had heard it all before. "You gave me six brothers who stole my dolls and laughed at me if I dared wear a dress," she said. "Besides, you're getting your boiler fixed, mama, so no complaints."

"You tell her," grinned Lorenzo. "Stand up for yourself, that's my girl."

Cam grinned back. "Thanks for the support, dad."

"No problem. But, you know, wearing a dress every now and again wouldn't kill you. And maybe a date with one of the nice boys around town?"

"Alright, papa, whatever you say," said Cam, escaping out the kitchen door and shaking her head. It was always the same.

It wasn't like she hadn't tried. Sometimes she felt like she'd dated every boy in the village, which, to be fair, she might have since there weren't that many of them and they'd all gone to school together.

Sometimes people acted like she wanted to be single, like she wanted to be living in a van. It wasn't true. She just hadn't found that magic yet.

That magic that made her mother's eyes sparkle when she looked at her father, even after more than forty years. That magic that made her father hold doors open and praise his wife to the heavens and blush fiercely whenever her mum won yet another award at the summer fete for her cakes.

She grabbed her tool box from the back of the van and then made her way down the creaky cellar steps to where the old boiler stood.

She hadn't been working long when she heard footsteps on the stairs. "Carmel, if that's you and you turn the lights out I won't be pleased," she shouted out.

"It's me," Donte said, appearing at the foot of the stairs. "I thought you might need a hand?"

Which was the other reason that she had a soft spot for him. He was the only one of her brothers that ever offered to help. Not that the others were mean or spiteful, just that they assumed she could do what she'd said she would do.

Which in a way was flattering and she knew that they supported her. Still, Donte was nice to have around.

"You can pass me that screwdriver over there," she said.

Donte did as he was told and then sat cross-legged on the ground next to her.

"What's up, kiddo?"

"Nothing much," he said. But he was starting to flush and Cam sat up so fast she almost bumped her head.

"Not much? You're terrible at lying, Don. What's up?"

He shrugged as though it wasn't important. "Just I might have a job lead, that's all."

"Seriously?" She clambered out from beneath the boiler and wrapped him in a greasy hug. "That's awesome, Don, I knew you could do it."

"At least it'll stop dad trying to rope me in to work around the farm."

"He's got five other sons to do that. There's nothing wrong with you making your own way," Cam said. "What's the job?"

"I don't want to say yet. It's not certain. But I've to go in this afternoon and have another interview, so I should know by tonight. Tomorrow at the latest."

"Then we'll celebrate," Cam said.

"Don't count your chickens, or my chickens in this case," Donte grinned.

Cam grinned back. It was one of their father's favorite sayings. Both their parents spoke English exceptionally well, and both were proud of the fact. But, unlike their mother who threw in Italian words when she couldn't be bothered to think of the English one, their father never uttered a word in his native tongue unless he was speaking on the phone to one of his brothers in Italy. He loved the English language and had an endless stock of proverbs and sayings.

"What about you?" Donte asked, accepting the screwdriver back and passing her a rag.

"What about me?" Cam said, peering again into the depths of the boiler.

"You. Work. Earning money. You know how it goes. If you don't get something soon, I'm pretty sure dad's going to marry you off to a cousin from Sicily or something."

Cam groaned. "Don't say that. I'm working on it, okay?" Which wasn't exactly the truth. She was trying to work on it though.

"Okay," Donte said. "Sore subject, I get it." He stood up and dusted off his pants. "Oh, I thought you should know, mum sent me down to the shop to get the papers this morning."

"And?" Cam said, frowning at the temperature gauge and tapping it so that the needle swung violently.

"Someone's moved into the Cromwell place."

She sat up so fast that this time she did hit her head and stars rolled in her vision as Donte winced in sympathy.

The new owner was here.

That changed everything.

CHAPTER FIVE

Piper stirred, blinked, then shot up in bed. Billy opened one eye, grunted, and closed it again, snuggling back down to sleep.

"Are you for real?" she said. "In the bed? Seriously?"

Billy only half-opened his eye this time and Piper sighed.

Okay, the dog was unexpected. She wasn't exactly sure what she was going to do about it yet. Not that she hated animals or anything, she'd just never been around them. However, Billy was the least of her problems.

She checked her phone and found that she'd slept straight through. "Christ, I must have been exhausted."

Throwing back the covers, she stumbled into the closest bathroom, then back out again, frowning. Experimentally, she opened the small door next to the bathroom and peered in. "Thank fuck," she said, and sat down to pee.

Then it was back to the bathroom again.

She stood for a long time peering at the bath-tub. But no matter how long she stared at it, no shower appeared.

Then she gave up and turned to the sink instead. She didn't have time for a bath right now. But the sink was no better. Rather than the single faucet she was used to, two stared back at her, one on either side of the sink.

Frowning, she turned one on and was rewarded with a clanking noise and then boiling hot water that made her snatch her hand away. Turning the second one on, she, unsurprisingly, got freezing cold water.

How to combine the two into something she could actually wash her face with was a mystery.

"Do these people actually bathe?" she mumbled to herself. Maybe they rolled in the dust like chinchillas or something.

Finally, she figured out that if she put the plug in she could run a sink of water and attempt to wash in it. Though how clean exactly she was after rinsing off in water that was still soapy was questionable.

"Bathrooms are first on the list," she said to Billy, who was now seated outside the bathroom door.

She'd been exhausted the afternoon before and had done nothing more than feed the dog and then fall into a dreamless sleep. Now that the sun was up, she was a lot more curious.

"We'll start from the top," she told Billy.

The top of the house was a large attic, stretching the entire floor-plan of the property, and filled with dustsheets covering old furniture, and trunks that looked designed to be on the Titanic. She sneezed, looked around, then closed the door, almost tripping back down the tiny staircase.

The second floor had bedrooms. Five of them. And two of the odd bathrooms with segregated toilets.

There was an endless supply of doors that opened into cupboards, strange little rooms that she couldn't name, and weird corners.

Then came the ground floor. A cozy living room, a dust-covered dining room, a room that looked like a living room again except she'd already seen one of those, a music room, and finally, a huge kitchen.

Billy whined, she opened up the back door and let him out into a garden that was a riot of flowers and weeds.

Piper stood and looked around her. It was odd. Like walking through someone else's life. This place was hers and yet every cupboard and drawer was crammed with reminders that this was someone else's home.

Someone she hadn't even known.

She wondered if she'd have liked her great aunt Lucy.

Then her stomach grumbled to remind her that she was starving. The kitchen cupboards contained vast hoards of dog food. But she guessed Billy needed vast hoards, given his size. Not much else lurked in there. There were blue and black cans that advertised themselves as baked beans, but when she opened one it didn't smell appealing.

The refrigerator contained one rind of cheese, a bottle of milk that had turned green at the bottom, and two out-of-date yogurts.

"Huh, guess we've got more in common than it might appear, Aunt Lucy," she murmured, closing the refrigerator door.

Still, at least this house had furniture. Which was a step ahead of her apartment at home.

This house. Her house.

Not for the first time, Piper wondered just what exactly she was going to do with the place.

Selling it had been her first, obvious thought. Just what was she supposed to do with a house on the other side of the Atlantic? Then one of the lawyers had mentioned using it as a rental property, which could provide a steady income.

She still hadn't decided.

What was clear though, was whatever the final decision, the house needed cleaning, sorting, and renovating. She wasn't about to be the evil landlord that rented out homes with faucets that didn't even mix the water for you.

There was a clattering and skidding of claws as Billy came in from the garden. Piper eyed him. His size still freaked her out, but he'd been nothing but gentle so far. The main issue seemed to be avoiding the massive amounts of drool he created.

"There's got to be a store around here, right Bill?"

He whined.

"There's plenty of villages like this on PBS, and there's always a vicar, a cricket team, and a village shop." Billy cocked his head to look at her. "And generally a body in the village pond as well," she added thoughtfully.

Billy whined again and she grabbed his leash so that his long tail wagged from side to side.

"Jesus, we'd better get you out of here, that tail might break a damn window."

Getting Billy out of the house was suspiciously easy. She was wary of his power, but as it turned out, he trotted along the sidewalk beside her quite obediently.

"We're doing alright, huh, Bill?"

He put out his tongue and she held the leash away from her.

"Less of the tonguing, if you don't mind," she said.

They reached the edge of the village green and Piper looked around. There was a church at one end. A traditional looking church, one that a child might have drawn, with a square tower and heavy wooden doors.

There was the pub, of course. And there, a red and white awning flapping in the breeze, was exactly the place she was looking for. A store. She hoped it wasn't full of black pudding or haggis or anything else that the Food Channel had taught her she didn't want to eat.

"Taking Billy for a walk then?" asked a voice.

She turned around and saw Arthur Slater ambling along the path behind her. "Good morning, Mr. Slater."

"Told you, didn't I? Always good manners, the yanks. You can call me Arthur, love."

Piper gave her best, friendliest smile, though she wasn't entirely sure how she felt about being called a 'yank'. "Good morning, Arthur."

He sniffed. "You ought to be careful with a big dog like that," he said. "I was always telling Luce, so I was. A slip of a thing like you and a big dog like that."

Piper drew herself up. "I'll have you know, Arthur, that I'm very capable of taking care of myself."

"No doubt, no doubt," he said, quickly backtracking.

"And Billy is being a perfect gentleman," she added, just as Billy started pulling at his leash. She yanked him back, willing him to make a good impression.

"No, no, love, it's not that, it's just that Billy likes to chase—"

The rest of his sentence was lost as Billy caught sight of something and pulled so hard at his leash that Piper almost lost her footing.

"Billy! Billy! Stop!"

But he was going, and since her hand was tangled in the leash, so was she.

She tripped, caught herself, then started to run to catch up with him, all the time yelling at him to stop. But Billy was on the scent and he veered across the grass as Piper's lungs struggled to keep up.

"Billy! Stop!"

But it was obvious now what he'd seen and where he was heading. Piper gave up trying to stop him and tried desperately to untangle her hand from the leash. But it was too late.

One cry, one splash, and one very happy dog bark, and the two of them were in the village pond. At the very last second, the leash slipped out of Piper's hand, making her gasp and inhale a mouthful of dirty water, then her feet slipped and she was rolling, disoriented, in the pond.

Which was about when a hand grabbed at the collar of her shirt and pulled her up.

Coughing and spluttering, Piper couldn't say a word. She was face to face with a woman with eyes the exact color of chocolate, with long dark hair, with an eyebrow quirked up, a grin on her face, and a smudge of oil across one cheek.

"You alright there?" the woman asked.

Still coughing, Piper nodded.

"You've got some duckweed in your hair," said the woman helpfully.

"What? What's duckweed?" Piper finally managed.

"Here." The woman reached out and pulled something from Piper's head, something green and slimy.

"Ew."

"The ducks seem to like it," said the woman. "And maybe it's good for you. Like those algae wraps that rich women get."

Piper finally laughed. Then she looked down at herself and laughed even harder. She was covered in mud and duckweed and pond water was dripping from every part of her. Billy gave a joyous bark and splashed over to sit beside her.

"You sure you're okay?" asked the woman.

"Absolutely fine," Piper said, embarrassed now. "I'm totally fine, no problem at all. I just need to grab a shower is all."

"Well, if you're sure," the woman said. She looked around. "I am in a bit of a hurry actually."

"Go, go," said Piper. "I'm fine, I swear."

The woman grinned and little wrinkles appeared at the corners of her eyes, making Piper's mouth inexplicably dry up, which was odd given she could still taste pond water. "I'll be going then. See you around."

Piper managed to pull herself up from the pond and grabbed hold of Billy's leash just as Arthur made it to the edge of the water.

"I was going to say that Billy likes to chase ducks," he said. "But I s'pose you found that out for yourself. You okay there?"

Piper groaned and nodded. Not the great first impression she'd wanted to make. And definitely not the best start to her first morning in town. Maybe she'd been wrong about her luck changing.

She squished back to the house in shoes full of water.

It wasn't until she was on the porch that she remembered there was no shower.

"For fuck's sake," she grumbled as she let herself into the house.

This was not turning out to be the first day she'd imagined. Though at least there hadn't been a body in the village pond. Not one other than her own, anyway.

CHAPTER SIX

Cam hopped up onto a stool at the cafe counter. "So, tell me all about it then," she said.

"All about what?" asked Beth, pouring them both a coffee.

"The new owner, Donte said they're already moved in."

"The new owner isn't an 'it', Cam," chided Beth.

"Well, I didn't know which other pronoun to use. Cheers," she accepted the coffee.

"And what makes you think that I'd know anything at all about the new owner anyway?" asked Beth.

"Because you know everything about everyone. After Arthur, you're the biggest gossip in the village."

"Arthur would be the smart person to ask, since he's the neighbor and all," said Beth.

"Yeah, I just couldn't do more scrapbooks today. Now come on, spill it. You must know something."

"Actually, Arthur was in this morning. And then Mary dropped in around lunchtime for a sandwich and she said that the new owner had been in the shop already, so I suppose I might know a little something," teased Beth.

"Then spill it!" Cam bounced up and down on her stool.

"Okay, okay. Let me see. It's a woman, I mean, *she's* a woman, she's lovely by all accounts and Billy seems quite taken with her, oh, and she's an American."

Cam's mouth opened of its own accord as she put the pieces together. "Oh shit," she said finally.

"What?" asked Beth.

"Um, I think I fished her out of the village pond this morning."

Beth choked on a mouthful of coffee. "Back up for a second there."

And Cam told her the whole story, how she'd been running to pick up her mother's chocolate and seen the dog drag someone into the pond. How she'd pulled out a woman with short blonde hair mixed with duckweed, and sparkly blue eyes, how she'd laughed and then seemed suddenly embarrassed.

"To be fair, I'd probably have been embarrassed too," put in Beth. "But didn't it occur to you that she must be the new owner? I mean, she had Billy with her."

Cam shrugged. "There's plenty of tourists around, plenty of Americans too. I just thought she was some poor AirBnB-er that Arthur had persuaded to walk the dog. I had no idea." She groaned out loud. "Why couldn't she have been a tourist?"

"You know, you say the word tourist with such disdain, if it weren't you, I might be taking offense here."

"You know what I mean," Cam said. "They take photographs all the time, want cottages for their summer homes, drive property prices up. There's a reason I haven't got my own place yet."

"And they spend tourist dollars which is good for the local economy," said Beth. "Besides, I used to be a tourist myself, remember?"

"Yeah, but you're Canadian, that's different."

"Different from what exactly?"

"She's an American," said Cam. "She'll be loud and brash and she'll throw money around like it means nothing."

"Uh, forgive me for interrupting what is likely to become a worryingly xenophobic rant, but isn't that exactly what you're looking for? Someone who wants to throw money around?"

Cam sighed and rubbed at her eyes. "Sorry. I'm being an idiot, I know that. I'm not xenophobic. Though, to be honest, with a mother like mine could you blame me for not liking foreigners?"

"Your mother is lovely," Beth said. "Just like this American will be. Give her a damn chance, Cam. You're pre-judging and that's not fair."

"You think she'll really want to give me that contract now?" Cam asked. "I mean, I did just fish her out of a pond and she looked horribly embarrassed."

"You saved her life."

Cam laughed. "The pond's about a foot deep, if that."

"She could have suffocated on mud and duckweed. She should be grateful," grinned Beth. "And you are only here because you're trying to put off the inevitable. You won't know if she'll hire you until you ask her. So how about you get your little ass in gear and go ask."

"Okay, okay, you're right. I just…"

"It's just scary," Beth said. "I get that. Decision time has come. Not knowing whether you got the job or not was sucky, but it was better than knowing that you definitely didn't have it."

"Right."

"And not as good as knowing you definitely did have it," Beth continued. "So go knock on the door. Introduce yourself. For all you know, you're exactly the person that she's looking for. Maybe she's making her way through the Yellow Pages looking for a builder right now."

"Does that still exist? The Yellow Pages?"

Beth shrugged. "Not really the point, is it? Go on. Go and visit and if you're a good girl I'll give you a ginger biscuit when you get back."

Cam got down for her stool. "Anything for a biscuit," she said, grinning even though her heart was beating double time.

The air was warm and the sun was shining as she stepped out onto the street. She was just rounding the common, Lucy's house already in sight, when someone yelled her name. Donte was running across the green.

"I got it, I got it," he was calling out.

Cam waited until he was close enough to talk to. "I'm guessing you mean the job?"

He beamed and nodded.

"Good work, kiddo. Um, what kind of job is it exactly?"

"Estate agent," he said. "Well, just like a beginner. It's with David Chancellor, you know, the one who puts his face all over the 'For Sale' signs? He's not as bad as I thought. He was quite nice actually, and it sounds like a fun job and the pay's alright and—"

"Jesus, Don, take a breath, why don't you?" Cam said. Then she grinned and slapped him on the shoulder. "You could be a pole dancer for all I care as long as it's something that's going to make you happy."

"I'm happy," he said. "And I'm just off to tell mum and dad."

"They'll be thrilled. Go on then, off with you. I'm a busy woman, you know."

Donte looked over at the Cromwell house. "Ugh, going to make the introductions?"

"It'll be fine," Cam said, with more confidence than she felt. After all, this was only the entire rest of her life that she was potentially talking about. Only a chance to stop living in a van. To finally make something of herself.

"Good luck, sis," Donte said, but he couldn't wipe the wide grin off his face.

"Go on, tell mum I'll be home in time for tea," she said, as though she ever missed a meal.

Then Donte was running off, his slight form slinking across the green, and Cam had no further distractions.

The garden path was so familiar and she was struck with a pang of sadness as she walked up it. She half-expected Lucy's gray head to appear from one of the windows, or for her tiny figure to walk around the corner in the enormous wellington boots she habitually wore.

Still, as her father said, it was a good death when you went in your own bed. Cam smiled a little as she thought about where Lucy might be now. Watching down over everyone and crunching on a biscuit, most likely, eager to know what was going to happen to her beloved house.

Cam's hands were sweating, so she wiped them on her pants before she rang the bell and waited. It was odd to wait on the porch when she was so used to just walking in.

"Hello," said a voice as the door opened. Then bright blue eyes widened. "Oh, it's you."

"Yes," Cam said. "It's me. Um, we didn't exactly meet before, did we?"

The woman grinned. "I think plucking weeds out of my hair counts as meeting. But we weren't introduced, if that's what you mean." She stood back. "Why don't you come in? I haven't quite mastered the kitchen yet, but I'm attempting coffee."

Cam followed her into the kitchen, where a pot of water bubbled on the stove. "I'm Cam," she said. "Technically, Camilla Fabbri. But everyone calls me Cam."

"Piper Garland. Pleasure to meet you again."

"Um, why are you boiling water on the stove?" Cam asked.

"For that coffee I was talking about."

"There's a kettle right there," Cam pointed out.

"A what?"

Cam shook her head and laughed. "Don't they have kettles in America? Here." She filled the kettle with water and turned it on. "It's a lot faster than waiting for water on the stove."

"Huh," Piper said. "I've got a lot to learn. And since you're such an expert, what exactly am I supposed to do with the faucets?"

"Faucets? Like taps?" Cam asked.

"Yes. Currently I'm torn between running a sink full of water and rinsing off in soapy water, or having one boiling hand and one freezing hand."

Cam laughed. "Okay, you've still got the old-fashioned kind of bathroom. Lucy wasn't much for modernization. Most of us use mixer taps now, but if you don't have one, then I guess running a sink of water is your best option."

"And what the fuck are baked beans?" Piper asked, then flushed. Her cheekbones were high and her eyelashes were longer than Cam had seen before. "Excuse my language."

"Uh, I think they might be an acquired taste," Cam said.

"Huh," nodded Piper as the kettle boiled and then switched off. She prepared two cups. "So you knew my great aunt then?"

Cam nodded. Her pulse sped up again and she had to wipe sweaty hands before she could take a cup off Piper. "That's actually kind of why I'm here."

"You're not just here to check that I haven't drowned in the bath or anything?" Piper joked. She reached for the other cup.

"No, well, yes, obviously I wanted to make sure you were okay. But actually, your great aunt and I had, well, sort of an arrangement, kind of. The thing is, that, well, um—"

She was rescued from her stumbling as Piper picked up her coffee cup and promptly dropped it, sending out a spray of scalding liquid and shards of porcelain.

"Fuck!" yelped Piper.

"It's alright," Cam said, already reaching for a tea towel. "No harm done."

"That was way hotter than I thought it'd be," Piper said, bending down with a roll of paper towels.

Cam grinned. "Easily done, it's happened to the best of us."

Then Piper was looking up and suddenly they were eye to eye. Close enough that Cam could see freckles on Piper's nose, close enough that she could smell coconut skin cream. Close enough that for a moment, inexplicably, she completely forgot to breathe.

"You're going to think I'm such a klutz," Piper said.

"God, no," said Cam, swallowing and tearing her eyes away, mopping at the floor.

"I'm not," said Piper. "Not usually anyway." She collected most of the pieces of cup and stood up. "You know, I've no idea where the trash is?"

"There's a bin under the sink," said Cam, collecting the wet towel and standing herself.

"A bin, right. Bin means trash, right?"

"Yep," Cam said. She was wrong-footed now, put off, unsure how to get back to the subject at hand. But she didn't have to,

Piper took care of it for her.

"So you and my aunt had some kind of arrangement?" Piper asked.

Cam blew out a breath and nodded.

CHAPTER SEVEN

How awkward. Piper rubbed her nose as she listened to Cam describe what her great aunt had wanted to do with the house.

So, just to be clear, she thought to herself, Cam had dragged her out of a fish pond, watched her spill a cup of coffee, and now she was expecting to be hired? It seemed to Piper like there was some kind of jinx going on.

If she let Cam into the house, she might be dead by dinner time. Her head cut off in an unfortunate window accident. Or her skull crushed by a falling chandelier. Or something.

And yet here she was, looking at her with those big chocolate colored eyes and Piper could feel herself melting, could feel herself wanting to please the woman, wanting to give her what she wanted.

"I get that the house needs renovating," she began.

Cam blew out a breath. "But you'd rather make your own plans?" she said.

Piper laughed, surprised. "You're trying to talk yourself out of the job?"

"No. No! But, well, I get that the contract I had with Lucy isn't binding anymore, and, well, I get that maybe you have your own plans and, yes, well..."

Piper leaned against the kitchen counter. She couldn't be a walk-over. Not anymore. She would not let people take advantage of her. What would Joey say? She had no idea who this woman was, not really, nor what she was capable of. Just hiring her seemed like a bad plan.

"Look, Cam, you seem really nice, honestly you do."

"But you'd rather I backed off?" Cam said, she was already stiffening up like she was going to walk away.

"I've just got here," said Piper. "Literally, just got here. Not to mention the fact that I'm still wringing pond water out of my hair, so to speak."

Cam smiled at this, showing a row of even white teeth like little pearls.

"I'm not saying no," Piper continued. "But I'm not saying yes either. Just give me a little time to get on my feet and then I'll get back to you. Fair?"

Cam looked down at the ground and Piper knew that she'd disappointed the woman, but she also knew that she was doing the right thing. She had to see what the competition was like. She had no idea how much builders were worth in this weird, funny-colored money.

"Fair," Cam said, then she smiled. "Just promise you'll consider me?"

"Absolutely promised," Piper said, somewhat relieved that she'd managed to get through this conversation without thoroughly offending the woman. Cam was, after all, the first female she'd really spoken to in the village. "So, here's a question."

"Shoot," said Cam, sipping at her coffee.

"Can I just walk into that pub? Or is it not safe for women or something?"

Cam spluttered, coughed, then wiped her mouth with the back of her hand. "Safe? I think the Duck and Pony is probably the safest place in the village. I mean, you stand the danger of getting your ear talked off, and you might get food poisoning from Rod's dodgy shrimp cocktails, but other than that, you'll be alright." She paused. "Are pubs dangerous in America then?"

"Depends on where they are," Piper said. "Sometimes. What

about the shop?"

"Definitely not dangerous," Cam said, solemnly.

"Yeah, not what I meant."

Cam put down her cup. "Sutton's Walk is about the safest place in the world. Not to mention boring. Nothing ever happens here. The pub is nice, the shop is nice, the people are nice. Everything is nice. I'm afraid the biggest danger here is that you're going to be bored to death."

"Bored sounds... Actually, bored sounds pretty good," said Piper. And it did. Bored meant no excitement, no firing, no cheating, no surprises. Bored meant safe. She could deal with bored.

Cam rolled her eyes. "Then you're definitely in the right place. Oh, don't forget that there's a cafe and bookshop just down the road. You might like that, especially since there's a compatriot behind the till."

"What's a till?"

"Uh, cash desk place? The bit where you pay," Cam explained.

"Huh, okay," said Piper, mentally adding it to her list of new words for the day. "Another American, huh?"

"Well, Beth's Canadian," Cam said, brushing her hands off on her jeans. "But close enough, right?"

Not really, Piper was about to say, but Cam didn't give her time.

"And I've been here long enough. I'll get out of your hair. I'm sure you've got things to do. It was lovely meeting you."

She held out a long, slim hand and Piper took it to find that it was stronger than she'd thought, that there were calluses on the palm. "Lovely meeting you too."

"I'll show myself out," Cam said, and then she was walking away.

Piper leaned against the kitchen counter and rubbed at her face. She'd barely had time to settle in and already she'd been reminded that she needed to do something about the house. Well, she was here for a reason, she supposed.

It wasn't like this was a vacation.

She sighed and turned on the electric kettle again. At least she could have some coffee for herself before she got started.

SHE HELD THE pencil between her teeth as she dialed the number on the flimsy page.

"Courtney's Builders."

"Hi, yes, hello, I was wondering if I could get a quote for a house renovation," she began.

"Ooo, I don't know about that love, we're run off our feet at the moment. Let me see… I could get someone out to you at the end of next month for an estimate if you like?"

The end of next month? "Ah, that won't work for me, sorry. Thanks and have a nice day."

She hung up, scratched the name off the list and moved on to the next one.

"Next week?" laughed the voice over the phone. "You'd be lucky to get a builder in by the end of the summer."

Another name crossed off the list.

Her third call went slightly better. At least at the beginning.

"A house renovation?" said the man on the phone. "Well, we are busy, but I suppose we could take a look."

"Wonderful," Piper said, breathing a sigh of relief.

"I could pop 'round tonight, if you like love?"

"Really?"

"Of course. On your own, are you? Just you in the house? Or will your husband be home?"

And she recognized immediately what was going on. She slammed the phone down, hand trembling. Yes, this was a nice village, and yes, the UK seemed far safer than the US. But that didn't mean there weren't bad people out there.

She scribbled through the name on the list so hard that the pencil went through the paper. The call had left a bad taste in her mouth. The man had been fishing, and God knows what he intended to do if she had turned out to be home alone. The thought sent a shiver down her spine.

She looked down at the list in front of her. She'd been lucky really that Lucy had been the type to keep an old Yellow Pages floating around, since there was no internet in the house.

Though, to be honest, it was beginning to look like her great aunt was the kind of person that kept everything lying around. She'd opened half the drawers in the living room to try and find the pencil she was now holding, and each time there'd been an explosion of papers or plastic bags or, on a more memorable occasion, a package of sewing needles that she'd had to scour the floor for. The last thing she needed was Billy eating a needle.

There were three more companies on the page she was on. She'd call them, she promised herself, before she took a break.

"COME ON, BILLY," she said. The tennis ball had been by the back door, and from the gnawed state of it, it was clearly the dog's toy.

She threw the ball the length of the garden and Billy shot off to find it.

"Dog like that needs plenty of exercise."

Piper's breath caught in her throat, then she turned to see Arthur hanging on the garden fence.

"He's a big dog, is what I mean," said Arthur.

"Huge," Piper agreed.

"Best to keep him away from the ducks though," Arthur chuckled.

Piper decided to ignore that. She didn't exactly need the reminder. She could still smell a vaguely fishy odor in her hair, even though she'd washed it multiple times. Arthur seemed to be everywhere and she could see how this might get annoying.

Still, all part of living in a small village, she guessed.

And it would mean that the man knew practically everything and everyone.

"Can I ask you something?"

"Fire away," he grinned. "I told you you'd be needing some advice."

"Do you happen to know any contractors or building companies in the area that might have time to come by the house?"

"Ah, so you're going to be renovating it then, are you?" Arthur said knowingly.

Piper looked back at the house and shrugged. It wasn't like she had much choice. Sell or rent, the place needed desperate modernizing.

"Well, there are plenty of builders around," Arthur continued. "But if I were you, and don't you go telling any of that damn family that I said so, I'd go with the Fabbri girl."

Piper frowned. "With who?"

"The Fabbri girl, Camilla, she was around here earlier, I saw her come up your front path."

"Really?" Not exactly the suggestion she'd expected from the old man.

Arthur sniffed. "Like it or not, she knows her stuff. She's a wee slip of a thing, but she's got a head on her shoulders and she's stronger than she looks. Luce had a contract with her, you know."

"I heard."

"And she might have been old, but she wasn't as dotty as she made out. Luce knew what she was doing when she hired the girl. Best around, though most won't give her a chance on account of her being a girl and young at that."

"A woman," Piper said automatically.

"What?"

"A woman, Cam's a woman, and she's got to be over thirty."

"Maybe she is at that," Arthur nodded thoughtfully. "Still though, you'd do worse than getting her out to look at the place again. She knows that house inside and out."

Billy's big head butted at Piper's hand as he deposited a drool-laden tennis ball at her feet. So Cam came recommended then, did she? She had to admit that she'd feel safer with a woman in the house than a man.

"Going to give her a ring and employ her then, are you?"

Arthur said.

Cam grimaced as she picked up the wet ball and hurled it as far as she could down the garden. "We'll see," she said, before she turned back to the kitchen to investigate another tin of baked beans for dinner.

CHAPTER EIGHT

Cam chewed on her last mouthful of lasagna and put down her knife and fork. "Brilliant, mum."

"A hard day's work makes for a healthy appetite," Lorenzo said. Then he raised a furry eyebrow. "Did you have a hard day's work?"

Cam blew out her cheeks and shrugged. She knew better than to lie to her father. "I had... an average day."

"By which she means that she spent half the day hanging around Beth at the bookstore," Carlos put in. He turned to his sister. "Anything we should know about you and Beth?" he leered.

Cam punched his arm. "Give over."

"If you're not going to work," her mother said. "We should find you a match. Then at least you can give me more grandchildren." She was feeding Lucas, Christophoro's son, with something that looked like pureed carrots. The baby pulled a face and spat out a mouthful.

Cam sighed and crumpled up her napkin. "I'm off to the pub."

"Drinking in bars will not set you up for success," said Lorenzo, wiping his plate with a piece of bread.

"But neither will sitting at home," Cam pointed out, bending to kiss his cheek. "You need help with the dishes, mum?"

"Oy," said Casmiro, his mouth still full.

"The boys are still eating," Isabella said, and clucked at the baby as he opened wide for another mouthful.

"Speaking of which, where's Donte?" asked Cam. "I'd have thought he'd be here crowing over us all about his new job."

"He already started work," said Lorenzo proudly. "He's going to be a hard worker that one, we should never have worried about him."

"Yes we should," put in Carlos. "He's a string-bean and a weakling, and if any of us are going to turn out not-quite-right then it'll be him."

"Your homophobia is disgusting, out-dated, and not at all funny," Cam scolded.

Carlos stuck his tongue out at her, but turned red. "You know I'm kidding. He can bring home who he likes, no skin off my nose."

"Then stop kidding, it's not funny," said Cam.

"Fine, fine," Carlos mumbled.

Cam was still shaking her head as she went out into the cool evening. She knew Carlos didn't mean it, she knew none of them did. But she worried about Donte. Mostly, she worried that with all the teasing from his older brothers he'd never have the courage to bring anyone home, male or female.

And she was worried about herself too. Not necessarily that her mother would marry her off, though she was sure Isabella would give it a damn good try. More that she desperately needed work and there was little going around.

She had her qualifications, she'd done her apprenticeship. She'd even freelanced for a couple of building companies. But no one was hiring right now.

If she wasn't careful, she'd still be living in a van in her parents' farmyard when retirement time came along. Not that she'd be able to afford to retire, but still.

The walk down to the village was as familiar to her as the back of her hand, and it took all of ten minutes before she was rounding the village green. From the corner of her eye she glimpsed the sparkle of the duck pond and grinned.

Yes, she needed Piper's business. But she wasn't going to force the woman. Besides, if today was any example, Piper would be calling for help soon anyway. Cam had the idea that the American might try her hand at a little DIY, something that could only end badly.

Maybe then she'd get a call.

Or maybe Piper would ask around for references.

Or maybe every single other building and contracting company in the entire county would be booked solid until Christmas.

She couldn't help but like the woman. She seemed confident, clear in what she wanted. And she was definitely exotic. That American accent made her sound like someone off the telly, and her haircut was about three styles ahead of the local barber's trends. Not to mention her eyes, deep blue and clear as the sea.

In fact, now that Cam was thinking about it, she rather thought that Piper was the kind of woman she'd like to be. She was willing to bet that Piper wouldn't have a hard time telling someone no, or telling someone anything at all for that matter.

The pub looked cozy and welcoming, the windows yellow with light even though it wasn't quite dark yet.

She pushed open the door to chatter and the smell of beer and smoke, even though there'd been no smoking inside now for years.

"Evening," Rod said from behind the bar. He was already pulling a pint and Cam nodded at him before spotting Beth at their normal table.

"So?" Beth said, as Cam got close enough to hear.

"So what?" groaned Cam, sinking into a chair. "And this round's on you. I've got a fiver to last until the weekend and you invited me, so fair's fair."

Beth grinned and got up to go to the bar. She came back a couple of minutes later carrying two beers. "Here you go then," she said. "Now, tell me."

"Tell you what?" asked Cam. She'd been staring off into space wondering if maybe Rod needed some help in the evenings. She could be a barmaid. She definitely had the boobs for it. A low cut t-shirt and she could probably make a fortune in tips.

"Did you get the job? Lucy's job?" Beth said, impatiently.

"Oh, uh, no, or yes, or maybe, I don't know."

Beth put both pints down and sat down. "You don't know?"

"She's thinking about it," Cam said. Would she like being a barmaid? She liked people. She liked beer. Those seemed to be two important qualifications.

Beth sighed. "Did you try to persuade her at least?"

"Persuade who of what?" Persuading Rod that he needed help would be the problem. The man ruled over his pub with an iron fist and a beer belly that made him look eight months pregnant.

"Earth to Cam, calling Cam!"

Cam blinked and finally turned her attention to Beth. "Sorry, I was just wondering if Rod needed help behind the bar."

"He doesn't," Beth said. "And even if he did, you're a builder, not a barmaid. Now talk to me, Cam. Seriously. Did you at least try to persuade the woman?"

"Her name's Piper," said Cam. "And I told her about the contract and all. But I'm not sure she wants me. I think she's probably going to look around, get some quotes, you know how it goes."

"And did you offer up references? Did you tell her that you could work a day for nothing so she could see what you can do? Did you push for yourself at all?" demanded Beth.

Cam sighed. Beth was frowning at her and with her curly blonde hair and freckle-smudged nose she looked like an irate child. "Beth, it's not like that here."

"What's not like what?"

"It's just not... It's not English," Cam said. "Putting yourself forward like that, pushing for something, it's not polite."

"It is effective though," said Beth. "And as far as I was aware, this Piper is American anyway, isn't she?"

"Yes."

"Then she's probably sitting over there wondering why in the hell you didn't tell her you were the right person for the job."

Which, now that Cam came to think of it, was quite a fair

point. "Do you think so?"

"Do you really want to work behind the bar with strangers ogling your boobs and only tipping you if you smile real nice?"

"No-oo," said Cam, drawing the word out. "On the other hand, I don't want to push my luck and talk myself out of a job before I've got one."

Beth growled. "You know, there's this weird thing that English people do, I don't know if you've noticed. But you all ask someone out or apply for a position or invite someone somewhere, and then you immediately give people an excuse not to come or hire you."

"That's ridiculous," Cam laughed.

"Is it?" asked Beth. "I'm having a birthday party next Saturday, would you like to come? Unless you're busy that is, which I'd completely understand."

"Ah."

"Ah indeed," said Beth. "I get that it's a politeness thing, and other English people expect it from you, hell, even I've found myself doing it now. But Piper's new here. She's American and will expect you to put yourself forward. Seriously, Cam, you need to push harder for this."

Cam reached for her beer, but Beth pulled it back. "Not until I hear you say that you're going to try harder."

"Fine. I'm going to try harder," said Cam.

"Perfect, off you go then."

"What? Now?"

Beth grinned. "Look, you're better off striking while the iron's hot and all that."

"Now you just sound like my dad."

"Wise man, your dad. And I know you, you'll have talked yourself out of this by morning. Go and do it now. Go and offer her a trial day or something, let her see what you're capable of."

Cam eyed the beer. "Can I have some Dutch courage first?"

"And show up at her doorstep smelling of booze?" asked Beth.

"You're not going to let this go, are you?"

"I'm your best friend and I'm looking out for your best

interests," said Beth. "Trust me. I'll look after your beer till you get back. I'll tell you what, I'll even buy another round in if you go talk to her now, deal?"

"Since when is the way to a girl's heart through beer?" Cam asked, but she was weakening. Beth was making good points and she needed the work.

"Since, oh, since the whole time I've known your broke ass," Beth laughed. "Now go on, go big yourself up and then come back here for a celebratory drink."

"Or a commiseratory drink. Is that a word?"

"How the hell am I supposed to know," said Beth. "You people make words up on the fly, I swear. You think aubergine is a word."

"It is," Cam said, standing up and pushing her wooden chair under the table.

"No, it's just a collection of vowels."

"Fine, fine, I'm going. Don't you move." She turned back after three steps. "And don't you drink my pint either."

Beth was still doing her evil laugh as Cam left the pub again and went out into the twilight.

CHAPTER NINE

The knock on the door sent Billy barking and Piper tried desperately to hush him as he bounced around the kitchen. Finally, she closed the door on him.

"I don't know what I'm worried about with a guard dog as big as that," she mumbled to herself as she made her way to the front door.

She opened up to find Cam Fabbri standing on her doorstep.

"Hi there," she said, finding that she was pleasantly surprised to see the woman. "I wasn't expecting to see you again so soon."

"Oh, right, yes, obviously." Cam's face flushed a pleasing pink. "Um…"

"Want to come in?" Piper said, taking a step back. She could hear Billy going mad in the kitchen.

"Uh, yes, yes, that's a good idea."

"You know you weren't wrong about those baked beans," Piper said cheerfully as she led the way to the kitchen.

"In what way?" asked Cam, confused.

"That they're an acquired taste," said Piper, opening the kitchen door to let Billy bound out and greet Cam. "Although, they're a damn sight better warmed up than they are cold."

"You tried to eat them straight out of the tin?"

"Um, yes. Maybe not my smartest moment. I think I'll be doing some real shopping tomorrow, rather than just the milk I picked up at the village store. I can't stand baked beans or dog food, and those seem to be the only two things my great aunt kept in the house."

She spotted the baked bean can sitting on the counter next to a crumpled square of paper towel she'd used as a napkin.

"And here's me leaving all my mess around for you to see," she said, grabbing the can and throwing it into the trash. "What can I do for you?" She threw the paper towel on top of the trash pile where it promptly fell off, so she reached down, picked it up and shoved it down on top of the rest of the rubbish.

"Well, here's the thing," Cam said.

Something was wrong but Piper's body and her mind were not communicating on the issue at all. It wasn't until she turned around and saw all the color leak out of Cam's face that she really realized that all was not well.

"What?" she asked.

"Uh, you're, um... You're bleeding," Cam said through white lips.

"I am?" asked Piper surprised.

She looked down and saw blood leaking down onto the floor. Puzzled she followed the flow up until she saw her hand and then her stomach rose just as Cam pushed a hand towel over the injury.

"Stay right there," Cam said.

"Uh..." She was losing herself, her vision was cloudy.

"Look at me," said Cam. She looked up, looked into Cam's dark eyes. "Everything's going to be fine. Just stay right here. Sit down, keep the pressure on using the towel. I'm going to be right back. Less than five minutes. Think you can do that for me?"

Piper didn't trust herself to speak. She nodded and clutched at the towel that was wrapped around her hand.

"Less than five minutes," Cam said, backing out of the kitchen.

* * *

"See? Was that so bad?" Beth said as Cam rushed into the pub.

"Keys," breathed Cam, panting hard.

"What?" Beth frowned and pushed a beer toward her. "Here you go, you can drink now."

"No." Cam swallowed, took a deeper breath, tried to calm herself. "I need your keys. Van keys. Please."

"Why?" Beth's face was starting to pale now. "What's happened? What is it, Cam?"

Another deep breath. It'd be faster to explain. "It's Piper. She's hurt herself, cut herself on a bean tin. Nothing serious, but I need to get her to casualty. It's too far to go get my van. Please can I borrow yours?"

"Of course," Beth said, fumbling in her pockets. "Do you need me to come?"

But Cam was already shaking her head, taking the keys, turning back to the door. "Thanks," she yelled over her shoulder as she left the pub again.

She ran as fast as she could to the cafe, finding Beth's small van parked outside as normal. The engine flooded and she swore as she tried to start it again. Finally, it caught and she moved the van carefully to the road in front of Piper's place.

Not that she was worried Piper was going to bleed out or anything. But she was definitely worried that the woman was going to faint, and knowing her, knock herself out on the way down.

Fortunately, she found Piper sitting exactly where she'd left her, pale and trembling.

"Come on, up you get," she said, helping her up. "The van's right outside."

"Van?" asked Piper.

"We need to get you to casualty."

Piper stopped. "Casualty?"

"Er... the hospital?" ventured Cam.

"But—"

"No buts, you're bleeding, you need stitches. It's a week night, there won't be much of a wait and it's not far," Cam said, all the while escorting Piper down the hallway, wrapping her arm around the woman's waist, making sure she kept moving.

"But—" tried Piper again.

"I said no buts," said Cam. "Come on, get into the van now, we'll be there in ten minutes. We're lucky around here, the hospital's close."

"Hospital."

"Yes," Cam said calmly, helping Piper into the passenger seat. She paused. "You're not going to be sick or anything, are you?"

"Sick?"

"Vomit?"

Piper looked down at her hand, still wrapped in the towel, went slightly green, swallowed in a determined fashion, then shook her head.

Cam groaned and ran back to the house, grabbing a washing up bowl from under the sink before checking that Billy had food.

"Here," she said, climbing into the van and starting the engine. "Beth'll kill me if you're sick in her van." She pushed the washing up bowl onto Piper's lap.

"I'm not going to be sick," Piper said.

"Then put your hand in it so you don't bleed over the seats," said Cam, starting the engine again. "And try not to hurt yourself again before we get there."

❋ ❋ ❋

"I've checked you in," Cam said, coming to sit beside Piper on a horribly uncomfortable plastic chair. "And I got you a drink. Thought you might need it." She handed over a cold can of Coke.

"Thanks," Piper said, looking around. This was a far cry from the hospitals she was used to at home. Much smaller, for a start. There were posters on the wall and the staff looked harried, though there weren't that many people in the waiting room.

"It's okay," Cam said, sensing her apprehension. "You'll get treated well here. Maybe not as fancy as in the States, but the NHS can get the job done, just you wait and see."

"NHS?"

"Um, National Health Service," said Cam. "And you won't need to pay or anything. No huge bills. Actually, no bills at all."

"I have health insurance," Piper said.

"Oh, well, I don't know how it works with stuff like that. I do know that anyone can walk into the hospital here and get treated."

"Really?" Piper asked, suspiciously. "That sounds like you're trying to scam me. And seriously, I do have health insurance through my job."

Cam settled back into her seat. "Through your job. Okay, so what do you do then?"

"I'm an editor," Piper said. Then she reconsidered. "I was an editor."

"Was?"

"I got laid off. Cut backs. You know how it is." She didn't look at the towel-wrapped hand in her lap. "Actually, this house thing all turned up at exactly the right time."

"Because you got fired?" asked Cam.

"Laid off," corrected Piper. "Yes. That and I just got out of a long term relationship." She smiled a little sadly. "I guess I was at something of a loose end." She sniffed, then looked at Cam. "You know you don't have to stay with me. I can always call a cab to get me home."

"Are you kidding?" Cam laughed. "If my mother found out I'd left a stranger sitting by herself at the hospital she'd have my guts for garters."

"What a pleasant saying," grimaced Piper. "Strict is she, your mom?"

"Italian," said Cam, with a grin. "Which explains the name and the horrendous number of siblings that I have."

Piper grinned back. "Thanks for bringing me," she said. "You really didn't have to, whatever your mom might say about things." Then she had a thought. "I didn't even ask you why you came knocking on my door."

Cam blushed and again Piper saw how her cheeks went a

pretty shade of pink that complemented her eyes. "It's nothing. Not a problem. Nothing for now, anyway."

Piper sighed and re-positioned her hand. "It was about the house, right? The remodeling?"

"You really, really don't need to think about that right now," Cam said.

"Yes, yes I do," said Piper. "The job's yours, if you want it."

"Are you kidding?"

"It looks like I kind of need you around. If I'm going to keep being as clumsy as I've been the last couple of days, I'll need you to drive me to the hospital, won't I?"

"I can definitely do that," beamed Cam.

"You sure you're not a jinx, right?"

"Me? A jinx?"

"It's just that I'm not usually this clumsy, I swear," Piper said.

Cam laughed and Piper grinned back at her. "I'd be happy to sign the same contract as whatever you had with Lucy," she said, glad now that she'd decided. "I'll need a couple of weeks, I guess. I'll need to clean the house out before you get started. God knows how that's going to work."

"Why don't I help?" Cam asked, suddenly.

"You?"

"Yes," said Cam. "I knew Lucy Cromwell my entire life. I can tell you what stuff's important and what's not, what to do with rubbish and where to donate things. And maybe I could tell you a bit about your great aunt too, since you never got to know her."

"If she was anything like my English grandmother, that might be a good thing," Piper said with a shiver. "You know, she used to feed me cookies that were flavored with ginger. Who does that to a kid?"

Cam sighed. "Yeah, I'd better take you shopping too. You've got a lot to learn about English food."

Piper held up her wrapped hand. "Hey, I already learned to avoid baked beans."

"The hard way," Cam pointed out.

"So, do we have a deal?" Piper said. "You get the contract to renovate the house, you'll help me clean stuff out?"

"And make sure you don't bleed to death or break any bones in the process," Cam said, grinned at her. "It's a deal."

She held out her hand and Piper took it with her good hand. For just a second that callused palm rubbed against hers and Piper had an inkling that maybe this was an important moment.

Then the feeling was gone and a nurse was calling her name.

"Go on," Cam said. "Get stitched up. I'll be right here when you're done."

CHAPTER TEN

Piper carefully climbed the stairs to the attic. She could feel Cam coming up behind her and was being extra cautious. The last thing she needed was to have yet another accident. Her bandaged hand throbbed as a reminder of how careful she should be.

"I thought we should start from the top," she said as she opened the attic door.

She stood back to let Cam in, seeing the way light streamed through the tiny roof windows and caught on Cam's hair.

"Okay," Cam said. "That sounds like a plan." She turned in a circle. "Well, I'd suggest that we get started with the clearing and tidying part of the equation whilst we talk about what you might want to do structurally."

Piper grinned and nodded to the corner where she'd already stocked a pile of trash bags, a broom, dustcloths, and anything else she could think of. "I'm all prepared. If there was one thing my great aunt had in abundance, it was cleaning supplies. Which is odd considering the state of her refrigerator and store cupboards, but there you go."

Cam laughed. "Okay, so lesson one about Lucy. She hated to cook. She kept the baked beans in for breakfast, but most of the rest of the time she ate at the cafe with Beth or at the pub."

"Beth would be my fellow North American, I take it?"

"She would. I'll take you over and introduce you if you like."

Cam peeled off the hoodie she was wearing, revealing a white tank top. "And we should open up the windows if we're going to be working up here. It's only going to get hotter as the day goes on."

She moved to open the first of the windows, then leaned out and yelled at someone. Piper looked down in time to see a large man grinning like crazy and waving back up. "Who's that?"

"My brother Cosmo," Cam said, hands on hips and looking around. "Alright, let's get started. Rubbish over by the door, donation pile on the other side of the door, anything you want to keep can go over there under the window. Okay?"

Piper nodded and decided that she rather liked someone else planning things for her. She opened up one of the trunks and found it full of books. Sifting through them, she decided they obviously needed to be donated and slid the trunk over to the door.

"So, why a builder?" she asked as she opened trunk number two. "I mean, it's not a popular choice with women, not that I don't think you can do it or anything, but..." she trailed off. Nice. Good start to a conversation.

Luckily, Cam just laughed. "It's what I'm good at. Good with my hands and I always have been."

Inexplicably, Piper found herself blushing at that comment, she buried her head in a trunk full of clothes. "Really?" she managed to mumble.

"What about you?" asked Cam. "An editor, huh? What is that exactly?"

"I work with books and authors," Piper said, happier to be back on familiar ground. "Or at least I did."

"Don't tell me you work with horror writers," Cam said, sliding a trunk over to the trash pile.

"You're a horror fan?" Piper said, sitting up fast enough that she bumped her head on the lid of the trunk she was working on.

"Someone gave me a Poppy Z. Brite book when I was far too young to read it and I've been hooked ever since," Cam said with a gleeful smile.

Piper grinned back. "Let me guess, Lost Souls?"

"Close, WormWood," Cam said. "You know them?"

"Are you kidding? They were my Bibles when I was in high school."

Cam screamed with laughter. "I cannot imagine you Goth."

Piper pouted. "For real? I'll have you know that I had a safety pin through my ear. As in an actual safety pin that I stole from my mom's sewing kit. She went ape-shit when she found out I'd stuck it through my ear lobe."

More laughter from Cam. "I can imagine. My mum'd probably cut my ear off." She darted a glance over that Piper just caught, holding her dark eyes for a second.

"They're dead," Piper said to avoid the inevitable question and because somehow it hurt less to bring it up herself. "My parents, in case you were wondering. My mom went first, breast cancer when I was in college, my dad in a car wreck just after I graduated."

Cam sat down on the lid of a trunk. "I'm sorry," she said. "That must have been... unimaginable."

"It was like someone had emptied all the air out of the world for a while," Piper said quietly. "I was unsteady for a long time. Then Lex came along and saved me. Or at least stopped me flailing about like a drowning kid in the deep end of the pool."

"That would be your ex?"

Piper nodded, then cleared her throat. "What about you? How does a whole Italian family end up living in a little English village?"

Cam grinned and got back to work. "My dad fell in love with the place," she said as she sorted. "He came over on a work exchange to learn better English, he and the old farmer got on famously, so my dad ended up staying and bringing my mum over. Eventually, the old farmer left him the farm, since he'd no kids of his own, and the rest is history."

"Do you speak Italian?" Piper asked curiously.

"Enough to swear at bad drivers and order a pizza," said Cam.

"It's an odd little place this, isn't it?" said Piper, standing up and stretching her back. "I can see how it might grow on someone. It's a bit like being outside of time, like a little oasis from reality."

"I think you might be romanticizing Sutton's Walk just a tad," Cam said. "There are definitely problems here. Unemployment, for one. Besides, you must have a life to go back to in America, I'm sure you can't afford to spend months gadding about the English countryside."

"You'd be surprised," Piper said quietly. Then she pulled something out of the trunk she was working on. "What's this?"

It was a dress, originally white, but with the lace yellowed with age. She held it up against herself, seeing the long train wrap around to the floor, and frowned.

"It looks like a wedding dress," she said, looking over at Cam.

"Can't be," Cam said. "Lucy never got married. She said men were more stubborn than donkeys and she'd rather have a donkey."

Piper laughed. "You know, I'm actually kind of sad now that I didn't meet her. What was she really like?"

"She was brilliant," Cam said fondly. "Definitely eccentric, but all the best old English women are. She was kind and generous, she always let us play in her garden and with her dogs. Billy is only the latest in a long line of monster-sized pets, trust me."

Piper had a vision of dinosaurs in the back yard.

"Lucy's is the house we all used to come to when we were kids and wanted some adventure, and she was always happy to oblige us. We dug in her flowerbeds, ran around her kitchen making mud pies. She was fun. Always fun."

"It seems strange, combing through her life like this," said Piper. "Someone that I never knew but who for the last decade has been my closest living relative."

"You'll get to know her," Cam said. "It won't be quite the same, but Lucy's still here."

Piper rolled her eyes. "We'll have none of that paranormal nonsense."

"If anyone's going to turn up as a ghost, it'll be Lucy," Cam said confidently.

"I thought we were supposed to be discussing what to do with the attic, not family histories," said Piper.

"Fine," Cam said, brushing some dust off her hands and standing upright. "I'd suggest you keep this space as is. The house will sell better if the attic is clean and in good shape. The new owners can decide whether to expand up into here or not. Have it be a clean canvas."

"Makes sense," Piper said. Cam was standing in a beam of sunlight and it caught in her eyes and hair and made her sparkle.

"We'll need to clean up a bit," went on Cam. She stamped on the floor. "And probably replace these floor panels."

"Bullshit," said Piper. "They're solid as a rock. They've supported all this junk for the last god-knows-how long."

"I wouldn't be so sure." Cam started stomping around the cleared area of the floor. "I'm seeing splintering, and this wood wasn't great quality to begin with."

"Are you one of those builders that's going to up-sell me on everything?" Piper said, suspiciously. Because she could have made the wrong decision here. Her bandaged hand was a reminder of the fact that she'd employed Cam when she wasn't necessarily in a clear-headed state.

"No!" Cam said. "Take a look for yourself."

Piper walked over to where Cam was standing. "Nonsense, this floor looks fine to me."

"It's your decision," said Cam, taking a step back.

"It is my decision, and I don't see anything wrong with this the way it is." Piper stamped on the floor, feeling the wood vibrate beneath her feet.

"But as your contractor, it's kind of my duty to inform you of things that could be unsafe," Cam went on.

"Unsafe? For fuck's sake, it's a floor in an attic that no one's going to use. You said yourself that the new owner will probably remodel it for his own needs. Let him do the floor."

"Again, your decision," Cam said, face starting to flush again, that pretty pink coming to her cheeks.

"This is safe as houses," said Piper. To illustrate her point she bent her knees and jumped as hard as she could onto the wooden floor, which creaked in protest but held just fine.

"Okay, okay," said Cam, holding her hands up in defeat.

Which was exactly the moment that Piper heard a crackling noise like electricity creeping along a wire.

She didn't have time to move, barely had time to breathe, before the floor disappeared from under her feet and her body plummeted through the hole, leaving her stomach behind to catch up with everything else.

CHAPTER ELEVEN

Cam's sides hurt from laughing.

"Get me out of here," Piper squealed.

"You look like a trapped insect," laughed Cam. Which was true. Piper's legs had disappeared through the floor, leaving only her torso in the attic. She was red with embarrassment, but obviously not hurt.

"Will you get me out," said Piper.

Cam put her hands on her hips. "What'll you give me if I do?" she teased.

"How about I don't give you a slap?"

Cam snorted another laugh. "You're in the position of weakness here, you do understand that, right?"

Piper sighed. "Fine. I'll buy lunch. Now will you help me out?"

Cam pretended to consider this with her hands on her hips. "Okay, I suppose," she said finally. She squatted down and held out her hand, just out of reach. "You know you really don't have to try so hard to impress me," she said.

Piper's blush deepened and a strange look crossed her face. "I've no idea what you're talking about."

Cam reached in, took both hands and yanked Piper out of the floor. "You don't need to impress me," she said out loud. Her hand skimmed the curve of Piper's waist to steady her as she came to her feet and suddenly Cam was feeling far too hot.

"I'm not trying to impress you," Piper said sourly. "You seem to be some kind of jinx on me. Every time you appear, I end up getting hurt."

"Are you hurt?" Cam asked, suddenly worried that she might have missed something.

"No," said Piper, looking down at herself. "Not hurt but definitely dirty. I'll need to grab a change of clothes before lunch."

"Sure," Cam said. "I'll finish up here and you go get changed. I'll meet you downstairs in ten minutes."

Piper walked across the squeaky floor to the door and Cam cleared her throat. "What?" Piper asked.

"Er, just wondering if we agreed that the floor panels need replacing?" asked Cam innocently. Then she ducked as Piper threw a roll of bin bags at her head, and laughed again.

As Piper disappeared to get changed, Cam dealt with some remaining rubbish, pushing some trunks to the walls so that she could see the real state of the floor.

It wasn't until she was right on the edge of the hole that Piper had made that she realized that the room below the hole must have been Lucy's, and therefore now Piper's, bedroom.

She glimpsed a curve of bare shoulder, skin delicate and white, before drawing back with a gasp.

Her heart started thudding in her chest and she swallowed hard. Peeking was wrong. Wrong in so many million ways that she couldn't even decide what was worse. She shook her head. Silly. Piper was a woman, she was a woman, it wasn't like it would be anything she hadn't seen before.

Something was pulling her toward that hole, dragging her gaze down, something inside her wanted to look and she had no idea why.

She battled with herself for what felt like forever, before finally, determinedly, walking away from the hole.

This was not Cam Fabbri, she told herself. She wasn't a peeper or a sneak or anything like that. She certainly wasn't about to spy on Piper through a hole in the floor. And why would she want to spy anyway?

"Cam?" Piper's voice drifted up the stairs.

Cam shook herself and blew out a hot breath. "Coming," she called back down.

The sun was shining down hot and hard when they got outside.

"Where's all this English rain that I've heard about?" Piper asked.

"You'd be surprised," said Cam, still slightly distracted by the mysterious pull of the hole in the floor. "We get our fair share of rain, but in the summer the drought's often bad enough that the government sets up a hosepipe ban."

"What's that?" frowned Piper.

"You know, you're not allowed to use the hosepipe in your garden? No watering the flowers, no washing your car, that sort of thing." Cam's eyes were on a figure loping across the common. "Sorry," she said. "There's something I need to deal with quickly. The cafe is right there, just go on in and tell Beth I sent you. She'll know my order."

Piper may have tried to say something, but Cam was already turning onto the grass and walking toward the figure.

❊ ❊ ❊

A little bell dinged as Piper pushed open the door to the small cafe and bookstore. Immediately she was assaulted by the smell of coffee and baking. Her mouth watered. A curly-haired woman looked up from behind the counter and then her face broke into a wide grin.

"You must be Piper," she said, coming out from behind her counter. "I should thank you for not bleeding all over my van. How's the hand?"

Piper relaxed immediately. Okay, so Beth was Canadian, but still, there was something about her that reminded her of home and she felt instantly at ease. "The hand's fine and I've got to apologize for Cam stealing your van. It was probably overkill to get stitches but..."

"But better safe than sorry," Beth filled in. "Come grab a seat at the counter and let's see what we can get you. I've got some fresh chocolate chip cookies just out of the oven and the lunch special is grilled cheese, what do you say to that?"

"With tomato soup?" Piper asked, stomach grumbling. She felt like she hadn't eaten properly in the last three days, which was probably true given the amount of empty baked bean cans in her trash.

"Can you serve grilled cheese without tomato soup?" Beth asked.

The bell over the door dinged again and they both turned to see Cam poking her head around, a brawny figure lurking behind her.

"Sorry, Piper," Cam said. "I need to deal with something at home. Are you okay having lunch here alone? Beth will look after you."

"Sure," Piper said, even though she felt strangely disappointed that Cam wasn't going to have lunch with her.

"Thanks," Cam said, quickly withdrawing her head and closing the door.

"And there you've uncovered our Cam's fatal flaw," Beth said, pouring a hot cup of coffee.

"What's that?" Piper asked.

"She never puts herself first. Ever," Beth explained. "That big guy behind her is one of her brothers, he'll be wanting her to move her van around or take a lamb to the vet or something. They always ask, and Cam always goes running."

"Another brother?" Piper asked. She was sure that the man behind the window wasn't the man she'd seen Cam waving at earlier.

Beth laughed. "There are six of them," she said. "The Fabbri boys are the local heart throbs, though two of them are happily married off by now."

"And what about Cam?" Piper found herself asking. "She's not a local heart throb?"

Beth paused, opened her mouth, closed it, then opened it again. "Cam's... picky, I suppose. She's definitely had her share of dates, but she's never found the one. Half of it's probably because the local boys don't like the idea of her being a contractor. The other half is probably because she's too busy running errands for her family to dedicate time to a relationship."

"She's never had a real relationship?" asked Piper. Her stomach was warm and she was being nosy, she knew that. Yet she couldn't quite stop herself from asking.

Beth laughed. "You can't ask me to spill all my best friend's secrets at once. Besides, you ask any more and I'll start to think you're interested. Let me grab a grilled cheese for you."

And it honestly wasn't until just that second that Piper realized that maybe she was interested. Then she immediately threw the thought away.

Sure, Cam was attractive. She was also fairly straight, or so Beth's comments about local boys led her to believe, an employee, and British. Not that her nationality disqualified her, but it did mean that she assumed Cam was rather attached to her family and her home and wouldn't be about to fly off to the States whenever Piper decided to go home.

What was she thinking? As if she'd ask Cam to fly home to the States with her. Of course she wouldn't.

Anyway, she was firmly on the rebound and busy changing her life, or so she told herself. Perhaps she was just busy being in the middle of a mid-life crisis. Either way, she shouldn't start a relationship.

Not that she was considering it.

"She is single though, if that's what you were asking," Beth said, coming back laden with delicious smelling plates.

"Oh, no, I mean..." Piper stumbled over her words.

"Dunno if she's into women though," Beth added thoughtfully. "It's never come up, though I don't see why she wouldn't be at least willing to give things a try. She's definitely open to new experiences. Still, I'd probably ask first at the very least."

"No, no," Piper said quickly. "I didn't mean that in the least, I mean, I didn't, not that she isn't attractive, I just meant, uh…"

Beth grinned. "Got it. You don't know what you meant. No problem. It's not like I'm going to say anything."

"You're not?" Piper asked suspiciously.

"My lips are sealed," said Beth. "You'd be surprised how much working here is like being the unofficial therapist for the village. I learned long ago that it's certainly not worth my skin to be going around repeating conversations I've heard. This is a small village, word gets around fast."

"I'll bet."

"Like I know you never met Lucy but she was your only living relative and you're modernizing the house and looking to sell it."

"Or rent it," Piper put in.

Beth shrugged. "We'll see."

"What's that supposed to mean?"

"It's supposed to mean that I came here nine years ago for a four day vacation," Beth said. "Now look at me."

"You could go home any time," said Piper, picking up a piece of grilled cheese.

"But I don't want to," said Beth. "Sutton's Walk grows on you. It's insidious. I don't think I could leave even if I did want to."

"I have a life back in the States," said Piper firmly. "And I'll be heading back in a few weeks." To find a new job and furnish that damn apartment finally, she added in her head.

"Please yourself," Beth said, picking up some silverware from a basket by her side and offering Piper a spoon. "Oh, she likes horror books and ginger biscuits."

"Who does?" Piper asked, confused.

"Cam, of course," laughed Beth. "She's not immune to a pint and she's endlessly generous and has a wicked sense of humor. Oh, and she adores animals. That should give you enough to work with."

"I'm not going to date your best friend," said Piper, taking a bite of her lunch.

"We'll see," Beth said again.

And Piper's mouth was too full to reply.

CHAPTER TWELVE

Cam walked up the front path in the early morning sunshine, her mind on what she was going to do to fix the house's bathroom problem, when a voice brought her up short.

"You're in and out of there like a dog in a butcher's shop."

"Morning Arthur," said Cam, forcing herself to smile.

"She hired you then, I suppose."

"She did." It had been a week now and Piper seemed to be happy with the arrangement, so Cam was too. Piper also had refrained from cutting, breaking, grazing, or blistering any part of herself for the last few days, something Cam was grateful for.

"So, when's she selling it?" demanded Arthur.

Cam sighed. "I don't know." For some reason the thought of Piper selling the house left her feeling bereft. Not like herself. She knew that the possibility was a very real one, but right now, right here, she had a job she enjoyed with a boss she enjoyed.

Why borrow trouble from tomorrow, as her father would say.

"It'll be to some outsider, no doubt," Arthur grumbled.

"Who do you know in the village that can afford a house like this?" Cam asked. "Besides, everyone you know already has a house because they live in it. So by default, the house'll have to be sold to an outsider, won't it?"

"Doesn't have to be one of them rich city bankers."

Cam rolled her eyes. "Then put a request in with Piper, maybe she'll take your views into account."

Arthur's wrinkled face brightened. "D'you think she will?"

"No, Arthur, no, I don't. But it's always worth a try."

He sighed and sniffed and Cam's heart jolted a little.

"You doing alright?"

"Fine, fine," he said, though he didn't really sound like himself. Cam cursed herself. She hadn't checked in on him and certainly hadn't visited him for the last week.

"Oh good," she said. "Because Piper was wondering if you want to come over for tea and biscuits later this morning."

"Really?" Arthur said, standing up straighter.

"Yes." Well, she would be as soon as Cam told her about it.

"Righty-o then, I'll see you then. For elevenses, would it be?"

Cam grinned, nodded, then escaped into the house.

The house was calm and quiet and she stood still for a second. The smell had changed now. Slowly, slowly Lucy's presence was being overtaken by Piper's. There was the faint hint of flowered perfume, the smell of toast, the smell of Piper, she guessed.

"In here," came a shout from the living room.

Cam followed the voice and found Piper curled up on an armchair, blonde hair tucked behind her ears, a batch of letters clutched in her hands.

"What have you got there?"

Piper looked up and her chin was sharp, her cheekbones high, her eyes sparkling blue and Cam suddenly realized that actually, Piper was very beautiful. Not in a traditional kind of way, she was a little too asymmetric for that, but beautiful nonetheless. Her heart wavered in her chest and made her feel a little light headed.

"You'll never guess what I found," Piper grinned. "Lucy's love letters."

"Love letters?" Cam said, dropping down into an armchair of her own. "No way. I told you. Luce had no time for men."

"And wanted a donkey," finished Piper. "I know, I know. But I'm not making this up. There was a bundle of them all tied up with a ribbon in the back of one of the drawers in that dresser.

They're definitely addressed to Lucy."

Cam got up and went to bend over Piper's chair to get a look. Sure enough, the letters were all addressed to 'My Dear Luce.' "Who are they from?" she asked.

"That's the mystery," Piper said, turning over the sheet she was reading. "They're all signed off 'Your Twinkle-Toed Lover.' I don't even know what that means."

Cam laughed. "Twinkle-toed means he was a good dancer is all."

"Whoever he was, this was pretty serious. I mean, look at these." She turned over another sheet and Cam had to bend even closer to decipher the cramped writing. Piper's hair brushed against her cheek and she felt a warmth as Piper breathed out.

"Jesus, there's some saucy stuff in there, alright," Cam said, snapping back upright again and blushing.

"What?" Piper laughed. "It's not like our generation invented sex, you know."

"Yes, but come on, I knew Lucy my whole life. She was like a grandmother to me."

"Right, right," said Piper, shuffling the letters back into order. "Sorry, I see how that could be awkward."

"A wee bit," Cam said, perching on the edge of the coffee table.

"It'd be nice to try and figure out who this guy was," said Piper.

"Are you serious?" Cam said. "Your aunt was ninety-odd when she died. Chances are that this guy is, well, worm-food, not to put too fine a point on it."

"Maybe he's not though." Piper flicked to the end of the pile of letters.

"What happened?" Cam asked curiously. "I mean, obviously Lucy didn't marry this lover, so why didn't they get together? What does the last letter say?"

"Nothing," said Piper. "It's like all the others, no sign that anything's wrong, or about to be wrong."

"Huh."

"Maybe it was the war or something," Piper said, then shook her head. "No, the letters are dated in the late forties, the war was long over by then." She sighed. "Maybe there are other relatives out there with Lucy's letters wondering what happened. We should try and track them down."

"You watch way too much telly. You don't honestly think that all English people know each other do you?" Cam teased just as her eye caught something.

"Of course not," Piper said. "But we could do a little detective work. Find something out for sure."

"Actually," Cam said, "you might not be wrong about us all knowing each other or of each other." She bent over to pick up an envelope that must have fallen out of the pile of letters. "Look at this," she said, holding it up.

"It's addressed to Lucy."

"Yes, but there's no stamp on it." Cam paused for a second, but when Piper didn't cotton on, she continued. "That means it was hand delivered. It must have come from someone in the village or at least from one of the neighboring villages. Whoever this man was, he wasn't from far away."

"So we could try and find him."

"You could try and find him," Cam said. "I have a job to do here, remember? Or don't you want fancy mixer taps and a shower?"

"Fine, fine," grumbled Piper. She reached for the envelope, took it and promptly dropped it.

Cam bent to pick it up at exactly the same time as Piper herself did. Their heads clacked together with a startling sound and Cam bit her lip as her eyes watered in pain.

"Ouch."

"Sorry," Piper said, rubbing at her own head.

"And here was me thinking you'd outgrown that clumsiness," Cam said. "It's fine, no harm done."

Piper stood up and the pile of letters that had been on her lap cascaded down onto the dusty carpet. "Oh crap," she said.

"I'm not sure I want to be bending down again now," said Cam, still rubbing at her head.

"You go on into the kitchen and make some coffee so we can get started with work. I'll get these," Piper said, her voice muffled as she bent over to collect the papers.

Cam was on her way to the kitchen when she remembered her impromptu invitation to Arthur and turned back to tell Piper about it.

Piper was bending over to pick up the letters, her long legs and behind tightly encased in leggings, a long shirt falling off one shoulder, her hair messed up, and for unexplained reasons, Cam's heart started to pound in her chest.

Piper stood up, cheeks flushing from being upside down and caught Cam's eye. Cam blinked.

"Keep looking at me like that, and I'll start to think you mean it," Piper said with a laugh.

It was on the tip of Cam's tongue to say 'mean what?' But she didn't. Mostly because deep down she knew exactly what Piper meant, she just really, really wasn't ready to hear it yet.

She cleared her throat.

"Uh, just so you know, I invited Arthur over for elevenses."

Piper frowned. "For eleven of what?"

"No, for elevenses. For tea and biscuits. At around eleven."

"Wait, you have snacks named after time? How does that work? Do we get twos and threes as well?"

"No," laughed Cam. "Just elevenses. I know Arthur can be a bit of a nosy old busy-body, but he's lonely really. He's a nice old stick when you get to know him. Interesting too." She grimaced a little thinking of the scrapbooks. "Well, mostly."

"I guess it pays to make friends with the neighbors," said Piper. "Especially when he's going to be living next to a building site pretty soon. Okay, sure. Why not?" She paused a second and wrinkled her nose.

"What?" asked Cam. The wrinkled nose thing was pretty cute. There was no harm in admitting that to herself, surely. After all, that was an objective thing. It was objectively cute.

"I'm going to have to brave the village shop," said Piper.

"I thought you'd already been," Cam said. "Please tell me that you're not still only eating baked beans and dog food."

"I never ate dog food. I swear. And I have been to the shop. Just

I bought normal things like ham and bread, frozen pizza, stuff that I knew what it was."

"And the problem now is...?" Cam asked.

"Now I'm going to have to shop in the biscuit section. You do know that in my country a biscuit is something entirely different and we eat it for breakfast, right?"

"I'd eat regular biscuits for breakfast given half the chance," Cam said. Then she grinned. "You can do it. Think of it as an adventure. Unless you really want me to come with you?"

She didn't know why she'd asked that. Piper definitely didn't need her help to go twenty meters down the road to the shops. It was just that, for a second, she'd thought that being with Piper, staying with Piper, would be nice.

They did have fun.

Piper had a good sense of humor.

She was wicked funny.

And, well, Cam was the one that had invited Arthur after all.

"No," Piper sighed. "I'd better do it alone. Besides, don't you have bathrooms to plan?"

"I do," Cam said, wondering why after all of that she now felt actually relieved that Piper didn't want her to come.

"Go on then. Coffee, then shopping, then a plan for the bathrooms." Piper stacked Lucy's love letters in a neat pile on the table. "Do you think we could fit in a jacuzzi?"

"What do you think this is, Essex?" Cam said.

"Huh?"

"Don't worry about it, it'd take too long to explain," Cam sighed. They were very different. Sure, Piper made her laugh. But there were far more differences than similarities. Which somehow didn't make her feel better at all.

CHAPTER THIRTEEN

"Just don't get him started on the war," Cam hissed as Piper opened the front door to Arthur.

Piper glared at her then smiled at Arthur. "Come on in, neighbor, it's good to see you."

"It's nice to be back in the old place," Arthur grunted with effort as he stepped over the threshold. "Been doing some cleaning, I see. Luce was a bit of a pack-rat. Mind you, we all are in our generation. The result of rationing, I s'pose. Or the threat of having your house bombed and everything you own blown up."

He tottered down the corridor to the kitchen and Cam leaned in close. "How did you do that?" she whispered. "I tell you not to get him started on the war and you manage it in one short sentence. You'll have your ear talked off now."

And Piper really did want to say something in response, but Cam was leaning in awfully close in the darkness of the hallway and Piper could smell her skin and she was suddenly having trouble breathing.

There was a second there when she was sure that Cam must be able to hear her heart beating, loud and echoing. But Cam just tilted an eyebrow upward and Piper plastered a smile on her face.

"Calm down, it'll be fine. And Arthur can talk about what he wants, he's the guest."

Cam stuck her tongue out, smooth and pink, then danced off down the corridor calling to Arthur that she was going to put the kettle on.

Piper leaned back against the cool wall for a second, getting her breath back.

She'd had a sneaky suspicion for a couple of days now. Ever since she'd assured Beth that she was certainly not going to date her best friend.

The truth of the matter was that she was developing the teensiest, tiniest crush on Cam Fabbri.

Which was understandable really, given the circumstances.

Here she was, fresh out of a relationship, her hormones already looking for new interest. And here was Cam, a single, attractive woman in a tiny village. It was natural really that Piper had developed an interest. Inevitable even.

Not that she had any intention of doing anything about it.

Well, probably not.

Not unless something happened to tell her that Cam was actually interested in women.

Not that she was.

Unless she was.

And then maybe...

Piper took a deep, cleansing breath. No. She was going to behave herself. She wasn't a schoolgirl and she certainly wasn't someone who played with hearts. Cam was a good woman and a good contractor, which was rather important just at the moment.

That was all she needed. Kiss the builder and have her run away and never return.

She snorted a laugh to herself and started walking toward the kitchen, nearly tripping over her own feet and having to grasp the wall to steady herself.

"I was just saying that you'll be selling this place now, won't you?" said Arthur.

The kettle was already close to boiling and Piper could hear the water bubbling. "Er, well, probably," said Piper.

"Want a biscuit, Arthur?" Cam said.

"Dunno, what you got?"

"Well, it might be a tough decision," said Cam. Piper could tell that she was close to laughing. Cam picked up a bag and put it on the table. "Take your pick," she told Arthur.

"Cripes, there's enough biscuits here to feed half the Foreign Legion," Arthur said, emptying out the bag onto the table. "Did Mary at the shop have a sale on?"

"No," Cam said, turning around and placing a large mug of tea in front of Arthur. "I sent Piper biscuit shopping. This is just what she came home with."

"Look, your biscuit selections are confusing," Piper said, feeling the need to come to her own defense.

"No matter, love," said Arthur. "Better to have too much than too little. I'll have a Garibaldi if you're offering."

Cam held out the packet to him before giving Piper her coffee and then settling down at the kitchen table with some tea of her own.

"Selling the place then," Arthur continued.

"Jesus, you're like a dog with a rat, Art," said Cam.

"Don't call me that," grumbled Arthur. "And I got a right to know what's going on, I'm right next door, after all." He glared at Piper. "Who're you selling to? Not one of them city types, is it?"

Piper blinked. "Uh, I have no idea actually. I haven't even put the place up for sale yet."

"Then watch what you're doing, young lady."

She looked from Arthur to Cam and then back again. "Why?"

Cam sighed. "Arthur's worried that you're going to sell the house to an outsider. Which is somewhat of an inevitability, as I've told him. What he doesn't want is you selling the place to someone as a holiday home or a weekend house, someone rich and from London."

"Someone who won't be part of the village and who'll drive up house prices," Arthur added.

"Oh, I had no idea that was a problem," Piper said. She hadn't put much thought into selling the house at all.

"Well it is," said Arthur. "These tourists come in and want to buy a house to use three weekends out of the year and then village people, our people, can't afford to buy a place of their own. Just ask Cam over there, living in a van in her parents' farmyard."

Piper's eyebrows rocketed up so far she was afraid she might lose them. "Is that true?" she asked Cam. "You live in a van?"

"It's a nice van," Cam said, blushing.

"See what I mean," Arthur said. "So just you be careful who you sell to."

"Yes," said Piper. "Of course. I'll be careful, I don't know how much I can control who buys the place, but I'll do what I can."

Arthur sniffed. "Well, it'll be easier now that you've got an estate agent in the family," he said to Cam.

"A what?" asked Piper.

"An estate agent," explained Cam. "Someone who sells houses. My brother Donte just started working for one in the next village over."

"Oh, a realtor," Piper said. She grinned. "Perfect. Get Donte to come over or send his boss or whatever and we can talk about the possibilities. That sounds far better than letting a stranger deal with things."

Arthur grunted in approval then began to feed pieces of his biscuit to a slobbering Billy who'd been waiting patiently. "What happened to your hand?" he asked Piper.

And Cam started to explain, much to Arthur's amusement.

LUCY'S LETTERS HAD been on Piper's mind all day. She just couldn't shake the thought of them. Or rather, she couldn't shake the thought of a lost love, a romance with an unhappy ending.

But then maybe all romances had unhappy endings, didn't they, she thought as she cleared the last boxes out of the large cabinet in the living room.

Dust spun in the air and the light was deep orange, fading

almost into gray as evening crept in.

She should have asked Arthur about Lucy, she realized now. He'd been in the village long enough, maybe he'd remember who Lucy's suitor had been.

Upstairs, she could hear Cam banging on pipes and otherwise making her presence known and it was surprising just how comforting it was to have her there. Or just to have someone else in the house.

She sighed as she flicked through old bank statements for accounts that no longer existed.

She did hope that Cam wasn't going to be a problem. Or rather, she hoped that she wasn't going to be a problem with Cam.

It wasn't like she was going to jump the woman or anything. It was just that every time she walked into a room Piper's heart gave a little pitter-patter. Which shouldn't have to be a problem. Piper scratched her nose. Maybe she'd sign up for some internet dating or something when she got back to the States. Put herself out there again.

"About done?"

The words made Piper jump and she turned to see Cam leaning against the door-frame. She grinned. "Getting to quitting time, huh?"

"Could be. A last cup of tea and then we'll start again in the morning?"

Cam's long hair was escaping from its bun, trailing pieces that tickled at her collarbone. Piper gulped, nodded, then busied herself brushing dust from her hands and pants so that she didn't have to look in Cam's direction.

"I'll get the kettle on then," said Cam, a touch of lightness in her voice that Piper thought might be a laugh.

By the time Piper got to the kitchen she found Cam standing in front of the kitchen table, a vast assortment of biscuits arrayed before her.

"It's really not my fault," Piper said. "I mean, there's biscuits named after Italian leaders, French kings, words that I've no idea what they mean. I just got the ones I thought would be okay."

"Well, you did get these," Cam said, holding up a packet of ginger biscuits. "So you didn't do too badly."

"They're your favorites," Piper blurted out without thinking. Then she blushed. "Beth told me."

"So you got them for me?" Cam asked, a strange look on her face.

Piper nodded and the kettle whistled.

"That's the sweetest thing…" said Cam, voice quiet.

For a second neither of them moved and Piper was entranced with the shiny thickness of Cam's hair and the delicate curve where her neck met her shoulder. The kettle shrieked insistently.

"I, uh, should get that," Piper said, swallowing and pulling herself away.

She switched the kettle off and reached up to pull down a mug. But as she opened the door and pulled at the first cup, another caught up in the jam and before she knew it, a mug was hurtling toward her face.

"Here."

Cam's hand shot out and caught the cup just in time, placing it gently on the counter. And when Piper turned to thank her she found that Cam was a whole lot closer than she'd thought.

Very close.

Too close.

Close enough that she could see each individual eyelash, close enough that she could smell sweat and soap, close enough that she could see the way soft down covered her cheeks. Close enough that it was far too dangerous and she should pull away.

But then Cam was standing up on tiptoes and coming closer and Piper didn't dare breathe for fear of disturbing the world.

Cam's dark eyes were wide open and Piper thought she might fall into them until Cam's lips brushed hers and then she knew she was going to fall into something and it scared the hell out of her and excited her all at the same time.

She closed her eyes and leaned in, wanting more contact, wanting more of this, more exploration, more of Cam.

Then Cam was pulling away, a look of absolute horror on her face and Piper couldn't say a word as Cam snatched her bag from the table and ran out of the kitchen. The front door slammed a moment later and Piper didn't move for at least another five minutes.

CHAPTER FOURTEEN

Every evening when the cafe closed up, Beth would walk herself over to The Duck and Pony and have a drink. It was her one vice, so she said, and she was very faithful to the habit. Which was why Cam knew exactly where to find her.

The pub was buzzing with early evening chatter as usual, and Beth was in her usual corner table. It was only Cam that was unusual.

"Oh my God, oh my God, oh my God," she blurted out as she sat down.

Her legs were shaking, her stomach felt sick and she hadn't allowed herself a second to think about what had just happened. She'd shot straight across the village green praying that this wasn't the one night that Beth had gotten ill or decided to take up yoga classes or anything else.

"Are you hurt?" Beth said, straightening up.

"No," said Cam. "Oh my God."

"You're a very funny color," said Beth helpfully. "Would you like a drink?"

Cam slammed her mouth shut to stop herself saying 'oh my God' one more time and nodded vigorously.

Beth got up and was back in an instant, pushing a glass in front of Cam.

"Whiskey?" Cam said, eyeing it doubtfully.

"Rod had already started pouring it," said Beth. "Said you

looked like you'd seen a ghost and wanted to know if Lucy was playing tricks on you up in the house."

Cam swallowed, shook her head, then decided that Rod was a wise man and she should trust his instincts. So she threw back the drink in one swallow, then started choking so hard that tears streamed down her face.

"Calm down," Beth said, handing her a tissue. "Want another?"

Cam shook her head. She could feel the whiskey burning in her stomach and her hands felt steadier. Well they did right up until she remembered why she was here and what had just happened, then they started trembling all over again. "Oh my God," she moaned.

Beth closed one eye and peered at her carefully with the other. "Let me guess," she said, opening her other eye again. "Piper hit on you."

Cam's eyebrows shot up in surprise. "No," she said slowly. "Not exactly."

"Then what exactly?" Beth asked.

"I hit on Piper."

"What?" Beth shrieked.

"Jesus, keep your damn voice down," said Cam looking over her shoulders. "You know what this place is like. It's all ears and wagging tongues."

"What?" Beth said in a whisper-shriek.

Cam swallowed and wished now she'd agreed to another drink. Beth sighed, got up and went to the bar.

What had she done? She had no idea why she'd done it. It had just been a moment of madness. Yes, that was going to be her excuse. If Piper ever let her in the house again, that was. Chances were she was going to be banned for life after pulling a stunt like that. So no job, no cottage, just life in a van in her parents' farmyard and...

"You're starting to hyperventilate," said Beth, putting a pint of beer down in front of her. "Now tell me what happened, slowly."

Cam opened her mouth and the words came spilling out so

fast that she couldn't stop them. "I kissed her. Just kissed her. Just right there in the kitchen out of nowhere I was standing there and she was standing there and a cup nearly fell on her head and then I caught it and then I kissed her."

"Right," said Beth, smirking a little.

"You don't understand," said Cam, calming down a little since she didn't want to be the only one freaking out and Beth was being oddly panic-free.

"Yes, I do. You kissed her."

"Yes, but, well, I shouldn't have. She's my boss, first. She's American. She's a woman. I'm not that way at all. I shouldn't have."

"So you don't kiss Americans then?" Beth asked. "What about Canadians?"

"That's not what I meant," said Cam. "I just meant that she's an outsider and she's going to be going home sooner rather than later, that's all."

"And all those excuses come before the fact that you're 'not that way at all' which I assume is a roundabout English way of you saying you hadn't considered bisexuality?"

"Uh, I, er..." Cam felt herself blushing. "I guess not."

"Right," said Beth. "Well, one thing at a time, I suppose. Did you like it?"

"What kind of a question is that?" Cam screeched. But her head was reeling with the memory of how it had felt when their lips met, of the pulse-pounding excitement of that one still second when she'd dared to move, dared to do something just for herself.

"A good one," Beth said. "Did you like it?"

Cam considered lying, but it really wasn't in her personality. So she shrugged and nodded.

"Okay, that's one thing dealt with. There's nothing wrong with being bi, or anywhere else on the sexuality spectrum and I'm sure you know that."

"I do."

"Would it bother you to be interested in women as well as

men?"

"I haven't thought about it."

"Well think about it now."

Cam sighed and rubbed at her face, the alcohol was definitely having an effect now. "I guess not. I suppose it doesn't matter, does it? Whoever you fall in love with is just a person inside a skin, what the outsides look like shouldn't be an issue."

"Great. So no huge coming out drama. Glad to hear it," said Beth. "As for the other stuff, well, did Piper like it?"

Cam frowned, trying to remember. "I don't know."

"Did she kiss you back?"

"I don't know."

Beth drank some of her beer. "Well, I guess in that case you have two choices. Either the two of you pretend it never happened and chalk it up to experience, or you talk it out. Either way, you'll find out tomorrow morning when you show up to work."

"Oh god," groaned Cam, thinking about showing up on the doorstep in the morning.

"Calm down, Cam. Things happen. And in the grand scheme of things, this was nothing. Less than nothing. Piper doesn't strike me as the kind of woman who's going to freak out that this happened, or that's going to spread gossip about you. So what's the worst that could happen?"

"She fires me."

"She won't. If she does, she's an idiot."

"It was just a moment of madness. I don't know what came over me. I've never done anything like that before."

"Well maybe you should," grinned Beth. "Live a little, experiment a little, you never know what you like until you try it."

Cam drank some beer. She was definitely calming down. She still couldn't believe what she'd done. Couldn't believe that she'd even thought about doing it. It was less the fact that Piper was a woman and more the fact that Piper was Piper.

Confident, funny, bright, beautiful Piper.

She imagined that she'd feel much the same way if she'd grabbed Brad Pitt in the kitchen and dared to kiss him. Not that Brad Pitt spent a lot of time in Sutton's Walk, but still.

"Come on," Beth said. "Drink up and we'll have another. You can drown your sorrows a bit. Leave tomorrow for tomorrow, it'll all get sorted out. Just you wait and see."

That was what she was afraid of, things being sorted out. She'd just have to apologize, that's all there was to it. Explain that she was an idiot and had gone briefly mental and that she was sorry and it wouldn't happen again.

She just hoped that Piper wouldn't be too angry.

❊ ❊ ❊

"What did I tell you," Joey squealed. "Ms. Right! And an Englishwoman. Is she a lady? Or, I don't know, a countess or something? Oh, is she an ice queen and you need to break through her shell?"

"Jesus, Joe, calm the fuck down," Piper said, lying back on the bed. "I'm trying to figure all this out."

"What's to figure out?" Joey laughed. "Making out is a good thing, a great thing, you deserve some fun after Lex."

Piper sighed. Maybe she shouldn't have called Joey immediately, but she'd panicked and wanted to talk and Joey was the only person she could call. "She's not a lady, she's just a regular woman. She's the contractor working on the house."

"Oooo, sexy. Is she all calloused hands and flannel shirts?"

"Not exactly," Piper said. "She is off limits though."

"Pooh! You're no fun."

"Joey, I'm here for weeks at most, I can't go getting involved with a woman just to have some fun. Who does that? I take what I want and then leave her here when I'm done? That sounds terrible."

"No, of course not," Joey said. "But you could have a mutually beneficial relationship where you both discuss the limits of what's happening and agree to both have some fun. That's what generally happens."

Piper groaned. "That's not my style."

"Then make it your style," Joey pushed. "Seriously, Pipes. You never have any fun. You're just out of a decade-long relationship, when are you going to sow your wild oats? And she was the one that kissed you, so she must be into this."

"I wouldn't swear to that," said Piper, closing her eyes and seeing the look on Cam's face all over again. "She ran away like she'd been scalded right after."

"Probably just freaked out that she'd dared to do it."

"Or weirded out because she's actually straight and some kind of magic or something forced her into it and now she's realized that it was all a mistake."

It was Joey's turn to sigh. "Okay, okay. I get that there are issues here. If you want my honest advice, Pipes, you need to talk to her. But you don't need me to tell you that. You can't go around wanting to be a mind reader and trying to figure things out by yourself. You need to start a conversation about this. With her."

"Or just ignore that it happened," said Piper. "I could do that too."

"You could," allowed Joey. "If that's what you both want, I suppose. I'm just saying that you shouldn't assume things are a certain way without talking about them first. Maybe it was all a mistake and you should forget about it."

"Exactly—"

"Or maybe she's looking for a little fun just like you are and you can have a great time together for a few weeks."

"Joe—"

"Or maybe she's the one and you're destined to be together and move into the Big House and have tons of servants and everyone will call you ma'am."

"I have mentioned that this isn't Downton Abbey, haven't I?"

"A girl can dream," laughed Joey. "And you need to talk things through with this Camilla. That or just screw her senseless."

"Bad taste, Joe," Piper said.

But Joey was right about one thing. Come the morning she was going to have to deal with the fall out here. And as much as she'd tentatively enjoyed that kiss, she knew that she couldn't commit to anything. It wouldn't be fair on anyone. Besides, Cam didn't want this. She'd seen the look on her face, she'd been horrified.

Billy climbed up onto the bed and Piper didn't have the energy to push him down again. So she curled up and put her head on his huge flank.

She really wished she could just disappear right now and leave that kiss as a beautiful memory. Instead, she was going to have to have a very uncomfortable conversation in the morning.

CHAPTER FIFTEEN

It took every ounce of courage that Cam had to walk up the garden path and let herself into the house. With every step that she took she was sure that Piper was going to open the door and shout at her, throw her out, fire her.

Instead, she got into the house like nothing had happened at all. Her legs were trembling and she felt like she might be sick.

"Thank fuck," came a voice from the dining room.

Cam frowned. "Piper?" She turned into the dining room and saw Piper with a towering pile of boxes leaning against a wall. "What on Earth are you doing?"

"Bit off far more than I can chew," Piper said from behind the stack of boxes. "Could you grab a couple off the top please?"

Cam took the top three boxes and put them on the dining table. "How long exactly have you been propping up the wall like that?"

"Can I plead the fifth on that?"

"You're not in America."

Piper pulled a face. "Ten minutes maybe?"

"Glad I came along at the right moment then," Cam laughed. "And I'd just like to say that it's probably a better idea to wait until someone else is around before picking up heavy things or climbing ladders, or, in your case, opening cans of beans."

"Very funny," said Piper. "I was going to drop the boxes, but then I couldn't remember what was inside them and didn't want to break anything. Besides, I knew you'd be here soon. Coffee? Tea?"

"Nice to know how much you depend on me. Tea would be nice."

It wasn't until she was following Piper through to the kitchen and stroking Billy's nose that she remembered that she was supposed to be terrified.

"Oh no," Piper said, turning to get cups and seeing her face. "You going to freak out again?"

"You should fire me," Cam said miserably.

"And be stuck holding boxes up against a wall all day? No, thanks."

Cam took a deep breath and pushed herself to speak. She'd been practicing, she'd practically been up all night, running through what she was going to say if she got a chance to speak, praying that Piper would at least hear her out.

And here was Piper making her tea like it was any other morning.

"I crossed a line and I'm truly sorry. I don't know what came over me last night, but that's absolutely no excuse, I shouldn't have done what I did and if you'd prefer that I left, I'd totally understand."

She looked up to find Piper frowning at her, kettle in hand. "Why would I want you to leave?" she asked. Then she shook her head. "No, hold on, back up a second here."

"Piper, I mean it—"

Piper put the kettle down and turned to face her. "You're talking like you did something horrific. Can we be adults here for a second?"

Cam nodded. What difference did it make? These were not the reactions she'd been expecting.

"Cam, you kissed me, and, let's be honest, I kissed you right on back. There was no coercion, no lack of consent, two grown adult women kissed each other and that's all there is to it. There's no reason for you to quit or even feel bad. We all make mistakes, Cam. I've definitely made plenty of them myself."

"You're being kind, but—"

"No, I'm being honest. Listen, this could be awkward, I get that. But it doesn't have to be. We've both got a good sense of humor, so why can't we laugh this off? Just chalk it up as one of those things that happens sometimes? We screwed up, but it shouldn't matter because we're both mature enough to handle it. Right?"

Cam took a breath to argue but then realized that she couldn't. There was nothing to argue. "You're right," she said. "I'm still sorry though."

"The English are always sorry about everything, though the Canadians might be worse," Piper said, picking up the kettle again. "There's nothing to be sorry for. Why don't we just forget it ever happened?"

Relief filled Cam's stomach. "Okay, I can do that."

"Perfect," Piper grinned. "Let's have that tea then and finish up. We've got a lot to do before this afternoon."

THE FIRST OF the big trucks pulled up outside. "They're here," Piper called out.

"Everything is ready, don't worry," Cam said, opening up the front door. She waved as the men climbed down off the truck.

"They're just taking the junk," Piper said. "Be careful they don't take anything from the donate pile."

"In that case, I'll take this one first," said a booming voice as Cam was lifted off her feet. She squealed and then saw a look of horror and confusion pass over Piper's face.

"Put me down, you eejit," she said, kicking her feet until Casmiro deposited her back on the ground.

"I'm guessing you know each other?" Piper asked.

Cam grinned. "Piper, this is my brother Casmiro, Cas, this is Piper."

"Pleased to meet you," Cas said, holding out a huge hand.

"Another brother?" Piper asked faintly.

"There are six of us," said Cas. "Well, six plus one, if you count this little one here." He rubbed Cam's hair and she grimaced which made Piper laugh. "I'm usually up on the farm, but Cam said you needed help getting all this to the tip, so here I am."

"What's a tip?" Piper asked.

"The place where you take all the rubbish. Trash," Cam hastily corrected herself.

"And we're in a bit of a hurry before it closes, so I'd better get on with it," Cas said. "It's all this stuff here, right?"

"Just up to the edge of the grass," said Cam. "Everything else is for the donation pile and they should be here any time soon."

"Got it," Cas said. "We'll get on with it then. See you for tea, Cam."

"He'll want tea too?" Piper asked.

"We must be thoroughly confusing for you," Cam said. "He means food, dinner. He'll see me at dinner time."

"At your parents' house?"

Cam groaned. "Yeah, I see how that looks. But we nearly always eat at home, all of us, even the married ones. Partly because of mum's cooking. But mostly because that's what we always do, it's just tradition, I suppose."

For an instant she imagined Piper sitting around the farmyard table, joking with her brothers, laughing with her mother, talking with her father, and her heart gave a jolt.

"Let's get out of the way and have some tea and biscuits," Piper interrupted the thought. "I'm getting used to this whole biscuit thing."

Inside the house, things were starting to change. With the junk and donation stuff out, the space was bigger, lighter and airier. The smell of wood polish and Piper's perfume was everywhere and Cam could feel the tightness in her stomach as she breathed in the scent.

A tightness that she couldn't help even though she knew it shouldn't be there. Piper had been so reasonable. So good-humored and nice about what had happened. Nicer than Cam thought she deserved.

"Penny for your thoughts?" Piper said.

She was standing by the kitchen window, a smudge of dirt on her cheek and her hair messed up. She almost took Cam's breath away and that made her feel even worse, even more confused.

"Have you done it before?" she asked before she could stop herself.

"Done what before?" said Piper, pouring water into the kettle. "Made tea? Yes. Definitely. Some might even say that I'm getting quite good at it now."

She should let it go. She should pretend she'd said nothing. Except she couldn't. She had to know. "Kissed a woman, I meant?"

There was a clatter as Piper dropped the kettle into the sink. "Obviously, I have."

"Obviously?"

"I told you about my ex," Piper said, turning around. She looked calmer than Cam thought she really was.

"About Lex?"

Piper's face creased into a frown. "Yes. Lex. Alexandra. My partner. My ex."

And now it was Cam's turn to frown. "I thought... I thought Lex was a man. You know, like Lex Luthor."

"You thought I dated a comic book super-villain?"

"No, well, kind of..."

But it was too late, Piper was laughing and then so was Cam. Laughing until they dissolved into teary heaps at the kitchen table.

"Jesus," Piper said, wiping her eyes. "Have a biscuit. Go on." She pushed the package toward Cam and got up to put the kettle on.

"What happened?" Cam asked. "If you don't mind me asking."

"With me and Lex?" Piper sighed. "She found someone else. A student of hers."

Cam could see how much that hurt just from the look on Piper's face. "I'm sorry."

"So am I," said Piper. "She was my life for ten years. That's a long time."

It was an intimate confession and one Cam felt the need to return. She looked down at the table. "I haven't," she said.

"Haven't what?"

"Before, when I asked you if you'd kissed a woman before." Cam swallowed. "I, uh, I haven't. Well, hadn't, I suppose."

"Well, you did well for your first time," said Piper.

Cam forced a laugh then changed the subject because the air was starting to feel heavy. Very heavy. "This place is looking good. I've almost got the renovation plans ready to go, so I'll bring them over tomorrow. We can get the last of the big cleaning done and then we should be good to start."

"Great," said Piper, pouring tea. "I can't wait to take a proper shower at last."

"It's going to be a while before that happens. Oh, and I asked Donte to come by tomorrow morning to take a look at the place. He said that they should be able to give you an idea of the worth of the house as well as how much rent you could expect if you decide to go that route."

"Excellent," said Piper, bringing tea over to the table. "In that case, we should have a toast." She passed one cup to Cam and held up her own. "To working together."

"To working together," Cam said.

And the light was catching in Piper's blonde hair and the summer air was coming in through the window and Cam knew that she'd been lucky. Someone else could have reacted badly to what had happened the night before. But with Piper, all was forgiven and forgotten.

She was lucky, but that didn't change the fact that something had changed. Something big had changed. Because sitting here right now, with Piper's dancing blue eyes and dimpled smile, there was absolutely nothing Cam wanted more than to kiss her again.

CHAPTER SIXTEEN

The phone call came at three in the morning and woke Piper out of a sleep so deep she couldn't remember where she was.

It was a scramble to find her phone, and when she did, her heart sped up and her stomach sank and then she buried the mobile in a pile of blankets and tried hard to ignore it.

Lex.

A month ago she'd have snapped up the phone. A month ago she'd have wanted nothing more than to hear Lex's voice. But now something had changed and she wasn't quite sure what it was. It was three in the morning, for fuck's sake, she didn't have the energy to analyze what had changed.

She screwed her eyes shut as the phone vibrated in the sheets and then stopped.

One breath, two breaths, and the phone started ringing again.

Groaning, Piper sat up properly, switched the light on and shoved the phone inside a pillow on the opposite side of the bed. At least that dimmed the sound. Then she folded her arms and rested her head against the wall.

What could Lex want?

She could see her now, dark hair tangled in the sheets, long fingers delicately holding a phone that seemed impossibly small in her big hands. She could feel the touch of those hands, could feel the softness of them, the insistence of them. She half-closed her eyes and let the memory of sensation take over.

Except when the hands touched her they weren't as smooth as she remembered. Her breath caught in her throat and a pulse pounded between her legs. The hands were callused, rough. The eyes looking into hers were dark and liquid and...

A deep, shuddering breath. And she really needed to derail this train of thought right now.

Her eyes opened and she reached for the pile of letters on the night table. She'd been through them once already, but it was comforting to read them again. Comforting to see that love like that really existed.

The letters weren't all passionate, of course. Mostly they were about the minutiae of daily life. About laundry and work and about meals and friends. But they were intimate and warm and Piper found herself envying Lucy that she'd had someone who loved her so much.

Right up until something had happened, whatever that was.

Billy whined in his sleep and Piper settled down to read through the letters again, letting the words soothe her until eventually she fell back to sleep.

"WAKEY WAKEY!"

Piper moaned and then her eyes flashed open. The letters were still splayed out over her bed, the bedside light still on despite the fact that sun was streaming into her bedroom.

"Rise and shine!" called the voice from the stairs.

Piper shot up in bed.

"Piper? Are you there? Are you alright?" The voice had a worried tone now.

"Fine, I'm fine," Piper managed to call back.

There was a light knock on the door. "You decent?"

Piper grabbed at the sheet and clutched it to her chest. "Yes?" she hazarded.

Cam's head popped around the door. "Oversleep?"

"Uh-huh." Of course she had. Her phone, which was

technically also her alarm, was shoved inside a pillow case.

"Shall I put the kettle on while you get dressed?" Cam asked. Her eyes were fixed very firmly on Piper's eyes, not straying even a millimeter downward. "Donte will be here in a few minutes. To look at the house."

"Yes," said Piper, her hand relaxing a little on the sheet, wanting suddenly to drop it, wanting Cam to come further into the bedroom. She swallowed hard and forced her fingers to clutch again at the sheet. "You go on, I'll be down in a second."

Cam took one last look into her eyes and then withdrew. Piper held her breath until she heard footsteps on the stairs.

No, she told herself. Just no. She'd be leaving soon. She had a half-life in the States. Cam was probably fairly straight, she'd admitted as much the other night. At least she'd never been with a woman before. This was too complicated.

A complication that absolutely wasn't necessary during what was supposed to be a relaxing and healing journey, a few weeks to herself, time to figure things out.

Piper took herself off into the ancient bathroom and washed with freezing cold water as punishment for the thoughts she'd been having about Cam.

DONTE WAS NOT at all what Piper had expected. A fine-boned, slim young man with hardly a shadow of stubble on his face, he was not like the other brothers that she'd met in the slightest. His suit looked a size too big and he took pictures with such earnestness that it was tough not to crack a smile.

"You sure he's your brother?" Piper whispered to Cam.

"Shh, let him do his job," Cam hissed back, watching him proudly.

"He does know what he's doing, doesn't he?" Piper was having second thoughts now. This kid couldn't be more than eighteen.

"He's taking a picture, how hard can it be?" said Cam. "And he definitely looks the part."

"Is your father missing a suit?" asked Piper sourly.

Cam glared at her. "You leave him alone, he'll do you proud. Go and make some tea."

"Tea, tea, tea, it's all you people ever think of," grumbled Piper as she went off down to the kitchen.

In truth, it was bothering her slightly having Donte taking pictures. It was making everything real. Not that the house hadn't been real before, but the thought of selling it, of leaving, had been far off and hazy. Now, suddenly, it was a lot more real.

Cam clattered down the stairs behind her. "Don says he's almost done, just a couple more pictures," she said.

"He is a professional, right?"

Cam blushed. "Well, this is his first job. But it's going to be fine. I'm sure he's just laying the groundwork, it's his boss, David Chancellor, that'll be doing the real work, I expect."

"Absolutely," Donte said, sliding quietly into the kitchen. "I'm just taking some pics. David will look at them and my report and then give you a quote for a good selling price."

"Right," said Piper, looking from one to the other. Up close it was clear that they were related. They had the same nose, the same arch of an eyebrow. "Um, about that, what kind of clients do you normally serve?"

Donte looked surprised. "Anyone that wants us, I expect."

"It's just that there's been some concern from the neighbors about outsiders buying holiday houses and the like," Piper added.

Donte flushed. "You mean Art Slater's on the war-path about that again?"

"Calm down, Don. You know what Arthur's like. And Piper's just asking is all," said Cam.

"I can't control who buys the house," said Donte. "But it's up to you whether you accept an offer or not."

"Then just don't accept offers from tourists," said Cam. "You'll sell the place to someone nice, right Don?"

Donte flushed an even deeper crimson. "Right."

Piper watched Cam scowl at him and knew that she suspected her brother was lying. But what choice did the kid have? He was in his first job, after all. And in truth, it was better that the house was sold or rented out. That way she could get back to the States.

Billy barked out in the garden.

"I'll get the kettle on," said Cam.

"No time," Donte said. "I've got to get back to the office." He held out a polite hand to Piper. "It was lovely to meet you."

"Likewise," grinned Piper, because Donte was charming and he very much reminded her of his sister.

"Oh, before I forget," said Donte. "Mum and dad said to bring Piper over for dinner tomorrow."

"They did?" Cam said.

"I couldn't possibly," put in Piper. "I mean—"

"There'll be no taking no for an answer," said Donte. "They were quite insistent."

"He's right," Cam said. Piper couldn't tell if she was upset with this turn of events or not.

"Dad went on about how he knew what it was like to be a stranger in a strange land and the least they could do was offer you dinner. And mum, well, you know mum," Donte said to Cam.

"She just wanted to meet the new woman in town and get all the gossip," filled in Cam. Cam looked at Piper. "What do you say?"

"Isn't it family time?" Piper asked desperately. She didn't want to impose, though a tiny piece of her was curious about just where Cam came from, what her family were like.

"They'll be offended if you don't come," Cam said. "But I can make excuses for you if you like?"

"No, no," said Piper. "Of course I'll come." She looked at Donte. "Thanks for bringing the invite. I'd be delighted."

"No problem," grinned Donte. "And I'm out of here. See you later, Cam. And catch you tomorrow, Piper."

Cam groaned as he left.

"What's that for?" Piper asked.

"Because he's being shifty and I don't know why. He can't hide the truth to save his life and did you see the way he blushed when you asked him about selling to tourists?"

"Leave the kid alone, he's just doing his job."

Cam pulled a face. "We'll see," she said. "And sorry about mum and dad. They do kind of want to know who I'm working for. You'll get a good meal out of it at least."

Piper laughed. "Don't worry about it. I think it's nice that they asked, and I'm looking forward to it now."

Cam groaned again. "Yeah, just wait until you meet everyone. And I've got a job to do so I'd better start doing it." She pushed herself off the kitchen counter and left the kitchen.

See, Piper told herself. This is easy. They're both adults, they can do this, she could definitely forget about the thoughts she'd been having last night. And it wasn't like she could fire Cam, she needed the help.

All she needed was a little self-control.

PIPER SWEPT THE dust bunnies and woodchips into a pile at the top of the landing. "I think this should do it for the night," she said, as Cam came out of the bathroom. "It's getting dark and you should be getting home."

"It's a lot quieter here than it is at home," laughed Cam. "It's almost restful being here. And that mixer tap is all installed, by the way. You can't shower yet, but you can wash in warm water."

"Thank God for that," said Piper. "Watch out for the dust."

Cam had been about to step right in the pile that Piper had just swept up. She avoided it at the last minute, taking a giant step that brought her right to Piper's side. Piper felt the warmth of her, could smell her scent and turned, broom still in hand, to avoid direct contact.

Turned and slipped and then one foot was hanging in mid-air and the broom was clattering down the stairs and a firm hand was holding on to the back of her shirt and pulling her back.

Pulling her back and in until Cam was holding her, arms wrapped around her from behind, breathing in her ear, body still shaking with shock.

And this time it was Piper's fault, if fault could be assigned.

This time it was Piper who spun them around, who pressed Cam right back up against the wall, who crushed her lips against Cam's, who lost all her breath and sense and anything else as they kissed and blood pounded and pulses raced and the evening grew warmer and darker.

CHAPTER SEVENTEEN

Cam could feel the blood pumping through her, could feel every atom of her body blending and merging with Piper's. Could feel her tongue, carefully exploring, could feel her hands cupped around her hips, could feel a longing she couldn't remember having felt before.

She moaned gently as Piper pulled away, sucking at her lip before closing her eyes and sighing.

"Cam."

"I know."

"This is a very, very bad idea."

"I know." Except pressed up against the wall like this, Piper's body against her own, it really didn't feel that bad at all.

Like she was mind-reading, Piper took a step back. "I mean a really bad idea," she said again.

"I know," said Cam, her voice small. She pressed her back against the wall and slid down so that she was sitting on the floor, looking at Piper's feet.

"In a different time and place," said Piper.

"I know."

With a sigh, Piper sat down cross-legged in front of her. "There's a lot that could go wrong here."

"And some things that could go right."

"Yes, but what's the balance? In the end, someone's going to get hurt. Starting something, anything, would be a mistake. I have to leave here eventually."

"Afraid you'll fail the language exam to stay?" Cam said, forcing herself to smile.

Piper laughed. "A little. But also afraid that if we started something then I might want to stay. You have to understand, Cam, I'm on the rebound here. I'm not in a position to start something new. You're technically my employee. My home is a thousand miles away. You've never been with a woman before and I'm a hundred percent only interested in women. We come from two different cultures."

"You eat biscuits for breakfast." She knew what Piper was saying and knew that Piper was right.

"Starting something would be a mistake."

"So you've said."

Piper sighed again. "You're very attractive."

Cam grinned. "I'll try to make myself uglier if you think it'll help."

Another laugh and Piper was rubbing at her eyes. "I shouldn't have done this."

"And I shouldn't have kissed you in the kitchen. So we're even, right? We've both made our mistakes."

"We're both adult enough to not pursue this, to act as though nothing happened."

"Yes," Cam said, swallowing hard and hoping that she was. She couldn't afford to lose this job, true. But equally, she didn't want to lose Piper. For some reason, the American had started to feel like a part of her life, a part she wasn't ready to let go of yet.

"In a different time and place," Piper said again. "This would be amazing, incredible, and I'd be the luckiest woman in the world."

"But the pieces aren't fitting together."

"Even if I want them to," agreed Piper.

Cam nodded. It wasn't like this was so perfect for her, she reminded herself. It wasn't like she was so ready to admit to her family and everyone she knew that she might not be as straight as they thought. It wasn't like she really, truly, actually knew what she wanted at this point.

"Right then," Cam said. "We'll go back to ignoring things."

"And I'll go back to paying more attention so that I don't fall down the stairs," said Piper.

For a moment it looked like she was going to hold out her hand, but then she reconsidered and Cam pulled herself up off the floor. "I'd better get going then. Don't forget about dinner tomorrow."

"Of course not," said Piper, pulling herself up.

Cam hesitated. "Unless you don't want to come, of course, I'd get that."

"I want to come," Piper said firmly.

And the words rang in Cam's head so hard that she flushed furiously and had to turn away, cursing herself for her dirty mind. "Be seeing you tomorrow then," she muttered as she walked down the stairs.

"IT HAPPENED AGAIN?" screeched Beth.

"No, I didn't start anything this time," Cam said. "It was all her. All Piper. I was being a good girl and pretending nothing happened and ignoring everything."

Beth put down her pint. "Let me guess. It's getting harder to ignore, isn't it?"

"A bit," Cam said miserably.

"Then stop ignoring it."

Cam shook her head. "Piper's right. She has to leave at some point, I need this job and don't want to fuck it up, and she's on the rebound. Plus, you know, I'm pretty new at this girl thing and I don't really know what's happening, if I'm sure this is what I want."

"Then I suggest you figure it out pretty damn fast," said Beth. "Though to be perfectly honest, I think you're making excuses."

"Excuses for what?"

"Excuses because you're nervous because you do actually know what you want. You're just afraid to ask for it."

Cam took a long drink. She hated how astute Beth was sometimes.

"Listen, Cam, for once in your life, why don't you do something for you? You spend all your time looking after other people and worrying about others. Why not, just this once, make a decision for yourself, just for you."

"Because it's a decision that involves someone else, someone else who isn't interested in what I want," Cam said.

Beth rolled her eyes. "I'm not suggesting that you jump the woman. I am suggesting that if you want her, which it seems like you do, then tell her so. Tell her what you want and then if she doesn't want the same, so be it."

"She has to leave."

"Not today," Beth pointed out. "Not tomorrow either. 'It's better to have loved and lost' and all that jazz. You want to spend the rest of your life regretting not taking this chance? Come on, that's ridiculous."

"You read too many romance novels."

"And you read too much horror, but that doesn't make you go around ripping people's faces off or haunting them, does it?" Beth asked with a raised eyebrow. "Stand up for yourself, ask for what you want, you might be surprised at what happens when you do."

She put her beer down again and leaned in.

"I'm assuming that you do want to sleep with her, right?"

Cam felt herself blushing. "Uh..."

"I'll take that as a yes then," laughed Beth. "It seems like you're both assuming this is going to be a relationship, but it might not be. It doesn't have to be. You could just have some fun and see where it leads. I mean, if you're not going to do something just because it might hurt later then you'd definitely have to stop drinking beer."

Cam looked at her drink and grimaced at the thought. "Yeah, I know."

"Then give it some thought. Give some thought to putting Cam first for a change, to asking for what Cam wants for a change."

"Okay, okay," Cam said, mostly just to stop Beth talking about it. "I'll think about it, okay?"

"Keep me in the loop," said Beth as a light hand landed on Cam's shoulder.

"Mum said that dinner tomorrow was going to be a roast except now she's all worried that Piper's a vegetarian," Donte said.

"I've been looking for you," said Cam.

"Which is my cue to hit the bathroom," said Beth, sliding her chair out and getting up.

"What?" asked Donte. "What have I done now?"

"I don't know," Cam said. "But you were shifty at Piper's. Especially when she asked you about selling the house. What's going on?"

"Nothing," said Donte firmly.

"Bullshit."

Donte rubbed his eyes. "Cam, please, come on, I'm trying to do a good job here. I want to succeed at this, I want to do well. I can't end up on the farm like the others, I'm not built for it and I don't want it."

"Fair enough."

"So let me do my job. I can't go around telling you everything, can I? There have to be some secrets, professional secrets, so let it go."

Cam scowled at him. "You'd tell me if something bad was going on?"

Donte scowled right back. "I'm not a kid anymore, Cam. I know I'm the youngest and all, and I know you all always think I need looking after, but I don't."

Cam thawed slightly. "I know, I know you're an adult now."

"You all want to take care of me all the time and I hate it," Donte said. "Just... just trust that you all did a good job and that I know how to make good decisions."

"Fine," said Cam. "As long as you remember that you can come to me with anything you like. Always. No judgment, no nothing. I'm here to help you."

"Got it," said Donte. "Now how about another drink?"

"My little brother buying me a drink, looks like there are definite advantages to you being a working man," Cam laughed. "I wouldn't mind another half."

Donte slid some money across the table to her. "I'll have a red wine," he said. "But you go up and get it."

"Because Rod still scares the trousers off you?"

Donte blushed and nodded which made Cam laugh as she took his money. "Good to see that there are still some things your big sister is good for."

"Don't tell me that he's still shit-scared of Rod," Beth said, coming back to take her seat. "He's just a man, Don, don't let him hold power over you."

"He's a big man who threatened to tell dad if he ever saw me drinking in here again," said Donte.

"Because you were fifteen," said Cam. "And he didn't do that to scare you, he did it to scare Carlos and Casmiro off for bringing you in here when you were a minor. Like he wouldn't notice."

"Still," Donte sniffed. "Better if you get the drinks in."

Cam shook her head but went off to the bar anyway.

Asking for what she wanted. Not exactly her forte. But maybe Beth had a point. Maybe. She'd just have to see. Maybe a big family dinner was just what was needed, maybe seeing the way Piper interacted with her family would give her some kind of clue whether this was something she really wanted or not.

Maybe it was just hormones clouding the issue, she thought as she remembered Piper pushing her back against the wall.

Or maybe not.

CHAPTER EIGHTEEN

"So that's the famous van, huh?" Piper said.
"The one and only," said Cam.
"It's bigger than I expected."
"Not as big as a cottage."
"Few vans are," said Piper.

They were walking across a farmyard that looked like something out of a PBS series. A stone farmhouse made up one side, smoke frothing from a chimney despite the heat of the evening. Barns and stables made up the other sides of the square, and Cam's van was parked up against a stone wall.

"This place is unbelievable," breathed Piper. "It's like time is lost, like the modern world never happened."

"Don't get too carried away. We've got a phone and telly and loads of other stuff," Cam laughed. "Though if we don't hurry up, there won't be much food left. Be prepared to fight for it, because six brothers means six hungry mouths."

"Got it," Piper said.

But she paused anyway, looking around at how the green hills spread away from the farm, how the blue sky crept down to meet the grass, smelling the fresh air. Yes, it was beautiful. And yes, she was stalling.

She was definitely curious about where Cam came from, but now, suddenly, facing the farmhouse she was shy. There would be so many people inside, people she didn't know, people who were already a tribe of their own.

"Come on," Cam said quietly taking her arm. "Don't be scared. It's just family, I swear."

It was a weird feeling, one she couldn't really remember having before. Maybe on her first day of work, walking into an office full of people who already knew everything and each other. Her palms felt sweaty, but she let Cam lead her in anyway.

The side door opened onto a mud room and immediately Piper could hear the clamor of people. A large dog sniffed around.

"Get out of it, Dex," Cam said, pushing the dog off to one side. "He's smelling Billy on you," she told Piper. "Just through here."

They went down a step and then through a door and then Piper stopped, Cam letting go of her arm.

In front of her was the largest table she'd ever seen, ringed with faces chattering and laughing, children and adults, food making the table groan with weight. And the noise of a dozen conversations was immense.

Until it wasn't.

All of a sudden, everything stopped and there was silence.

Piper shifted under the gaze of everyone and she felt Cam take a deep breath.

"Okay, this is Piper," she said. Another deep breath. "And Piper, this is..." She started pointing her way around the table. "Christoforo, Jeannie and Lucas, my dad Lorenzo, Carlos, Casmiro and Donte who you've already met—"

"Cam, *amore*, poor Piper will never remember all these names. Besides, the food will be cold by the time you've finished introducing everyone."

"And that's my mum, Isabella," Cam grinned.

"There's going to be a test at the end," said a big man at one end of the table, a small girl perched on his lap. "So I'm Carmel, just remember that one."

Piper laughed. "I'm afraid Donte's the only one I'm going to remember," she said.

Donte flushed with pleasure at being singled out.

"You're not even going to remember me?" Cam said.

"Sit down, girls," said Isabella. "And Piper, you're very welcome here. Please, make yourself at home."

"My home is your home," Lorenzo said with a wide grin. "Come, sit next to me." He patted a chair.

Within minutes, all her nerves were gone and the chatter had started back up. Isabella was piling a plate high with food for her and Lorenzo was asking her questions about America and baby Lucas was being passed around from hand to hand.

And Piper wondered just what she'd been nervous about in the first place.

Across the table, Cam grinned at her. "Okay?" she mouthed.

Piper grinned right back and nodded.

IT WAS LATE in the evening when Piper finally was able to excuse herself.

"You must come back," Lorenzo said, shaking her hand firmly. "Please, you're very welcome here. Perhaps next weekend?"

"Yes, please," cried out Angela, one of Carmel's two daughters. "I want you to teach me the names of all the states."

"Book worm," joked her uncle Carlos.

"I'll take you up to see the horses next time," Cosmo said. "If you're early enough we can fit in a quick ride."

"And take some leftovers," Isabella pressed. "Please. My refrigerator won't hold them. Here, *patatina*, take these." She handed over a bag of food.

"Patatina?" Piper asked.

"It means little potato," Carmel said.

"It's a term of endearment," Cam put in hastily. "And will you let this poor woman get out of here? She still has to walk all the way back down to the village."

"Want me to drop you off in the car?" Carmel offered.

"I could use the walk," said Piper, rubbing her over-full stomach.

"I'll walk you down," said Cam. "Don't want you getting lost and wandering the moors for the next month or so. Everyone, you've got precisely thirty seconds to say your goodbyes and then we're out of here."

There was a loud chorus of goodbyes that wasn't finished by the time Cam opened up the front door and ushered Piper out into the night.

"You don't have to walk me," Piper said, once the door closed and they were in the silence of darkness. "I think I know how to get home from here."

"And let you fall in a ditch and break your leg?" Cam said. "The chance'd be a fine thing. Come on, the walk'll do us both good."

"I'm not that clumsy," said Piper as they began to walk away from the farmhouse. "Honestly, I'm really not. It's just since I've been here."

"Something in the English air?" asked Cam.

"Something like that," Piper said.

"So, what did you think? A bit overwhelming when you see them all together like that, isn't it?"

Piper laughed. "I can't imagine growing up in a place like that, surrounded by so much…"

"Noise?" put in Cam.

"So much love," said Piper quietly.

The air was cooler now and the narrow lane they were walking down bristled with sweet scented flowers, the moonlight bright and white on the road.

"I think I'd forgotten," said Piper.

"Forgotten what?"

"What it was like to have people, to be surrounded by them, to have a family. I'd forgotten what it was like to not be alone."

"You don't have to be alone, Piper."

It hurt, suddenly. Piper knew that grief never really went away. But it had been so long since her parents had died that she'd thought she was used to the shape of the sadness already, thought that it could no longer surprise her. And yet it did right then.

"Maybe you're right," she said. "I find it hard to let people in.

Hard to trust maybe. I don't know. I got used to being alone."

"I couldn't imagine that," said Cam.

They walked in silence for a while and Piper didn't feel the need to talk, didn't feel like she had to fill the space.

"Piper?"

"Mmm?"

"I'd like to say something."

"Go ahead then."

"I'd like to say something and then have it forgotten if you choose to forget it, I mean, if it's not the right thing to say."

Piper looked from the corner of her eye and saw Cam's regular profile against the moon. "Complicated," she said. "Why don't you just tell me?"

Cam laughed. "Because I'm afraid of making another mistake."

"Mistakes are how we learn," Piper said gently.

"Okay then." Cam didn't stop walking so neither did Piper. "Here's the thing. I want you."

"You want me?"

"I do," Cam said. "And I get all the arguments about why we shouldn't start anything, but here's what I don't understand. If we're both mature and adult enough to pretend nothing happened and keep working as usual, why aren't we both mature and adult enough to let something happen and keep working as usual?"

"Cam..."

"Yes, you have to leave at some point. And yes, I'm totally new at all this. But why should we stop ourselves having fun? That makes no sense. I can handle this if you can, Piper. If you don't want me then I get that. But I want you to know that I do want you."

They were entering the village now, the moon streaming onto the duck pond on the green.

"I have to leave one day," Piper said.

"I know that just as well as you do. But how about not being alone for a while?" Cam asked. "You don't have to be alone, Piper.

I'm right here knocking and waiting to be let in. So open the door. You can always throw me out later, or maybe I'll decide to go home. But you'll forever be alone if you don't open the door."

"And what if I don't want my heart broken or I don't want to break your heart," said Piper, the thought of it making her stomach clench.

Now Cam did stop. She stopped and turned and looked directly at Piper until Piper had to blink. "What if my heart is already broken?" she asked. "What if yours is? What if denying this, not following this, is what breaks hearts?"

Piper shook her head. "I can't promise you anything."

"I'm not asking you to," said Cam. "But for once, I'm putting myself first, asking for what I want. And what I want is you, Piper. Regardless of the future, regardless of anything else, I want you."

Piper breathed out, looked at the moon, and then started to walk again. There was silence for a second until she heard Cam's footsteps chasing after her.

She hadn't wanted to let someone in for such a long time. Not since Lex. But tonight, seeing Cam's family, seeing the bond they had, the love that they had, had made her feel more alone than she'd ever felt in her life.

And she had no one to blame for that but herself. She couldn't go around blocking people out, couldn't ignore the fact that there was someone here who could, maybe, mean something to her.

Okay, there were problems, but that didn't stop the fact that she was feeling something here. And maybe she was ready to feel something again. Maybe she had to stop ignoring and start noticing.

She opened up the garden gate and let Cam step through it first before following her. She walked up the steps to the front door, stumbling at the second to last until Cam's hand reached out and caught her elbow to steady her.

She took a second to get her breath back, then said: "You know, I've just realized something."

"What's that?" Cam asked, dark eyes shining in the moonlight.

"I don't think I'm clumsy at all," said Piper, reaching up to stroke Cam's face. "I think I'm blinded by you."

Cam's head tilted to nuzzle into Piper's hand. "Then ask me in," she whispered. "Ask me in, Piper."

For a long moment, Piper didn't move. Her decision was already made, she already knew what she had to do. But she wanted to watch Cam for just a minute longer, she wanted to drink in the sight of her before everything changed for the better or worse.

Then she pulled back her hand and took her key from her pocket.

She was trembling as she unlocked the door and opened it.

"Well then?" she said, half-turning back to Cam. "Are you coming in or not?"

CHAPTER NINETEEN

Cam stepped into the dark house, moonlight streaming through the windows and Piper gently closed the door behind them.

She took a deep breath and turned to Piper.

"You don't have to do anything," Piper said quietly.

"I don't?"

Piper smiled. "I invited you in, Cam. I understand the euphemism. I also understand that you've never been with a woman before and you might be nervous."

Cam's heart was beating in her stomach and her hands were sweating. She had a sudden, overwhelming, urge to run. But she stood her ground, knowing that she was only nervous and that the feeling had nothing to do with Piper herself.

"So you don't have to do anything. There are no expectations here, Cam."

She nodded, mouth dry, unsure of what to do next.

Piper grinned. "Tea?"

And Cam snorted with laughter. "Tea? You've definitely been in England too long if that's what you're thinking about."

"Do you want some or not?" Piper asked, skirting past her to get to the kitchen. "There might even be some biscuits left."

Cam followed as Piper went into the kitchen and let an excited Billy out into the back garden. She watched as Piper filled the kettle and plugged it in. She watched every movement, every breath that Piper took.

Before, pushed up against the wall upstairs, she'd wanted Piper unquestionably. Now that there was time and possibility, she still wanted her just as desperately, but she was also afraid. Afraid that she didn't know what she was doing, afraid she'd make an idiot of herself.

Afraid to ask for what she wanted.

"Biscuit?" Piper asked conversationally.

"Mm-hmm."

She understood that Piper was taking a step back, that Piper wanted her to be sure, wanted her to act, wanted to make sure that this was what she really wanted.

Which meant that she was going to have to be the one who started this.

She gulped down a lump in her throat and Piper reached up into the cupboard to get biscuits, standing on tip-toes, the curve of her waist clearly visible and Cam had to move.

She stepped in quietly, so close to Piper that her breath stirred her hair, and then slowly, gently reached out to trace the curve of her breast down to the curve of her waist and the curve of her hip.

"Jesus," Piper said, jumping back and unleashing a flood of biscuits from the cupboard.

"Sorry!" cried Cam. "Sorry, sorry." Biscuits fell all around her.

"You made me jump, I didn't hear you coming," Piper said.

"And now I've ruined all the biscuits," Cam said, mouth twitching.

Piper snorted this time, then Cam joined in, then they were laughing as the kettle began to boil.

"Come here," Piper said, holding out her hand.

"But the kettle..."

"Ignore the fucking tea," growled Piper.

Her eyes were darker, her lips looked bitten and swollen, and Cam felt a roiling heat in her stomach. She obeyed, taking a step toward Piper and taking her hand.

Piper pulled her in and slowly, carefully, cupped her face. Then those lips were on hers and Cam lost her breath all over again. She disappeared into Piper's kiss, pressing herself up against her body, feeling every inch of her.

Piper pulled back a little. "I'm not sure how patient a teacher I am," she said.

Cam bit her lip and said nothing, but she took Piper's hands and placed them on her waist. Piper growled again and pulled her in and Cam let it happen, let the warmth rush over her, let the heat build up inside her until she could take it no more.

Pulling away she struggled out of her t-shirt, unbuttoned her jeans.

"Getting a little impatient, are we?" Piper said.

But she leaned up against the kitchen table and watched, eyes heavy, arms folded, as Cam stripped down to her plain white underwear.

"Fuck."

"Fuck what?" Cam said, flushing.

"You," Piper said simply.

"I thought that was what we were here for?"

Piper gave a half-smile. "I meant fuck you're beautiful. Fuck you're the sexiest thing I've seen in years. Fuck I daren't even touch you in case you change your mind."

Confidence made Cam stand up straighter, made her raise an eyebrow. The very idea that someone like Piper, someone so together and beautiful and sexy would find her attractive was enough to let her finally take what she wanted.

"Then allow me," she said.

She stepped up to Piper and with steady hands unbuttoned Piper's shirt. A black, lace bra was revealed and she could see the pale curves of the tops of Piper's breasts. She had to swallow her mouth was so dry.

Then Piper was moving too and they were kissing, pressed together again skin to skin until Cam felt wetness pool between her legs until she was gasping for air until she could barely hold herself back.

Piper reached down, pulling down her jeans, hesitating for

just a second as she was on her knees in front of Cam, looking up. "You sure you want this?"

Cam had to clear her throat before she could speak. "Absolutely definite and if you don't start now then I might have to start without you."

She was already pulsing, already breathless, the only thing holding her back was that she didn't know what she was doing. But Piper took over, Piper reached up and pulled down her underwear, Piper pushed her back until she was perched on the edge of the kitchen table, Piper parted her legs oh so gently.

Cam sucked air in between her teeth. Piper stroked the delicate skin on the inside of her thighs and a shiver went up her spine.

"Still okay?" Piper checked in.

"Mm-hmm," Cam said, incapable of words.

Piper chuckled. She leaned in, carefully kissing her way up the inside of Cam's thighs until Cam thought she'd actually die it was so hard to take a breath.

She watched as Piper parted her legs further, watched as Piper got so close that she could feel her breath on her wetness, watched Piper's blonde head bow toward her.

Then she had to close her eyes as Piper's tongue found her spot immediately.

Cam's legs started to shake, her knees too weak to hold her up, and she had to cling on to the side of the table as Piper began to lick her, at first gently and then in insistent circles.

It was like someone else had taken control of her body. Cam thrust her hips up toward Piper's tongue, begging for more without saying a word, and Piper knew exactly what to do.

Cam's breath came faster and faster, her heart was pounding so hard she could hear it in her ears, her legs still wouldn't hold her up and she was so close to the edge that she was afraid she was going to fall.

Piper reached up with both hands, grabbing her from behind, steadying her, supporting her, her tongue never stopping as Cam began to squirm and moan.

And the heat washed over her, her muscles reached their limits, she jumped into the pool of relaxation and wave after wave of sensation overcame her until she was taking juddering breaths and holding on to Piper's head between her legs.

"Easy, easy," Piper said, drawing back.

Cam slowed her breathing, let the stars fade from her vision, and Piper started to get up.

"Where do you think you're going?" Cam said, finally opening her eyes.

Piper raised an eyebrow, but settled back to the floor as Cam sank down to join her.

And Cam wanted to do this right, she truly did, she wanted to be gentle and skilled like Piper had been. But then she also wanted this right now, she wanted to feel Piper move in her arms, she wanted to touch her, to take her, and she didn't know which side of her was going to win. Gentle or forceful.

So she kissed Piper soundly and let her hands wander over her body until she found the clasp of Piper's bra. Then she bent further, feeling the softness of breasts, brushing her lips over pale skin and hardened nipples until she heard Piper gasp.

The floor was hardly comfortable, but she wasn't about to stop now. She shuffled over so that she was sitting with her back against the kitchen cabinet, then she pulled Piper to her, so that Piper was sitting between her legs. Then her hands could wander as much as they pleased as her mouth littered kisses on the back of Piper's neck.

It was Piper that took her hand and guided it down though, Piper who pushed her fingers beneath the waistband of her underwear.

Cam's breath started to come faster again as she found wiry hair, as her fingers searched for and then found slippery wetness.

Instantly, Piper gasped and her hips moved and Cam giggled behind her. "Slowly and gently," she teased.

"I'll kill you," muttered Piper through clenched teeth as Cam's fingers found the spot they needed and began to work.

"Better let me live until we're done here," Cam said, feeling Piper straining beneath her, feeling every nerve taut as Piper gasped for breath.

She let her fingers glide in the slick wetness and pull Piper toward orgasm the same way she'd touch herself alone late at night. She kept a steady rhythm as Piper moaned and wetness sprang up between Cam's legs yet again.

Then Piper stilled for a split second before she cried out and her thighs clamped around Cam's hand. Cam held her pressure as Piper bucked against her and then slowly, slowly became still again.

"Not bad for a beginner, right?" Cam said, pulling her hand away from Piper's stickiness.

"Eight out of ten," Piper said sleepily.

"Eight!"

"Fine, eight and a half." Piper laid her head back on Cam's chest. "There's always room for improvement." She wriggled a little. "Particularly in location. The kitchen floor wasn't quite what I had in mind."

"Oh, I don't know," said Cam airily, holding up something that had been tickling her leg since she'd moved. "There are biscuits."

Piper laughed and took the biscuit from her. "Safe to eat?"

"Depends on how clean the kitchen floor is."

"Better not risk it."

Piper stirred then moved, getting up and Cam's heart sank. She wasn't ready for this to be over, she wasn't ready to be without Piper in her arms. But Piper simply held out a hand.

"How about round two in the bedroom?" she asked. "If we can make it that far."

"I thought you promised me tea," said Cam as she let herself be pulled up. "And there was mention of biscuits."

"You're welcome to wait while I prepare both," Piper said politely, putting her hands on her hips so that her breasts rose up and her curves were fully visible.

"No," said Cam, mouth dry again. "No, that's fine. We should probably concentrate on trying to make it to the bedroom."

"That's what I thought," Piper said primly, before taking Cam's hand and leading her toward the stairs.

CHAPTER TWENTY

Piper turned over and opened her eyes to see a grinning Cam watching her. "That's only slightly creepy."

"What?"

"You watching me sleep."

"Well now I'm watching you wake up," Cam said, still grinning. Her hair was tousled and her eyes were sparkling and Piper couldn't remember ever seeing anyone so beautiful.

"No regrets?" she asked lightly, far more lightly than she really felt.

"Not one," said Cam. "You?"

"Are you kidding?" Piper's stomach flipped as the weight lifted off her shoulders. "Although, we did only do it twice last night, so maybe I regret not hitting that third time."

Cam laughed. "Who says we have to stop now?"

"Well, there is work to be done," said Piper, but her hands were already reaching out for Cam's body, already anxious to feel her.

Ten minutes. That was all it took. Piper was breathless at the very sight of Cam and it wasn't exactly difficult to climax when Cam's fingers started their journey. It amazed her all over again that Cam was there, that this was happening.

Sure, the dark thoughts were still there. But she was getting better at banishing them, better at pretending this could be their forever.

"Stay right there," Cam said, jumping out of bed.

Piper slid up the bed so that she was sitting up and Cam came out of the bathroom carrying a bottle of disinfectant and some nail scissors. "What are you doing?"

"Give me your hand," Cam instructed.

Piper held out her hand and then spotted the black stitches still marking her skin and snatched her hand right back again. "Oh no you don't."

"Seriously? Six brothers and a whole farmyard to play in and you think this is the first set of stitches that I've taken out?" Cam asked, sitting on the edge of the bed. "They're ready to come out and you can either let me do them or go sit in Casualty for the entire afternoon and wait for a nurse to do it."

"Fine," Piper said, holding her hand back out again.

There was silence for a moment as Cam started working, and when she spoke she didn't look in Piper's eyes. "I don't regret anything," she said. "But I'm not sure how my family are going to react to all this."

"I'm not forcing you to come out," Piper said immediately. "That's your business, not mine, I'd never make you tell anyone you didn't want to."

"I know," Cam said, head still bent over Piper's hand. "But I have to tell them. We don't keep secrets from each other, it's not our way. Besides, they should know. This is a good thing, even if it does end up being a short thing. They deserve to know that you make me happy. You deserve for them to know."

"It's really your choice," Piper said.

Cam let go of her hand. "All done. And I know it's my choice."

Piper studied her hand, now stitch-free. "Nice."

"And you have no excuse not to do the washing up anymore," Cam said. "Want to wash first or second?"

"Whichever."

"Your house, you go first," Cam said.

"You just want extra time in bed before you need to get to work."

"Plus, you can make me tea while I'm washing," Cam shot back with a grin.

CAM WAS SITTING up in bed with Lucy's letters on her lap when Piper came back from the bathroom. "These are kind of addictive."

"It's killing me not knowing what happened to Twinkle Toes and Lucy," Piper admitted.

Cam put down the letter she was reading. "Maybe Twinkle Toes was a woman," she said.

"Why would you say that?" Piper sat down on the bed.

"I don't know. It would explain things, I suppose. Explain why things didn't work out, why no one in the village ever talks about it. Maybe explain why no one else even knows."

"Yes, that's called projecting," Piper said smiling at her. "It's okay for you not to feel comfortable with this yet, Cam. It's okay to feel conflicted or worried or nervous."

"I'm not, really, I'm not. It was just an idea."

"A wrong one, unfortunately," said Piper, taking the pile of letters from Cam's lap and flipping through until she found the one she wanted. She handed it to Cam, pointing out one paragraph in particular.

Cam blushed. "Oh, yes, I see. That's definitely not a woman. Got it."

"I thought I'd protect you from the spicier parts," grinned Piper. "But you needed proof. And I need breakfast. Let's go eat."

PIPER WAS WASHING down the painted walls in the living room when her phone rang. She studied the number before answering, but didn't recognize it.

"Hello?"

"Piper? It's Donte."

At least Lex wasn't stalking her from an unknown number. Piper put down her cloth. "Hi Donte, what can I do for you."

"Just seeing if you're home. David would like to drop by this afternoon and talk about selling the house, if that would work for you?"

"David your boss?"

"That's the one," Donte said. From the background noise he was obviously driving. "I'd come myself, but he's sent me to look at a property a couple of villages over and I won't make it back in time. Besides, I think he wants to put a face to the name and meet you himself."

"Sure," Piper said, knowing that she should be happier about this. She did want to sell the house after all.

"Great," said Donte. "He'll be with you around three."

"Perfect." Piper hung up.

"Everything okay?" Cam asked, sticking her head around the door.

"Yes, absolutely," said Piper, tucking her hair behind her ear. She should say something, but she didn't. The phone call sat in her stomach heavy.

"Great, listen, I've got to get some shopping done. I need some stuff for the bathroom and I promised dad I'd pick up a tool he's rented and that he needs this afternoon. It'll take me most of the afternoon, I'm afraid. Fancy coming and keeping me company?"

Those eyes, the way they shifted from chocolate to hazel and back again. Piper was in half a mind to take Cam right there and then. She took a breath and shook her head. "I can't." The truth, she had to tell the truth. "David Chancellor is dropping by. It's probably nothing, he probably just wants to talk about prices and things, nothing important."

But Cam's face dropped slightly anyway. "Right, sure. Well, I'll be off then."

She was turning away and Piper hated to see her go. "Will I see you later?"

Cam turned back, face brightening again. "You want to?"

"You don't?"

"I'll think about it. I mean, if you happen to be in The Duck and Pony at around seven then I suppose there won't be any avoiding you."

Piper laughed. "It's a date."

ENJOY THE SUNSHINE, smell the flowers, take today for today, she reminded herself as she dragged Billy away from the ducks on the village green.

"We're getting lunch, Bill, come on."

She should be happy. She was happy. Thinking about her night with Cam made her bounce inside with excitement. She couldn't remember the last time she'd felt like this. But then there was the darkness lurking behind everything.

Deep inside she knew that they were going to get hurt. She knew that she had to leave. They were living on borrowed time and having fun, but reality would intrude at some point.

Yet she couldn't force herself to regret letting Cam in last night. She couldn't force herself to promise that she wouldn't kiss her again and again, that she wouldn't want more.

"You can't bring Billy inside," Beth said when she spotted Piper and the dog. She was straightening books outside the shop. "He drools over everything. But there's a bowl of water for him over there."

Piper tied Billy up in the shade and followed Beth into the shop. "I just want something quick to go if that's alright."

"More than alright," Beth grinned. "A sandwich suit you?"

"Great," said Piper, clambering up on a stool to wait.

"So how go things with you and Cam then?" asked Beth as she got a paper bag ready.

Piper narrowed her eyes but it was clear from the fake-innocent look on her face that Beth already knew far more than Piper would have guessed. "Cam told you?"

"She might have mentioned something."

Piper rubbed at her nose, then shook her head. "You know, I think you should probably ask her rather than me."

"A woman of discretion," beamed Beth. "I like it. Correct answer. What about a cookie to go with that sandwich?"

"Absolutely," Piper smiled back. She couldn't help but like Beth.

"Find anything juicy in the house when you were clearing out then?" Beth asked as she wrapped all the food up.

"Nothing really," said Piper. "No unexploded hand grenades or Picassos in the attic." Then she paused. "There was one thing though, we found some old love letters of my great aunt's."

Beth raised an eyebrow. "Lucy was the stereotypical spinster, I wouldn't have expected her to have surprises like that."

"That's what Cam said. But now I'm intrigued, but I've got no idea where to find out more information."

"Huh." Beth leaned on the counter and blew out a breath. "Don't know if I can help you, I don't have much of an idea myself. It's not like there's records of people who fall in love, not if they don't get married anyway."

"Yeah," Piper said, taking funny colored money out of her pocket. "That's what I was afraid of."

"You can try asking Arthur Slater," Beth suggested, taking the money and making change. "He's the oldest person in the village, he might remember something if there was scandal at the time."

Piper nodded, it was a good idea, one she'd considered herself. She made a mental note to bring up the subject with Arthur the next time she saw him. Then she took her sandwich, thanked Beth and picked up Billy on her way out.

It was late for lunch and Donte had said that David Chancellor would be there at three. She supposed she'd better find out what he wanted.

CHAPTER TWENTY ONE

Cam walked into the pub with her heart in her mouth. For an instant she thought that Piper wasn't there, but then she saw the familiar blond head and her heart sank back to its regular place, though it pounded all the more as Piper grinned at her.

Then she saw Beth and realized that Piper was sitting at their usual table.

Her hands started sweating, which was ridiculous since Beth already knew almost everything. Still though, Cam felt wobbly as she went to join them.

"Come, join the toast," Beth said.

"A toast to what?" Cam asked. Her arm brushed against Piper's as she sat down and her pulse thrummed, but Piper made no move to kiss her or greet her in any intimate way. Cam's stomach settled a little.

"A toast to Piper being a smart, smart lady. Not to mention a very moral one," said Beth.

Cam felt her cheeks flush. Moral wasn't exactly the word she'd have used to describe Piper last night. Or this morning.

"She's overstating things," said Piper.

"Am not," Beth said. "Tell Cam everything right now, I demand it, while I go and get drinks in for us all."

"I didn't mean for us to sit with Beth if you don't want us to," Cam said as soon as Beth was gone.

"I like her," said Piper. She leaned in a little. "Not as much as I like you though," she added in a whisper that set Cam's blood on fire.

"You'd better tell me what went on with David Chancellor," Cam said, turning away slightly out of fear she might just grab Piper and kiss her then and there.

She'd been trying not to think about the meeting all afternoon, but she had to ask, she had to know. She might not like the idea of Piper selling the house, but she'd agreed to all this, she knew the reality of the situation.

Piper beamed. "Well, he came over and I invited him in and he drinks coffee, not tea, so I was wondering if he's actually English or not and—"

Cam lightly punched her arm. "You're playing with me," she said. "Get to the point."

"Okay, okay. He already had an offer for the house."

Cam's vision faded a little at the edges and she felt dizzy.

"Hold on," Piper said. "He had an offer, a good one. But I asked him who the offer was from and it turns out it was from a developer."

"A developer?" Cam asked, confused.

"Some guy who wants to split the house into three holiday apartments, except David called them flats, and rent them out," said Piper. She took a breath. "So I turned it down."

"You turned the offer down."

"Yep."

Cam swallowed and licked her dry lips. "You didn't turn him down because, well, because of us, because of me, did you?"

"No," Piper said firmly. "I turned him down because both you and Arthur, and now Beth, have told me about house prices in the village and because I don't want to sell the house to a developer. I want to sell it to someone who'll live there, someone who'll love it as much as Lucy obviously did."

Cam found that she was blinking fast against tears that were forming. She didn't know if she was touched or relieved, but either way, she was glad.

"Isn't it brilliant?" Beth said, sliding back into her seat and depositing glasses onto the table. "She's a little star, aren't you, Piper?"

"Yes," Cam said, voice thick. "Yes, it's brilliant."

CAM PILED HER plate high at breakfast the next morning. Spending time with Piper was great, but the food did leave something to be desired. So she'd made it home for breakfast, not to mention a change of clothes.

She'd felt odd walking into the kitchen though, like she was different, maybe like everyone would notice.

She knew she had to say something. She wanted her family to know, she truly did. But as she ate, it was hard to find a good opening.

In the end, she thought she'd better force one. She cleared her throat. "So..." she said.

Carmel was bickering with Carlos about who was going to move the cattle and Cosmo and Donte were fighting over the last fried egg and nobody stopped to listen to her.

"So..." Cam tried again.

Still nobody stopped. "More bacon, *amore*?" her mother asked.

"No, mama, thanks."

Cam looked around at the faces at the table and she knew they loved her, she knew they knew her and adored her and she told herself that they would all understand. Of course they would.

But why was it so difficult to tell them?

She took a deep breath and stood up. Maybe later, she told herself. Maybe tonight or tomorrow. There wasn't a hurry, not yet. Besides, who made big announcements at the breakfast table? Breakfast wasn't for announcements, they were definitely an evening meal kind of thing. Plus, she had to get to work.

So, tomorrow it would be then.

CAM WAS RINSING out a cup at the kitchen sink when Piper sidled up behind her.

"Hello there," she whispered so close to Cam's ear that goosebumps raised on her arms.

"Why, hello," Cam whispered back.

"Miss me?"

"Since early this morning?" Cam said. Piper's hands were on her hips, thumbs circling over her hipbones. "Only a little."

"Only a little?" asked Piper, letting her right hand move slowly around to the button on Cam's jeans.

"Maybe slightly more than a little," Cam gasped. Piper's fingers flicked the button open.

Two weeks it had been. Two weeks and the novelty still hadn't worn off. Piper still made her feel like she'd run a marathon just by looking at her, just by touching her. Cam moaned a little as Piper tickled at the elastic of her underwear.

She could feel Piper's breasts pushed up against her back, could feel her own longing, wanting, and it took a long, long second before she remembered that they weren't alone.

"The plumber's just upstairs," she hissed.

"So?" Piper said, fingers creeping down under the elastic of her underwear now. "You're not suggesting he join us, are you?"

Cam hiccuped a laugh as Piper slid her hand further down into her pants. "Not at all."

"Then just stand there like a good girl and pretend nothing's happening," Piper said, sliding her fingers into Cam's wetness.

Cam swallowed and parted her legs a little to give Piper easier access. She was right in front of the kitchen window. Anyone walking into the garden could see her, see them. But as Piper began massaging her, fingers deft and strong, Cam's eyes started to close and she couldn't bring herself to care if they were seen.

IT WAS GETTING to the point that Cam was feeling bad about

walking into her own home and that, she told herself, was ridiculous. She just needed to spit the news out, just say it. And yet she found an excuse every time not to mention Piper.

"You're not around much, my love," her father said as she slipped into the kitchen for dinner.

"Just busy, that's all," Cam smiled but her heart was beating furiously. It wasn't a lie, not exactly. But it tasted like one.

Still though, she was beginning to wonder whether it really was worth saying anything. If Piper was going to leave anyway, maybe she should protect her family. Was it necessary to tell them about a relationship that was going to be so short?

Which made her feel even worse because then not only was she thinking about hiding things from her family but was also thinking about Piper actually really leaving.

"And speaking of people who aren't around often," her father said. "I've almost forgotten your name."

Donte blushed bright red. "Sorry, dad, I've been working."

"Such a busy, busy family," said Lorenzo, but he was smiling proudly.

She was busy, in her defense. The house was coming along nicely. But she was also coming home for dinner, going out again to the pub or to meet Beth, and then sneaking back into Piper's house. Then she was just as sneakily coming home before breakfast for a change of clothes.

"Busy doing good," Donte said. "Right, Cam?"

"Right what?" she asked as her mother passed her a plate of spaghetti.

"You mean Piper hasn't told you?" Donte asked, accepting a plate of his own. "Oh, hold on a second, I almost forgot." He pulled a paper out of his jacket pocket and slid it across the table to Cam.

Automatically, Cam opened it. "What's this?" she asked.

"A cottage," Donte said. "Well, the bare bones of one anyway. We just got it in, it hasn't been made public yet. It's a bit of a wreck, but you're the construction expert. I figure you could do it up, keep living in the van until it's ready."

Cam looked up at him. "Are you serious?"

"As a heart attack," said Donte. "You can put an offer in. I'll put it in for you if you like. This place could be yours. It's up on the road to the hospital, used to be a part of the Baker farm until they split the land up. It's a good price even if it is in need of a ton of work."

Cam looked back at the picture. A place of her own. A place she could make her own. With the money from Piper she could definitely afford it, or at least the down payment. She could hardly believe it.

"Thank your brother," Lorenzo said.

Cam shook her head. "I just can't believe it."

"Why isn't Donte getting us all houses?" Carlos said.

"Right," said Cosmo. "I'm going to need a place too. I'm thinking six bedrooms..."

Cam tuned him out and looked back at the paper again. A place of her own. Then she remembered what Donte had said.

"Hold on a sec, Piper hasn't told me what?" she asked.

Donte took a huge forkful of spaghetti. "That there's been another offer on Lucy's house," he said.

CHAPTER TWENTY TWO

Even though Cam's back was to her, Piper could tell something was wrong. There was something in the way she was holding herself.

"Tea?" Piper asked.

"I'm just making some," said Cam. There was a pause. "You want some too?"

"Sure," said Piper. She sat down at the kitchen table and waited quietly until Cam was done. It wasn't until Cam put a cup down in front of her that she spoke again. "Are you okay?"

Cam blew out a breath and nodded.

"Okay, wanna try that one again?" Piper asked, smiling gently. "Are you okay?"

Cam sat down and put her head in her hands. "I want to be okay. I should be okay. I agreed to all this, after all."

Piper wrapped her hands around her tea mug. "Why don't we start from the beginning?"

"Donte told me about the offer on the house." Cam looked up and Piper saw pain in her eyes. "Were you going to tell me?"

"I was about to tell you right now," said Piper calmly. "David called right after you left yesterday and then you didn't come back last night so I haven't really had the chance to say anything."

Another big breath. "Is it a good offer?"

"Better than the last one," said Piper. "And it's not a developer, David assured me of that."

Outside birds were singing and she could hear Arthur pottering around in his garden. But she couldn't leave Cam to go and talk to him, not right now.

"I was going to tell you, Cam, I wasn't keeping this from you."

"Are you going to take it?"

Piper looked into her tea. "I haven't decided yet."

The offer was a good one. She should take it, she knew that. There was no reason for her to have a house here, no reason for her to put things off much longer.

The idea of keeping the house and staying had occurred to her, of course it had. On those long summer nights in Cam's arms she couldn't think of anything more perfect.

But she had no job and the money was running out. She wasn't allowed to work in the UK and couldn't afford to stay that much longer. She needed to go back to the States and start looking for a new job.

"I shouldn't be upset," Cam said. "It's stupid, I feel stupid. I know that you have to leave, I knew that from the very beginning."

"We both knew this had to end, Cam. I don't want you to think that this isn't hurting me too." It was. It hurt just to think about it. Not that she had much choice. "But even if I do accept the offer, I'll still be here for a little longer, a few weeks at least while we get everything sorted out."

"That should make me happy."

"It doesn't?" Piper asked. She put her elbows on the table. "We can quit this now if that's what you want, Cam. No hard feelings. We can go back to being just business."

"How is that supposed to help things?" Cam asked.

"Alternatively, we go on as we are, enjoying the time that we have left together," Piper said. And ignoring the fact that we have to split apart, she added in her head.

"That's easy for you to say."

"It's not easy for me to say, and it's definitely not easy for me to do."

"Does it have to end?"

Cam's question pricked at her, pricked and then twisted like a knife wound. "How can it not?"

"We could try to keep this going long distance."

Piper nodded. "We could. But to what end? I mean, even long distance we'd have to have some kind of goal in sight. Could you see yourself moving to the States? Leaving your family?"

Cam screwed her eyes tight shut and shook her head.

"And I can't stay here without working," Piper said gently. "We hardly know each other, Cam. Upending our lives for something so fresh, so new would be a mistake."

"Maybe you're right," Cam said. "But could we try at least? Could we be long distance for a while after you leave? It would give us a chance to think about things, some distance, some clarity perhaps."

Piper sighed. "I don't want to hold you back, Cam. I don't want you to deny yourself someone or something else because you're counting on me."

"Think about it."

Cam's glare was so ferocious, so pleading that Piper began to bend. "I'll think about it if you agree to try and make the best of the time we have left here together."

"Okay," Cam said, flashing a short smile.

Piper reached out across the table and took Cam's hands in her own. "I don't want you to think that I don't have feelings for you, Cam. I don't want you to think that it'll be easy to leave you."

"I know," said Cam. "I know."

There was the sound of floorboards creaking and then someone called out and Cam snatched her hands away from Piper just as Donte walked into the kitchen.

"Don't you know how to knock?" Cam barked.

Donte blushed. "I'm sorry, I did call from the door but no one answered. I thought you were probably drilling or something and couldn't hear me. The door was open."

"And you sensibly came in," Piper said, smiling at him. She liked the boy and didn't want him to feel bad. "What can I help you with?"

"Uh, nothing," Donte said, flashing a look at his sister. "I just wanted to drop off this paperwork. David said you were considering an offer, so I thought I'd bring you our FAQ brochure, since, you know, you might not know how selling houses works in England or whatever." He ran his fingers through his curly hair.

"That was thoughtful, thank you," said Piper.

"Yeah," Cam said, with a sniff. "Yeah, it was nice of you, Don. Thanks."

"No worries," said Donte. "I'll, um, get out of your way then. See you later Cam."

Piper waited until his footsteps were echoing out of the hallway and then onto the porch before she turned back to Cam.

She felt slightly sick, her blood pumping faster than normal, her mouth tasting bad.

"You didn't tell them, did you?"

"What?" Cam asked.

"You snatched your hands away like that because you didn't want Donte to see us, because you didn't tell your family, did you?"

Cam frowned. "But you said it was my decision. You said you'd never push me to come out. You said it was up to me."

"And you said that you were going to tell them." Piper could feel the anger in her veins and tried to tamp it down, tried to be reasonable.

"I haven't found the right time," Cam said miserably. "And then I started thinking that maybe it wasn't worth it, what with you leaving soon and all. Maybe I shouldn't disturb them with something like this." She looked up, eyes flashing. "And you said it didn't matter."

Piper took a calming breath. "It doesn't matter. It's your decision. What does matter, on the other hand, is that you told me you were going to do something and then you didn't. That's a matter of trust, Cam, and that's important to me."

"I don't see why it's such a big deal."

"What if I'd have met one of your brothers on the street and I thought that you told everyone when you hadn't and ended up mentioning something to him about us? What then? I'd have outed you, which is a terrible thing to do to someone."

Cam looked down at the table. "Right," she said.

Piper took another calming breath. "And trust is an important thing in a relationship. An important thing to me anyway. Lex cheated on me, I've told you that, and that feeling of being lied to, of being betrayed, never quite goes away."

"I wouldn't betray you," Cam broke in.

"I'm not saying you would. I'm just explaining why it's important to me that we have trust, that we do what we say we're going to do," Piper said. She reached out again and took Cam's hands.

"Lex really hurt you, didn't she?"

Piper had a flash of the grinding, bone-breaking pain she'd felt when Lex had finally told her. She nodded. "She did. But she isn't a bad person, not really. Lex also saved me when I most needed saving, after my parents died. She helped me build a life, she and I made something that I was very proud of. Something that I'm not sure I'll ever have again with anyone."

"Okay," said Cam slowly.

"I'm telling you that because I want you to know that the majority of our relationship was good, was great. It was just that one little thing, that one little betrayal of trust that was our undoing. That's how important it is."

Cam sighed and blinked twice, then swallowed. "Alright," she said. "Alright, I get it. Then I'll be honest. I'm not sure about telling my family about all this until I'm comfortable with where we're going and what's going to happen to us."

"That's fair," Piper said.

"And now I need to get on with some work. I'm not angry with you, but I could use a little time on my own to process things."

"Also fair," Piper said with a smile. "How about you go up and get started and I'll bring you some elevenses later?"

Cam smiled. "Sounds like a plan."

IT WAS AN hour later, more or less, when it happened. Piper was distracted maybe. Or perhaps she just wasn't paying attention. Later she wasn't entirely sure what exactly had happened. She did know that one moment everything was fine and the next… it wasn't.

CHAPTER TWENTY THREE

The crash was so loud that Cam heard it over the radio playing in the background. For a moment, she hesitated, sure that Piper was going to yell up the stairs that everything was alright.

But she didn't.

Cam's skin prickled and she dropped the wrench she was holding and sprinted down the stairs.

The first thing she saw was Piper's body lying on the ground, her face pale, her limbs twisted as though she was in the deepest sleep. Cam's heart started to race and she knelt beside Piper, picked up her hand.

"Piper? Pipe? Come on, Piper, wake up."

She clutched at that hand like it was a life raft, like letting go would mean the end of something, of everything.

"Piper?"

Why had they argued? Why hadn't she been here to help, to save her? Why had she insisted on going back to work alone instead of having Piper chatting merrily away as she helped?

"Piper!"

Long eyelashes started to flutter and Piper groaned. Cam's internal organs settled back into their regular positions as she took a breath.

"Piper, what the hell happened?"

Piper's eyes flickered open. "Ouch."

"Ouch? Ouch what? Where? What happened?"

"I don't know."

Desperately, Cam looked around. Beside the doorway to the living room there was a large cabinet. It had been crammed full of hats and coats and boots, but was now almost empty and smelled faintly of cedar. And one of the doors was half-open.

"Did you run into the cabinet door?" Cam asked incredulously.

"I don't know," said Piper.

"Jesus, you're worse than a Chaplin film. How could you not see the door? It's huge, I mean, it's a door."

Piper was already struggling to sit up and Cam helped her, hauling on her upper arms until she was propped up against the wall. With deft fingers she palpitated Piper's head. "No blood," she said. "But I'm not sure if there's any bruising or anything worse."

"I feel like I've been punched in the head," said Piper.

"You're not going to like this, but you know what has to happen next, right?"

Piper groaned. "No, come on, Cam. I'm fine. I'm going to have a splitting headache, but I'm fine, really."

"Nope," said Cam. "You lost consciousness. There isn't a choice here, Piper. I'm going to go and get the van and you're going to sit right here without moving."

"No, seriously, Cam I don't want—"

"I don't want you dying of concussion. Sit tight. I'll be right back."

"THIS IS ALL a fuss over nothing."

"You sound more English by the day," Cam said with a grin.

"I feel like I'm getting more English. I mean, I've participated in your healthcare system twice in a month. That's got to count for something."

"That's what it's here for," said Cam. "And it's better safe than sorry."

She sat on her hands on the uncomfortable plastic chair and felt extra uncomfortable because she should have been there. This morning had not gone as planned. And it was her fault.

"Listen, Piper."

Piper turned her head, her face still pale against the white of the examination couch. "That sounds ominous."

"It's not," Cam said. "I swear it's not. I just... I'm sorry."

Piper frowned. "Sorry for what? Please don't tell me you did this. I don't actually remember hitting my head on that cabinet, and if you say now that it was really you smacking me over the head with a wrench then I'll have to believe you."

"Yes," Cam said gravely. "It was me, in the living room, with a wrench."

Piper snorted a laugh then groaned. "That made my head hurt."

"Sorry," said Cam. "And sorry for this morning. It was silly. I knew what I was getting into when I made the move and it's wrong of me to press you for more. If you'd like to try long distance, then I'd love that. But if you need to walk away clean, I get that too. That was always the plan and I should be grateful for the time we have together rather than just wanting more."

Piper reached out a hand and Cam took it. "I'm sorry for reacting the way I did about you telling your family. I don't want you to do something you're not comfortable with. And I realize you weren't lying to me or anything, it was just circumstances that stopped you telling them."

"Ha!" cried Cam. "Look at that, our first fight and we're making up. That wasn't so bad."

"Speak for yourself," Piper said. "You're not the one with an egg on your head."

"Oh calm down, I'm sure it's nothing. We're just here for a check-up," chided Cam. "But I am astounded at what can happen to you when I'm not around to fish you out of ponds or stop you falling down the stairs."

"I told you, that has nothing to do with me. You're the entire reason that I'm clumsy. You blind me."

"With my stunning beauty," Cam said. "So I've heard."

"Knock knock."

Cam turned and saw Carmel standing in the door, a bag in his hand. "Well, well, a brother that knows how to knock."

He stuck his tongue out at her. "Mum said that hospital food is awful and that I should bring you two lunch," he said. "How are you Piper?"

"I'm fine," Piper said. "Just under observation for the next couple of hours and then I can go home."

"And I'll stay with her overnight," Cam said. Then she felt the heat rising in her cheeks. "Just to make sure she's okay, she's not supposed to be alone." The last thing she wanted right now was Carmel connecting the dots.

"I heard there was a patient in the village," Beth said, appearing beside Carmel, a bag in her hand. "So I brought sandwiches since hospital food is so pants."

Cam laughed. "Great minds think alike, right Car?"

"Get in line," growled Carmel. "Mum's lasagna came first."

Beth grinned. "Can't have too much lunch. Everything okay in here?"

Piper smiled but Cam could see she was tired. "I'm fine, everything's fine, I just feel like an idiot is all."

"Shouldn't let Cam go around hitting you with hammers then," said Beth.

"Exactly what I thought," Piper grinned. "But thank you. Thank you both. It's kind of you to check on me."

"You're part of the village now," said Beth. "We look after our own. Arthur wanted to come too, but I persuaded him to stay at home and look after Billy. Hope that's alright with you?"

"Perfectly fine," said Piper.

"And that's enough visiting for today," Cam said. Piper really was looking tired and she was supposed to be resting. "So everybody out. I'll let you know when we're on our way home."

She chased everyone out of the cubicle and drew the curtains properly before sitting on the edge of Piper's bed.

"It's sweet of them to check on me," Piper said.

"We're nice people. There are definitely worse places to live than Sutton's Walk."

"I know," sighed Piper. "I've lived in them."

"There's always a place for you here," Cam said, then bit her lip. "Sorry. I didn't mean it like you should stay, I just meant it like…"

"Like I should stay," Piper said. "And it's fine. You're not being pushy. I get that this is an option. It's just not a great one, that's all. I've got no job, only a little money, and no chance of getting any kind of visa to stay here. It's not like I haven't thought about it, but it just makes no sense."

"Understood," Cam said, deliberately pushing away the darkness she felt. She forced herself to smile. "At least we've got plenty of supplies. I mean, if the doctor forgets about us, we can probably eat for a week with what Carmel and Beth brought."

"It was kind of them, and kind of your mom too, I'll have to thank her."

"Dad's been asking when you're coming for dinner again. They like you, you know. The whole family does."

"They like me right now," said Piper.

And Cam could fill in the rest of that sentence for herself. Though she didn't think her family would hate Piper if she told them what was going on. They might not be quite so welcoming though.

"I've been putting them off," she said. "But you're welcome to come over for dinner."

"I know," Piper said. "Thanks." She reached out a hand again and Cam took it.

Just the touch of her made Cam's mouth water. She shifted a little on the bed, stroking Piper's palm with her thumb, making herself feel warm and liquidy inside. Until her other hand came up and started stroking Piper's thigh.

"I've never done it in a hospital bed before," Piper said, voice low and full of promise.

Cam's insides flipped over and her mouth went dry.

And a ringing started from somewhere.

"My phone," Piper groaned. "Can you get it? It's in my bag."

"Just as well," said Cam, jumping off the bed. "We almost got into some real trouble there."

"I'm supposed to be resting," Piper said primly. "You're taking advantage of me in my weakened state."

"I'm taking advantage of you later, consider that a promise," laughed Cam as she searched through Piper's bag.

Finally, she found the phone and it was still ringing.

She didn't mean to see the screen, she barely looked at it. But the name was short and written in big letters and she couldn't help but see it, not really.

Lex.

Her hands started to sweat, but she pasted a smile on her face and handed the phone over as though she'd seen nothing.

She really didn't want to fight again today. This was none of her business. Piper could speak to who she wanted.

Yet she still felt the darkness coming back, still felt like she was losing Piper already and she couldn't help that.

She put Piper's bag back on the chair and turned just in time to see Piper ignore the call.

"Here, put this back in my bag," Piper said. "I've switched the volume off. It shouldn't bother us again."

And Cam's heart lightened. Piper didn't want to talk to Lex. Of course she didn't. She gave a sigh of relief as she put the mobile back into Piper's bag.

"So, about that trouble," she said, climbing back onto the bed.

"Mmm, about that," said Piper, with a grin.

CHAPTER TWENTY FOUR

Piper pushed the back door open to let in a flood of sunlight. Billy barked joyously and ran out into the garden. Wanting to feel the warmth on her skin, Piper followed him.

Her head only ached a little now, and she wasn't sure how much of that was from her stupid accident and how much was from fretting over Cam.

She shouldn't have started this, she knew that. Hell, she'd known that from the beginning. But Cam was funny and kind and smart and beautiful and just for once, Piper had given in to what she truly wanted to do. She'd let herself not be sensible for a change.

Yes, she'd known that she was setting herself up to get hurt, not to mention Cam. Yes, she'd somewhat kidded herself that they could sleep together and have it just be fun. And no, she didn't want to leave.

But choices had been made and the situation was what it was. She could hardly change immigration laws. Nor could she win the lottery. She sighed as the sun stroked over her. It had been worth it though, hadn't it?

Worth it to feel Cam's hands on her skin, worth it to see Cam's smile in the morning, worth it to have those few moments where she felt like she could do anything, be anyone, be happy.

"Heard you've been in the wars."

Piper jumped. "Arthur, you gave me a fright."

"Sorry about that, love," he said, appearing over the back fence, leaning his sun-spotted arms on top of the railing. "Been in the hospital again, I hear."

"Uh, yes," Piper said, blushing. "A silly accident is all."

"Lucky that Cam was there to catch you when you fell then, weren't you?" he said.

Lucky. Yes, she had been. More than once. She might be clumsy when Cam was around, but she was lucky that the woman didn't seem to mind stepping in to save her. "Mmm," was all she said to Arthur.

"Billy'll have them geraniums all dug up before lunch if you're not careful," Arthur said.

Piper whistled and Billy barked, leaving his digging and going sniffing after the scent of a rabbit. And Piper remembered that she had something to ask Arthur. How to go about it?

"You, er, you must know a lot about the village," she ventured.

"That I do," said Arthur, cloudy blue eyes looking out over the garden. "Lived here my whole life and don't see that changing any time soon. I'm almost ninety four, you know."

"Impressive," said Piper. "I was wondering if you might help me?"

He eyed her suspiciously. "I might."

"It's just that when I was clearing out the house I found a lot of my great aunt's things, obviously. And, well, I never really knew her. I'd quite like to though."

He grinned. "Lucy was a laugh, she was. Everyone thought she was eccentric, a bit batty, you know. But she just let 'em think that. Sharp as a tack was Luce. Clever, independent, sure of her own mind. She was a good one."

"You two were close?" said Piper, coming closer to the fence.

"Close as could be, we were neighbors," Arthur said. "She was the last one of our generation left, excepting me, of course. I'll miss her."

To her horror, Piper saw that his eyes were misty. Only then did she think that maybe, just maybe, Arthur might have been the one. Maybe he was Twinkle Toes. It was a stretch, but...

"Do the words Twinkle Toes mean anything to you?" she asked.

He blinked and turned to her, frowning then laughing. "Only in as much as I don't have 'em," he said. "Two left feet, me."

Piper let out a breath. "There's something in particular."

"Thought there might be," interrupted Arthur. "I told you I'm almost ninety four, didn't I?"

"Yes."

"Then you'd best get on with asking whatever it is that's on your mind. Otherwise I might just keel over waiting for you to find your tongue," he said sharply.

Piper smothered a smile. "Alright then. I found letters. Love letters. From someone that signed himself off as Twinkle Toes. It looks like my aunt was very fond of this person, loved him maybe. But obviously they didn't end up together. I just wanted to know..." She tailed off.

"You're just nosy is what," Arthur said. "Wanted to know about Luce's private life and all."

"If you know anything," said Piper. "I mean, it's an intrusion, I understand that. I just wondered if maybe you could tell me more."

Arthur sniffed and looked up at the sky. "More hot weather," he said. "Plants'll be dying of thirst before long."

"I'll take that as a no," said Piper, disappointment settling in her stomach.

"Don't take it personal, love," said Arthur, a little more kindly. "But I barely know you. You're not from the village. Some things are best left amongst those that might best understand them."

Piper didn't quite know what to say to this and Arthur was already hobbling away from the fence. Then she heard someone calling her name from inside. Billy bounded back into the house and she sighed.

She'd have to let this go for now. Maybe she should tell Cam to ask, maybe Arthur would tell her more.

"Coming," she said, going back to the kitchen and expecting to see Cam's dark head bent over the kettle.

Instead, she found Donte standing stiffly by the table, hands fussing with some papers that he'd brought.

"Donte, Cam's not here yet," Piper said.

Cam had gone home for a change of clothes and breakfast, a habit that Piper tried hard to understand. It'd be easier, of course, if Cam just moved a few things into the house, but neither one of them had suggested as much.

"I was looking for you, actually," he said, smiling awkwardly.

"Me? Well, I'm honored. Tea? Coffee?"

He shook his head. "It's more of a business thing."

"Okay," Piper said. "Shoot."

Donte cleared his throat. "It's just that, well, we wouldn't want you to miss out on this offer. It's a good one, even given the rising house prices in the village, and we're a little worried that if you spend too long thinking it over then, well, then the buyer may decide to look elsewhere."

Piper raised an eyebrow at this. "You are?" she asked. "Both of you, that is. Not just David Chancellor?"

Dante cleared his throat again. "I'm his deputy."

"Right," Piper said. She did not want to talk about this. Not in the slightest. She didn't want to make any of this real even though she knew she had no choice. "Who is this buyer then?"

"As you know," Donte said, face flushing. "The buyer would like to remain anonymous."

"Mm-hmm. Not a developer though, David assured me of that," said Piper, thinking.

"Mmm," said Donte, but his skin was flaming hot now and Piper thought about offering him a glass of cool water.

"Are you alright?"

"Perfectly, thank you," said Donte, voice cracking a little.

Piper sighed and rubbed her eyes. "Can I be honest with you?"

"Sure." His hands still scrabbled with the papers he was holding.

"I'm really not sure yet. I need time. The renovations aren't finished and aren't likely to be for another few weeks yet. I thought that I'd have a bit more time to decide what to do."

"But surely it's better to have a sure sale, a definite thing, money in your pocket and all that."

Piper grinned. "Quite the little salesman now, aren't you?" she said. "And I get your point. And yes, the money would be good."

"You know that this doesn't happen immediately," said Donte, stepping in closer. "I mean, it's not like you'll have to move out tomorrow or anything. We could get the process started, go through the financials, start talking time-scales, and move on from there."

"None of that is binding?" Piper asked.

Donte shook his head. "Even accepting the offer isn't binding until contracts are signed. There'll still need to be a survey done and all kinds of other things."

And maybe it would be better to hurry things along. Like ripping off a band-aid. Maybe she should bite the bullet and stop things going too much further.

She had to leave. Perhaps a little sooner was better than a little later.

She still needed to find a job, after all. She still needed to buy furniture for her apartment. She still owed Joey a night of drinks, apart from anything else.

"Okay," she said slowly. "Okay, you can get the process started."

Donte let out a breath like he'd been holding it and nodded. "Perfect, wonderful."

"As long as it's not binding," Piper said again. "This is just to hurry things along in case I do decide to make this for real."

"Understood," Donte said.

Piper smiled. "Then tell your boss that you succeeded."

His grin faltered slightly.

"Now, do you want that tea, since business is out of the way? I've even got biscuits," Piper said. "Cam's got me trained well, as you can see."

She sensed his hesitation.

"I don't bite."

"No, uh, I'd better get going. Cam'll be here soon and I've got to get into the office."

"Busy, busy," Piper teased.

He smiled and made as though to leave but paused when he got to the door.

"Yes?" Piper asked.

He bit his lip. "Nothing, nothing," he said. "Just, well, just be sure this is what you want is all. You can still cancel all this right now."

"I know," Piper said. "You've made it perfectly clear, don't worry. I'm going into this with my eyes wide open."

He stared at her for a moment, then nodded and finally left.

Piper put the kettle on and busied herself getting cups. Cam would be here soon, she thought. Except, now that she thought about it, she had said she was stopping to pick up some bolts that she needed. Piper put one cup aside and made only one coffee.

It didn't feel good to sell the house. But it did feel like she was moving forward again, something she realized she'd been missing. This had been a nice vacation, a nice interlude, but she had to get her life on track.

So maybe it was a relief to finally start making some decisions, even if it did hurt more than she'd really like to admit.

Her phone started ringing and she groaned. It had to be Cam. She practically sprinted into the living room and picked the phone up without thinking about it.

"Everything's fine," she began.

"Oh," said a familiar voice. "Well, I'm definitely happy about that."

Piper's mouth dried up and she felt a little sick. She really should have checked before picking up the phone. But then, she was getting her life started again, wasn't she? Tying up loose ends. Getting back on track. And ends didn't come much looser than this.

"Lex," she said. "What do you want?"

CHAPTER TWENTY FIVE

Cam pushed through the half-broken wooden door.

"You mean all this could be yours?" Beth said, gazing around at the broken windows and puddles on the floor.

"If I want it," said Cam. She'd wanted to see the place, wanted to be sure, but she was having a hard time drumming up any enthusiasm,

"Wow, are the windows included?" asked Beth. "Because that would be a deal-breaker for me if they weren't. They really set the tone, you know?"

Cam forced a smile on her face. "It's for sale as is."

"Complete with spiders and... is that mouse poop?"

"Uh... dunno," Cam said, studying the floor. "Maybe."

Beth grinned. "I'm kidding, you know that, right? This place could be amazing. It will be amazing, when you've applied your talents to it. Sure, it'll take a while, but the bones are there."

Cam nodded, looking around, trying to imagine what the cottage could be instead of what it was. "I suppose," she sighed in the end, completely unable to picture anything other than the ruin she was standing in.

"Alright, enough's enough," said Beth, folding her arms. "What's going on?"

"Nothing!"

"Bullshit. I've known you your whole life, Cam, I—"

"Um, no you haven't."

"Well sometimes it feels like it," said Beth. "I certainly know when something's wrong. And I'm going to assume that you brought me here because you need to talk about whatever it is and now you're being too damn English to bring it up."

"Not true."

"Very true," said Beth. "So spill it."

Cam screwed her eyes tight shut. Maybe if she tried hard she could pretend that she hadn't heard anything, hadn't eavesdropped, hadn't spent the whole day with her stomach turning over and a sick taste in her mouth.

"I will torture it out of you if I have to," Beth threatened.

"I heard Piper on the phone this morning," Cam said quickly, not because she was afraid of Beth's threat but because if she said it fast enough maybe the memory would hurt less.

"So?" asked Beth, leaning up against a dirty wall.

"So she was on the phone with her ex."

"How do you know that?"

"Because she said her name."

Beth scratched at her nose. "That'll do it. And what did you overhear with those big ears of yours, my dear?"

"Nothing. Something. I don't know."

Nothing, in truth. It wasn't like Piper had promised undying love to the woman or even really said anything. At least not in the tail-end of the conversation that Cam had heard. It was nothing more really than what seemed like small talk.

Piper had mentioned the house, the name of the village, the fact that she was sticking around for a few weeks. Nothing more, nothing less. Even their goodbyes hadn't exactly been loving.

So it should all mean absolutely nothing.

Except Cam just couldn't shake the feeling that it meant *something*. She'd spent all day expecting Piper to bring it up, expecting her to say something about the call, but she hadn't. Maybe she wanted to hide it.

"Cam, I think you might be building this up into something

that it's not," Beth said quietly. "You know that Piper has an ex. Probably more than one, if we're being honest, she's an attractive woman. You have exes. That's what happens when you're both in your thirties. You have baggage."

"I know, I know. But this... Lex is different."

"Lex being the ex, I assume?"

Cam nodded. "Lex saved her. Piper's said as much. Her parents died when she was young and Lex was the one who helped her put her life back together again. Then Lex cheated and they broke up and Piper came here to try and put herself back together again."

"Okay," Beth said. "It's okay for her to share something with someone else. Are you jealous?"

Cam took a second to think about this, then shook her head. "Not jealous, at least I don't think so. Just... afraid I think. Afraid that this is the end of something that I don't want to end."

"Jesus," said Beth. She stood up straight and came over to Cam, taking both her hands. "Look me in the eye, Cam Fabbri."

Cam blinked but did as she was told.

"Are you in love with Piper?"

The question caught her off guard when really it shouldn't have. She should have considered it, privately at least. She should have thought about how she was feeling, what she was feeling. But she hadn't. She hadn't because she knew that this wasn't supposed to work and that labeling it would make it harder when it ended.

Now though, with Beth staring at her, holding her hands, it was very difficult not to think about it. Very difficult not to answer the question.

"What's love?" she said, pulling her hands away and rolling her eyes. "I mean, I like sleeping with her, obviously. She's nice. We have fun together. But that doesn't make it love, does it?"

"You wake up wanting to see her face," Beth said softly. "You think of her every time you turn around. Your heart misbehaves when she looks at you and suddenly you know what it's like not to be lonely. Suddenly you realize that even though you've been surrounded by people your entire life, you've been alone. Until now."

Cam's eyes stung. She blinked.

"Every moment without her seems wasted," said Beth. "And every moment with her seems too short. And every time you close your eyes…"

"I see her face," Cam finished.

For a long, long moment there was only the sound of the breeze blowing through the long grasses, of the birds chirping, the soft rustle of leaves swaying. And Cam knew the truth of it. Not that the truth made things easier, or changed them, but it was still the truth.

"You're in trouble girl," Beth finally said, lightly. "You've got it bad."

"And what am I supposed to do about it?" Cam asked. "She's going to leave. She has to leave. She's said as much."

"And you don't want to follow her?" asked Beth.

Cam shrugged. "I don't know. No, I think. I love my family, I love my village, I love what I do. But then, when I think of all those things without her, it feels like they won't be enough any more."

"So you'd think about it?"

"She hasn't asked me to," Cam pointed out.

Beth rubbed at her face with her hands. "Jesus, Cam. You really need to figure this stuff out. You have to think about it, make some decisions, decide what's best for you."

"And what's best for Piper."

"This could be yours," Beth said, gesturing around her at the wrecked cottage. "And I mean that with zero sarcasm. You could build something here, Cam. A home. Take the money you have and the money you'll get from Piper and buy this place and you'll have a home of your own. Something you've wanted for as long as I've known you."

"I know."

"Or maybe your needs have changed. That's okay too. Maybe you want something different now."

Cam closed her eyes. "I don't know. I really don't, Beth. I can't just demand that she stay. I can't demand that she give up her whole life to be with me here. And I can't demand that she take me with her."

"You can talk with her."

"I don't think talking will change anything," Cam said sadly. "I've tried talking to her about being long distance, but we ended up arguing. The fact of the matter is that we both agreed to something knowing that it would end, knowing that this moment would come, and by fighting it I feel like I'm betraying the agreement that we had."

"But you didn't intend to fall in love with her," said Beth.

"Didn't I?" Cam asked.

Beth raised an eyebrow at her and Cam felt her skin turn hot and red. She remembered pulling Piper out of the duck pond, the soft warm feel of her hand, the way her heart had beat harder and her mouth had dried up at the sight of her.

"I don't think I had any choice in the matter," Cam said. "I think it happened long before I realized it and completely outside of my control."

"That bad, huh?"

Cam nodded. "But I do have control over how I act now, over what I do and what I decide."

Beth looked around the cottage again. "Can you give up everything for a woman you barely know?"

"I don't know."

Beth took her hands again. "I'm here for you. If you need to talk about things, if you need help, you know that, right?"

"I do. But I think I need to deal with this alone."

"Then I'm here for you when you've decided," Beth said, leaning in and quickly giving her a peck on the cheek. She let go of Cam's hands. "I'm not here for spider clean up duty, however. And it's almost drink time, so we should be getting on."

"We should," grinned Cam.

Beth left and Cam took a last look. And just for a moment she could see it. She could see the cottage with a fire crackling in the hearth, could see a battered leather couch and a wall full of bookshelves, could see a dog on the mat and dinner on the table.

She smiled and turned a little until she could see Piper, sitting in an armchair by the fire, hair tucked behind her ears and a book open on her lap. Cam's heart stilled until she shook her head and the image disappeared and the cottage was just a broken-down old ruin once again.

"You know what Piper told me at lunch?" Beth said as they walked down the overgrown path to the van. "She asked Arthur about Lucy's letters and he wouldn't tell her a thing. Said that basically she wasn't a villager and these things are best left to those who'd understand better."

Cam snorted. "Seriously? I'll ask him then."

"He'll probably tell you," said Beth. "It's us outsiders he doesn't like."

"You've lived here for years."

"Don't kid yourself," Beth said. "I'm still an outsider. You English can be very funny about things like that."

"We're welcoming," Cam said, bristling. "It's not like we're xenophobic and racist or anything."

Beth pulled a face but didn't pursue the conversation. She jogged around to the passenger side of the van and opened the door. "It's drink time, come on."

Cam took her time pulling her keys out of her pocket. Beth's comment had surprised her. She hadn't thought that Sutton's Walk was anything other than lovely to visitors. In fact, she was sure it hadn't been.

The village was her home, all she knew, and the thought of maybe leaving it filled her with sadness.

Her head felt full and she really, really wished that she could just hand all these decisions over to someone else to make for her.

She climbed into the van and started the engine. One drink. One drink and then she'd drive herself home, park up in the farmyard, and give some serious thought to solutions to the situation she found herself in. She'd leave Piper alone tonight.

SIENNA WATERS

She needed no distractions at all.

CHAPTER TWENTY SIX

"Come on, you big beast," Piper said, yanking on Billy's leash.

She'd taken to walking him three times a day, figuring that he needed plenty of exercise. What she hadn't thought about was just who was going to take care of Billy when she was gone. Something that she really did need to plan for.

"What about Arthur?" she suggested to Billy.

But Arthur was old and didn't have the energy for looking after a big dog like Billy, not really. She could ask Cam, she supposed. But it seemed like an imposition. Or Beth? She sighed. Arthur had been right when he'd intimated that she was an outsider here.

A real villager would have tens of people to leave the dog too.

Just for a silly little second she found that she was blinking away a tear.

She'd never wanted a dog before, in fact had never had a pet before at all. But Billy had grown on her. She didn't like the idea of leaving him behind. But what the hell could she do with a dog the size of a small pony in the city?

All of which just brought back the idea that she was leaving.

She had to leave.

Which made her feel depressed again.

This really hadn't been the point of this trip at all, she thought, as she pulled Billy onto the sidewalk. She was supposed to come here and get her head straight. Not come here and complicate life even more.

There were options though, weren't there? She just hadn't wanted to see them she'd been so set on her idea of what was supposed to happen.

She'd been thinking, ever since Donte had come asking for an answer about the house.

Okay, maybe they weren't perfect options, but they existed. After all, plenty of Americans lived in the UK. There had to be some system of getting a visa or something. And maybe she could talk herself into a job.

Or even freelance.

That way she could stay with Billy. She had a house already, so she wouldn't need to pay rent. There were bills though, food too, the UK wasn't cheap. Far from it.

There were options that she'd dismissed, being so sure that she needed to go home and fix the life that she had. But what about starting a new life over instead? Wasn't that a possibility? The idea frightened her.

"Watch out, if he sees a duck he'll have your arm off," said a voice.

Piper blinked out of her thoughts to see a large, brawny, dark-haired man grinning at her. Then she searched her memory. "Cosmo?" she ventured.

"Nice try," he laughed. "Christophoro."

She shook her head. "I'm sorry. It's not that I'm terrible with names, though I'm not great, it's that—"

"We all look the same except Cam and Donte," Christophoro filled in with a grin. "I know. We don't take it personally, don't worry. How's the house coming along?"

"Great," Piper said. Clutching on to Billy's lead. She felt weirdly nervous, afraid that she might say something that would give her and Cam away.

"She's a good worker is Cam," Christophoro said proudly.

"Don't tell her I said so, but she can put the rest of us to shame. Mum won't trust anyone else with the boiler."

Piper smiled politely.

"Oh, I did stop you for a reason," he said, running his hand through his short hair. "There was someone looking for you."

"For me?" Piper asked, confused.

"Yeah. I sent her up to the house," said Christophoro. "Hope you don't mind, but she looked about done in and I figured she could sit on the step and wait there for you if you weren't around. Promised I'd keep an eye out for you."

"Oh," said Piper, brain quickly doing the math and not liking the answer she came up with. "Er, thanks. I should be going then."

"Right," Christophoro said. "Have a nice night then."

But Piper was already hurrying off down the sidewalk, stomach dropping at the sight she was sure she was about to see.

Billy raced ahead and paused only long enough for Piper to open the gate. But when she did, the garden was empty and no one was there. She let out a breath. She was being stupid. She'd jumped to a conclusion, and an unrealistic one at that.

She was just about feeling herself again, reaching in her pocket for the front door key, when a figure appeared from around the side of the house.

Her stomach dropped all over again.

"Well," grinned Lex. "Aren't you going to invite me in?"

HER HANDS HAD stopped shaking enough that she was able to carry the tea tray without spilling the tea. Not that she was clear on what was happening here, or on how she felt about it. But she knew that tea was in order. She'd lived in England that long, at least.

"How did you find me?" she asked, as she deposited the tray on the coffee table.

"You told me the name of the village," Lex said, turning away from the bookshelf that she'd been studying.

"But that was just this morning," said Piper.

"And I was already in the UK," grinned Lex. "Surprise."

Lex had always been spontaneous. It was something that Piper had loved about her, the way she could just pull people out of their routines, how she could make life special all over again.

"But why?" Piper asked.

Lex came and sat down, crossing her long legs and reaching for a cup. "I'm teaching a summer semester class at London University," she said. "It was a last minute thing. And I knew you were here."

"Joey," Piper said, mentally cursing her friend.

"Hey, don't be too hard on her. She didn't tell me exactly where you were. She didn't really intend to tell me at all. In the middle of yelling at me for being an asshole she let it slip that you were out of the country and that I'd never find you."

"And you always liked a challenge," said Piper.

Lex sipped at her cup then pulled a face. "What the hell is this?"

"Tea."

She put the cup down again. "Jesus, it tastes like something that came out of the toilet. And I was, by the way."

"You were what?" asked Piper.

Lex was just sitting there. Her Lex. Her face as familiar as the back of Piper's hand, the little scar on her cheek, the rings on her fingers. She was wearing the boots that they'd bought in that little store by the beach on their anniversary. She smelled just the same, like home.

"I was an asshole," Lex said, re-crossing her legs.

Piper blinked. "What do you want?"

"To tell you that I was an asshole and that I fully acknowledge the fact and that you should know that I know," Lex said. She leaned forward a little. "I was, and am, the biggest, stupidest, most horrendous asshole in the world. You deserve better than me and you're better off without me."

Which took Piper aback. "You came all this way to say that?"

"Not exactly," said Lex.

Piper had the idea that she might not want to hear what Lex had to say next, so she steered the conversation in another direction. "You cheated on me."

"Which is unforgivable." Lex closed her eyes for a second and looked so old that Piper realized she'd almost forgotten just how long they'd been together. "I can't undo what happened, Pipe. I'm not sure I can even really explain it. It was wrong on so many levels. I don't know what I was thinking except… Except we had a life, Pipe. A whole life. And I didn't know any different life from the one we had and suddenly I got to thinking that maybe there were other lives…"

"And maybe you'd prefer them?"

"And maybe I needed something more." Lex looked down at her hands. "Pipe, I was wrong. I don't know what else to say. I should never have done it."

"You shouldn't have."

"You needed me," Lex said, looking up with deep blue eyes. "You needed me so much, Pipe. And I got used to it, I got used to being needed. I was proud to help you. But then, over time, you stopped needing me. You stood on your own two feet, and I was happy for you. But I missed being needed. Then Kyla came along and she was so young and so sweet and so lost. But that wasn't why I did it. It had nothing to do with age or looks or anything like that. I did it because she needed me."

Piper took a breath, trying to find the anger that she'd had for Lex. But all she found was hurt and the smallest, tiniest amount of pity.

"It felt so good to be needed."

"I needed you," Piper said softly. "I did. I was lost without you. You know, I haven't even furnished the apartment that I rented? I might not have said it, I might not have shown it, and that's on me. But I did need you, Lex."

"I fucked everything up."

"You did."

Lex twirled a lock of dark hair around her finger. "That's what I came for. To explain. To apologize. To tell you that none of this was about you. It was all me."

"Thank you," Piper said. "I needed to hear that." It didn't make things better, but it made things more understandable.

"There's something else," Lex said.

Piper nodded. She didn't want to hear it, but perhaps she needed this too.

"I have no right to ask. You hold all the cards here, Piper. But I have to say this because I'll regret it forever if I don't. If there's any way, anything I can do or say, just any chance at all of us building something together again. Well, I want you to know that I'm here for it."

Six months ago, a month ago, that would have been enough, it would have been all Piper wanted to hear. But now she just nodded. She checked her watch.

"You're not going to get a cab out here at this time of night," she said.

"Really?" frowned Lex. "It's not even eight yet."

"Trust me," Piper said. She got up. "I'll get some blankets and sheets. You can make up a bed on the couch and spend the night."

"I've booked a hotel," said Lex quickly. "I didn't expect you to put me up."

Piper smiled. "It's fine. I know you didn't. But you can't walk country lanes at night. It's not a problem. You go into the kitchen and make some coffee and I'll get those sheets for you."

"Right," said Lex, standing up. She hesitated for a second before reaching out for Piper's hand. "Are we okay?"

They shouldn't be. Piper couldn't remember ever hurting as badly as she had when Lex had left. But now she could barely remember how that pain had felt. She did remember how much she had loved Lex, she remembered how comforting she could be, how familiar and comfortable. And she remembered that Lex had saved her once.

"Yes," she said. "Yes. We're okay."

CHAPTER TWENTY SEVEN

Cam took a deep breath and then opened the garden gate.

A whole night of thinking.

A whole night of trying to put herself in Piper's shoes, of trying to figure out what was the best thing to do.

A whole night of possibilities and endings and everything in between.

And here she was. Ready to admit that she knew nothing, had decided nothing, but that that in itself was a step forward. Because she was ready to talk, ready to be honest about her feelings, and ready to unveil herself in front of Piper.

If Piper wanted to pursue this, then they would just have to find a way, they'd just have to compromise and get things done.

Just for once, Cam was going to do what everyone always told her to do, and put herself first. She had feelings and she was about to explode with them. Piper could choose how to deal with that as she wished.

One way or another there was going to be resolution here.

So why was she grinning as she walked up the garden path? Why couldn't she stop herself smiling? This was terrifying. Terrifying, she realized, and thrilling all at once. Which was about all she could imagine love was supposed to be.

The front door was unlocked so she let herself in and was half-way down the corridor to the kitchen before she realized that there were voices. She slowed her step.

Piper's voice was instantly recognizable. The other voice was American. She slowed even further. Slowed and then stopped just as she came to the door, just as she was able to see who was sitting and having breakfast.

Lex, because it had to be her, was taller than she'd imagined. Her eyes were deepest blue and her nose was a little crooked but in a sweet way. She had a wide smile and when she laughed, her whole face lifted with it.

She was pretty, Cam thought. Pretty and confident. They made a nice couple. Lex reached over and took a napkin, passing it to Piper who rolled her eyes and then wiped jam from her lip.

There was such familiarity in the gesture, such naturalness and openness that it made Cam's heart stop.

Then Piper laughed at something Lex said, and Cam could see it. She could see how they fit together, how they shared something visceral. She could see how Lex had rescued Piper, how Piper had needed saving. She could see a whole history between the two of them in the space between them and it made her hurt so badly she almost cried out.

And at the same time it made her so happy for Piper, so happy that something like this, a relationship like this, could exist, that she could almost weep with it.

She stood and watched for what could have been hours, just drinking in the sight of them, seeing how two people could be together, seeing the private moments that could only exist between two. She stood until her legs ached as much as her heart.

Then she forced herself to take a step, then another, until she was standing in the doorway.

Lex's eyebrows lifted, then she grinned. "Wow, you're quiet as a ghost. You've gotta be the contractor, Cam, right?"

Cam nodded, not trusting herself to speak just yet.

"Fuck," said Piper. "I totally lost track of time." She stood up, knocking over a pot of jam as she did so.

Lex reached out and righted the jar. "Calm down, you're always in such a snit about things happening on time."

"I just—" started Piper.

"I'm already all packed up," Lex said. Outside, a car horn beeped. "And that'll be my cue."

She stood up. "Pleasure to meet you, Cam," she said, bumping past her on the way to the living room.

"Just a second," Piper said, watching Cam with careful eyes. "I didn't mean..."

"You didn't mean for me to see this," Cam filled in.

"Yo, Pipes, I'm out of here," called Lex from the front door.

Piper bit her lip then jogged down the hallway. There was a whispered conversation that Cam couldn't hear and then Lex was opening her arms and Piper was disappearing into them and she couldn't watch any more.

She went to the sink and started to fill the kettle. She heard the front door close and knew that she and Piper were alone again.

"You're right, I didn't mean for you to see that," Piper said, coming into the kitchen. "But not in the way that makes things sound. I just meant that I would rather tell you about it than have you walk in and see it without warning."

Cam turned the kettle on and looked out into the garden. Arthur was shuffling along his path to the vegetable patch. She really needed to look in on him, make sure he had enough shopping to last a few days.

"Cam?"

She wanted to turn around. But as long as she didn't, everything was still okay. As long as she kept looking out of the window, all those possibilities still existed.

"Cam, I feel like I might need to explain things," Piper said.

One last deep breath, then she moved. "Don't worry," she said, turning around. "We're not about to have one of those rom-com grand misunderstanding moments."

Piper lifted an eyebrow. "You think we're in a romantic comedy?"

"Well, I did fish you out of a duck pond," Cam said. The kettle whistled. "Tea?"

"That was Lex."

"I figured as much."

"She's teaching a course in London, I didn't know. She just showed up at my door. She slept on the couch. That's it. There's no more to the story."

"That's fine," Cam said. "Tea?"

Piper nodded and sat back down at the breakfast table. "I should have said something, I knew you were coming. But she was going to catch an early train and I thought she'd be out of here before you got here. I absolutely was going to tell you she was here though."

Cam poured the tea and took the mugs to the table, along with a plate for the teabags when they were done brewing.

"Piper, it's fine. You don't need to be defensive about this, you don't need to feel bad. I have no doubt that Lex was an unexpected guest and that she slept on the couch. I don't know you that well, but I do know you well enough to know that being cheated on hurt you enough that you'd never do it to anyone else."

"No," Piper said. "No, I wouldn't."

"Did she want to get back together?" Cam asked, because she had to know. Not that it would make a whole lot of difference. But she wanted to know.

Piper nodded. "She apologized."

"You should accept the apology."

"I did," sighed Piper.

"Then what's the problem?" Cam asked.

Piper laughed grimly. "Yeah, I think you know the answer to that."

"I'm the problem," said Cam.

"No. Yes. No. I'm the problem."

"Then let's solve all this right now," said Cam. "We're adults. We knew this was going to end. So it needs to end."

"I'm not going back to her," Piper began.

Cam's heart broke into tiny pieces as she said: "You should."

Piper gripped her mug.

"No, listen to me, Piper. You're right about so many things. What you and I have together is new and isn't worth risking anything for. What you and Lex had, have, is a whole life together. If you can find it in your heart to forgive her, then you should at least try again. You can't just throw everything away."

"I never wanted things to be this way," Piper said.

"I know. But I also know that Lex saved you. You told me as much. And I'm not sure that I can save you in the same way. I'm not sure that I can build something with you in the same way that you and Lex built a life."

"Cam, you're an amazing woman, you're—"

"I know," Cam broke in. "I don't need to be flattered. I'm not here because I want you to tell me how special I am. You have a life in the States, you can have a life with Lex. You once told me that you didn't want to be long distance because you didn't want to stand in the way of me finding something or someone else."

"It's true."

"Yes, but now I actually understand what you mean," Cam said. "I don't want to stand in the way of you reconciling with Lex if that's the best decision for you. And let's face it, it probably is. You can go back to your life, Piper. You can go back to that life that you already put so much work into."

Piper tapped her fingers on the table. "And you?"

Cam smiled. "A cottage just came on the market. Donte told me about it. With what I have and what you owe me for the work here, I should just about be able to make a down payment."

Piper smiled. "I'm happy for you."

"So we're both moving on with our lives, we're both getting what we wanted, right?"

"You're a good woman."

"So people tell me," Cam said.

"And I can tell you that I didn't mean for things to end this way, but I think you know that."

"I think we both knew from the beginning that we were going to get hurt," Cam said. "But if I'm honest, I have to say it was worth it."

Piper nodded. "Yes," she said. "It was, wasn't it?"

All the pain in the world would have been worth just one kiss, Cam thought. "So, what now?"

"Well," said Piper. "I suppose we'd better get on with things. Assuming we're both still mature enough to do what needs to be done."

"I've got plans to finish," Cam said. "An electrician is coming in tomorrow to take a look at the place."

"And I've got an offer that I should accept," Piper added. "So I should get contracts and the like signed."

"It'll be a few weeks yet until everything's done and dusted."

"I'd like to spend more time with you," Piper said awkwardly. "I mean as friends. I hope we are friends."

Cam had to swallow hard to get rid of the lump in her throat. She had to do this. It was the right thing for Piper. Whatever Cam herself might want. Piper and Lex were a good couple and could be again. It was only right that Piper picked up her life again.

No drama. No fighting. No tears.

"Yes," she said. "We're friends."

CHAPTER TWENTY EIGHT

Piper laid back on the bed. "I get it," she said. "I mean, I do get it."

"Really?" Joey said. "Because you're not sounding great, to be honest. Do I need to come over there? Buy you pints in the pub?"

Piper managed to laugh into the phone. "No, no. I'll be fine. The last thing I need is more Americans showing up here. Any more of you and the village will think I'm invading."

"You're joking, that's better."

Outside it was still warm, the birds were still singing. The room was starting to be familiar now, starting to feel like home.

"I'm ruining her life," Piper said.

"That's a bit dramatic."

"Well, it's true. I am. I turn up here and all of a sudden she's interested in women from a million miles away. Of course she wants me to leave. It makes sense. Without me here she can go back to her regular life. Go back to being with men, go back to living with her family, working on buying herself a house. Go back to normal."

"Is that how sexuality works then?" Joey asked. "Because if it's just a matter of being around the right people then I think I might need to move in Sarah Paulson and Holland Taylor so that

I can stop falling for asshole guys."

"You know what I mean. I disrupted things. It'll be easier for Cam if I'm not here. I've put a lot of thought into this, Joe."

"Will it be easier for you if you're not there?"

"Maybe." Piper's stomach hurt just thinking about it.

A whole week had gone by since Cam had told her that they should break things off, since Lex had showed up unexpectedly. A week was a long time to think about things. And now that the initial hurt was wearing off a little, she could see that Cam was probably right.

"You're still working together though, right?"

"Mm-hmm."

"Is that awkward?"

"Not really." Only when she temporarily forgot and reached out to touch Cam's arm or stroke her hair and then remembered that she was no longer allowed to do such things.

She heard Joey sigh. "Listen, Pipes, you guys sound like you were perfect for each other. Mutual attraction, comparable senses of humor, the whole nine yards. But I get that there are problems. No relationship is perfect, you know?"

"It's not. This is more than that though. We were doomed from the start."

"More of the drama."

Piper laughed. "No, I mean it. We both knew this was never going to work in the long run, we both tried anyway, and now Cam has finally come to her senses and been the grown up and decided we need to end this before things get more painful. I can respect that."

"I'm not sure I can."

"She hasn't even told her family about me, Joe. I just walked in here like I owned the place and up-ended her life and now she's decided that enough is enough. Which is fine. Painful, but fine."

"And all this has nothing to do with Lex showing up out of thin air?"

"She might have been a catalyst. But this was going to happen sooner or later. Maybe it's better that it's sooner. And maybe the sooner I get out of here the better. There's no point in dragging things out."

"Okay, here's a question then."

"That sounds ominous."

"I've known you a long time, Piper Garland. I'd like to kid myself that you're my other half, the twin I never had. I've held back your hair while you barfed and wiped your tears and drunk to your achievements and met every last girlfriend you've ever had."

"I thought there was a question here?"

"There is," Joey said. "My question is, do you love her?"

For a moment the world stopped spinning and Piper lay on her bed with the phone pressed to her ear and couldn't breathe. Then everything snapped back into place.

"Don't be ridiculous."

"I'm not," said Joey. "And you know I'm not. I can tell from the tone of your voice, I can tell from the way you speak about her. Not that it necessarily changes anything, you can be in love with someone and not together with them. But if you can't admit that even to yourself, then yes, you're right, you guys need to stop this and get on with your lives."

Piper swallowed.

"Are you going back to Lex?"

"Are you about to lecture me about that?" Piper said. "Because I'm really not in the mood, Joe. Things have been tough enough the last week or so. I can't deal with you dissing Lex and—"

"Hey, hey, since when have I spoken badly about anyone you've loved?" Joey interrupted. "If that's your choice, then so be it. Lex has made mistakes, we both know that, but a mistake doesn't make someone a bad person. Just a flawed one."

"Right," Piper said, knowing that Joey was right and knowing that she'd over-reacted.

"So, are you?"

Another deep breath. "Yes, I think so. Temporarily at least. I mean, I'm going to join her in London for a few days. We'll see how it goes."

"You guys were together a long time. It's worth seeing if there's something there worth saving."

"That's my thinking," Piper said, though she was more and more sure that there was nothing there to save anymore.

Still, she owed it to herself and to Lex, and to the life they'd built together, to give it a try.

"Here's me thinking that you were going to England to have a break, think things over, get away from things. And you end up making even more trouble while you're there," Joey said.

"I know, I know."

"And I'm not even there to buy you a drink," said Joey. "Stay strong, Pipes. You've got this. I'm sorry that things weren't as relaxing as you thought. And I'm really sorry that things didn't work out with Cam. She sounds nice."

"You'd like her," Piper said, staring out of the window. "Maybe you'll meet her. Maybe she'll come over for a visit."

"Jesus, are all lesbians like this? You know straight people just want to murder their exes in their beds, right?" said Joey. "You guys rent cottages together for the summer and go on retreats."

"That would seem to be a flaw in straight people rather than lesbians," Piper said.

"You could be right there," laughed Joey. "Alright, I've got to go. I'll see you soon, I hope."

IT WASN'T WHAT she wanted. But Piper was old enough to know that life wasn't all about what you wanted.

Cam came in and worked. They had tea and chatted. They were friends, friendly. But there was always the feeling of something more in the air. And it was that that made Piper think that she needed to do everyone a favor and move things along.

Cam had done the hard thing, she'd broken things off. So now maybe it was Piper's turn to do something tough.

She listened to Cam walk away, heard the front door close, and her heart hurt at the sound of it. All she really wanted was to curl up in a cozy cottage with Cam at her side. But too much stood in their way.

Seeing Lex had been a surprise. Hearing her apologize had been more of a surprise. And the lure of maybe having her old life back was, well, alluring.

And all this was just a dream, just an oasis, a nothing, not real, not sustainable. She opened up the back door and let Billy leap out, then followed him into the garden.

"Love-lorn are we, my dear," Arthur said, straightening up from his vegetable patch.

"What?" said Piper.

The old man laughed. "It's clear as day. That Cam Fabbri walking around with a face like a wet weekend and you wandering around like you're lost. The two of you are on the outs."

Piper opened her mouth then closed it again. She wasn't exactly sure what to say.

"What? You thought I'd be prejudiced just because I'm old? That's prejudice itself, I'd say." He sniffed. "The two of you make a nice couple. You're good for each other. It was nice to see Cam putting her own needs first for a change, wanting something other than to please others. Can't speak about you, of course, haven't known you that long."

Piper suddenly realized that any gossip about this could ruin Cam's life in the village. She stepped forward. "Arthur..."

"Say no more, love," he said, holding up a wrinkled hand. "I'll not say a word out of place, on my honor. I'm old enough and ugly enough to know better than to mess with love. No one will hear a thing from me."

"No words of wisdom for me?" Piper asked, smiling a little.

"Watch too many films, you do," said Arthur. "Just because I'm old doesn't mean I'm going to suddenly give you the secret to success or anything. Look at me, I've been single for neigh-on ninety years. What do I know about love?"

He started shuffling down his path toward the house. Then he stopped.

"I do know one thing," he said. "Love or not, just a general rule of life. Things tend to work out for the best in the end." Then he went in his back door.

Piper sighed. Maybe they did. Maybe they would. Who knew?

But she knew that she couldn't go on doing this. Couldn't see Cam every day. Couldn't keep worrying that she was ruining Cam's life for nothing. Even Arthur could see that they'd had something. It was time to do this for real.

She pulled her cell phone from her pocket and dialed.

"Donte?" she said, when he picked up. "I think it's time to get that contract ready. I need to sell the house."

CHAPTER TWENTY NINE

Cam tightened the last bolt then stood up, stretching out her back. "Done."

"One down, one to go," Piper said. But she was smiling as she looked around the modern bathroom. "It looks amazing though."

"Don't worry, the plumber is starting the second bathroom on Monday," said Cam, washing her hands in the sink that she'd finished installing.

"Good," said Piper. But she sounded distracted.

Cam could understand that. She could understand how difficult it was to see someone that you wanted every day. She could understand how complications complicated things. She could understand all that in a way that a few days ago she really hadn't got.

But every time things got hard, every time she wanted to reach out and touch Piper, she just reminded herself that she was doing the best thing.

The best thing for Piper, and that was what counted.

Maybe too, the best thing for herself. She honestly wasn't sure about that yet. She was sure that she missed Piper's arms around her, missed laughing with her and touching her.

"Everything okay?" she asked as lightly as she could.

Piper sighed. "You know, for someone who's known me a month, you're awfully good at reading me."

"Consider it a special talent," said Cam.

"Listen, I was just about to take Billy for his walk. Want to come?"

Cam shrugged. Why not? It wasn't like her evenings were suddenly full and lively. It wasn't like she had much to do other than eat at home, drink in the pub with Beth, or sit in her van with a book.

Besides, said a little voice in the back of her head, every moment with Piper is extra special, isn't it?

"Sure."

"I'll let you finish up in here while I get Billy's leash on."

By the time she was coming downstairs she wasn't so sure that she should go at all. It was getting harder to be around Piper. Harder knowing that she was going to leave any minute. But Billy was raring to go, and Cam didn't have the heart to change her mind, so she went anyway.

"There's something you should know," Piper said, as they made for the village green.

"You're leaving," said Cam, suddenly sure this was true.

Piper sighed. "I think it's for the best. I know that the house isn't quite finished yet, but I trust you to do what's right. You don't need me around getting under your feet all the time."

"I don't mind," said Cam. "I honestly don't."

"Okay," said Piper. "A little more honest then. You don't need me around making all of this any harder than it really needs to be. It's time that I left. Donte's getting the papers together so I can sign off on the sale of the house."

"When?" asked Cam.

Piper let out a breath. "Tomorrow."

Something stabbed Cam in the heart and the pain made her lose her breath. "Okay."

"Short notice, I know. But I honestly only decided yesterday." Piper stopped on the edge of the grass. "I think it's best that I go. Don't you?"

"Are you going home?"

Piper shook her head. "I'll go to London for a few days to see Lex. Then I'll fly home from there on Thursday. I just... I need to see her. Figure out if there's something there to save."

"I hope there is," said Cam, desperately not wanting there to be but hating herself for being selfish.

"I don't know," Piper said, starting to walk again. "I'm starting to feel like I don't know anything anymore."

"It has to be worth trying," Cam told her. "After everything that you've shared, it must be worth the effort."

"Perhaps," said Piper. She cleared her throat and made an attempt to sound brighter. "And what about you? What about your cottage?"

"I've put an offer in, well, Donte has. So we just have to wait and see," said Cam, wishing she was more excited about the prospect of having her own place.

"I hope things work out for you, Cam, I truly do."

"Me too."

They walked in silence for a few meters, Billy pulling at his leash. "I, uh, wanted to say thank you," Piper said finally.

"Thank you? For what?"

"For everything. For all the work you've done, obviously. I've transferred money to your account, so you should be all paid up and ready to pay that down payment as soon as your offer is accepted."

"Thank you," said Cam, knowing the money wasn't the issue.

"And, uh, thank you for everything else," Piper said quietly. "For the laughter, for the fun, for making me feel welcome. I hope you don't have any regrets, Cam, because I certainly don't. I know that this hurts, that I'm definitely hurting, but that's the price we have to pay sometimes, isn't it? The sacrifice we make for having something that's worth having, even if it's for a short time."

Cam nodded and her hand brushed against Piper's. Quickly, she snatched it away and put it in her pocket.

"I should thank you too," she said. "And no regrets, really."

Was that true? If she could undo all this, would she? She really didn't know. She couldn't imagine her life now without Piper in it.

"Jesus, this walk is turning into a misery fest," Piper said.

"Well, you started it," pointed out Cam.

"You're right, I did. My apologies. This doesn't have to be a final ending. You could come and visit, you know. My best friend Joey is dying to meet you."

"A holiday in America?" Cam said, knowing full well that she'd never set foot on the plane, that she couldn't hurt herself by seeing Piper in her element, Piper with Lex. "We'll have to see about that."

"When your cottage is all done, of course," Piper said. "You're always welcome."

"And you're always welcome here," Cam said.

"I might have to come back just for the biscuits. You know, I'm not sure American ones are going to cut it anymore? I'm going to have to fill up my suitcase at Heathrow."

Cam laughed. "I could send you some, you know."

"That sounds like a plan," said Piper, stopping again. She looped Billy's leash over her wrist and took Cam's hands.

As much as she didn't want to be touched, Cam let it happen. No, that wasn't true. It wasn't that she didn't want to be touched. It was that she didn't want to be untouched again after. But Piper's warm, dry hands were already in hers and there was nothing she could do about it.

"This has been wonderful," Piper said.

"You're starting to be miserable again," said Cam.

"You're right, but this needs to be said," Piper started.

But then Billy began barking and pulling at his leash and Piper stumbled. Cam yanked her hands back and the leash flew off Piper's wrist as Billy made a break for it, a madly quacking, flapping duck steps ahead of him.

"Jesus Christ," Piper said, looking down at her wrist.

Cam giggled, then broke out into a full laugh.

"Hey, at least I had the smarts to let go of the leash this time,"

Piper protested, before starting to laugh herself.

"We'd best go catch Billy before he eats the local wildlife," Cam said, starting after him. Then she paused. "What's going to happen to him?"

"Arthur is going to take him," Piper said. "Maybe not the greatest option, but they're quite attached to each other."

"I'll stop by," Cam said quickly. "Make sure he gets long walks and that kind of thing. Don't worry about him."

Piper looked over to where Billy was splashing around at the edge of the duck pond. "Come on then, let's fish something out of the pond one last time."

"He's not as muddy as you were," said Cam, smiling at the memory.

"Don't remind me. Though at least if I fall in again I've got a real shower to use."

IT WAS ALMOST dark by the time they got back to the garden gate.

Cam's whole body felt heavy.

"So, uh, I guess this is goodbye?" she managed.

"And I guess this is you being just about the most English person in the world right now?" Piper said, hooking Billy's leash onto the gate.

"What's that supposed to mean?"

"It's supposed to mean that this is an emotional moment and that it's okay to actually show some emotion," said Piper.

"Yeah, not something I'm great at."

"Then let's practice right now," said Piper, taking her hands again. "This is goodbye. And I'm so lucky and privileged to have spent time with you, Camilla Fabbri. I'm honored to have known you and to have had this time with you."

"Wow, and you want me to follow that up?" Cam said, blinking away what might be a tear. "I, uh, I'll miss you."

Piper smiled. "There you go, that wasn't so hard, was it? I'll miss you too, Cam. But we're friends, remember? Stay in touch."

Cam nodded. "I'll try."

"I need you to send me pictures of the house. And of your new cottage of course. Oh, and of Billy. So you don't have much of a choice in matters."

Cam sincerely wished this moment was over. Not that she didn't want to be standing in front of Piper. But she wanted the agony of saying goodbye done, she wanted it to be a painful memory, something she could shut away, rather than a painful present.

"I should go," she said, voice hardly cracking at all.

Piper hesitated for a moment and looked as though she might be about to draw Cam into her arms. But she didn't. She let go and took a step back. "Good bye, Cam," she said gently.

"Good bye," said Cam, voice definitely cracking.

After a long second, Piper took Billy's leash and opened the gate. She walked down the garden path and into the house without looking back.

And it was just as well. Because Cam didn't think she had the strength to walk away. So she just watched it happen. Watched and felt her heart shred into a million pieces.

CHAPTER THIRTY

Piper crammed a pair of socks into the case and zipped it closed. That was it. Everything. She looked around the bedroom and her heart sank. She wouldn't be back here again.

"You're on to new things," she told herself. "You're reclaiming your life. It's exciting." Which should probably be easier to believe than it actually was.

She lugged the case down the stairs and left it by the door. She was about to put the kettle on for the last time when the doorbell rang.

"Donte," she said when she opened the door. "You're early." She looked at him with narrowed eyes. "And you rang the doorbell."

"The door wasn't open this time," he said defensively. "And I'm only five minutes early." He hesitated. "I could, uh, drive around the green or something for a few minutes if you'd like?"

Piper laughed. "No, come in, come in. I was about to put the kettle on. Tea?"

Another hesitation and then he stepped over the threshold. "Yes," he said. "Yes, please."

He grinned at her and his smile was so much like Cam's that Piper's heart tried to explode in her chest. She caught her breath, sniffed, turned and walked away down the corridor. "This is exciting," she hissed to herself under her breath.

"What's that?" asked Donte.

"Nothing," Piper said. "Milk and sugar?"

"Milk, no sugar," he said.

He laid his briefcase on the table and started to go through papers as Piper made tea. Only when they were sitting opposite each other, steaming mugs on the table, did he slide a document toward her.

"The sale contract," he said. His hand stayed on top of it. "This is binding. There's no get-out clause on this one."

Piper's heart misbehaved again. "I know," she said. She reached for it and tried to slide it toward her side of the table, but Donte's hand still lay on top of it.

"Cam really likes you," he said.

Piper raised an eyebrow at him. "I know," she said carefully, not wanting to give any secrets away and not sure at all what Donte knew.

"She thinks you're amazing. Clever too."

Piper gulped. "That's nice," she managed.

Donte was starting to flush pink and then in one movement he pulled the file back and away from Piper.

"Hey!"

"Can you trust me?" he said.

"Why should I?" Piper asked, frowning and wondering just what the hell was going on.

"Because... because you trust Cam and I'm her little brother?" he said unsurely. "I know it's not much, but it's all I've got right now."

"What are you talking about?"

Donte sighed then cleared his throat. "You shouldn't sign this contract," he said. "At least not right now. Not this second. It's not a great plan. A better offer might come along, an easier sale. You're hurrying things and in real estate that's never a good idea, whatever my boss might say."

"It's not exactly like I have much choice," Piper said, amused now at his sincerity. "I'm leaving the village, leaving the country in a few days."

"There is a choice," he said. Another clearing of the throat and Piper remembered how young he was. "I've got a power of attorney form here. You could sign that instead and give me the right to sign a contract on your behalf. It's a limited power, so I won't be able to do anything else. But it'll give you time to think things through a little, time to make sure you hear all the offers. As long as you trust me enough to sign it."

"I don't know," she said. She was getting used to the idea of this all being over, of making a clean break.

"It costs you nothing," Donte said quickly. "You've got until the beginning of next week to decide on the sale. But there are other interested parties. I'm not supposed to say anything, David definitely wouldn't want me to. I am looking out for you though, please, Piper. I wouldn't ask you this if I didn't think it was important."

Piper bit her lip then accepted the piece of paper he was offering her. She should just sign the contract, just finish things.

Out in the garden, Billy barked and she could hear Arthur talking to him over the fence.

"You'll ensure that the house is sold to the best person for the village?" she asked Donte, eyeing him fiercely.

He nodded. "I swear."

Then she took his pen and signed it.

She probably shouldn't have. She realized that as soon as it was done. But he was believable, he was sincere, and maybe, just maybe, the idea of having a tie to the village for just a few more days appealed to her.

If she found the strength to walk away from here, maybe a few days in London would give her the strength to walk right back to here. Who knew?

She just wasn't quite ready to sign it all away right now, that was all she could say.

"Tea's lovely," Donte said, taking a sip. "Got any biscuits?"

And Piper laughed. "You're too much like Cam," she said getting up and finding a package.

"Everyone says that. Cam and I are the outcasts, the two not like the others," Donte said, taking a biscuit.

"Outcasts is a strong word, you know," Piper said.

Donte shrugged. "It's harder for Cam, she's the girl. She gets stuck doing the stuff no one else wants to do, she's the one mum turns to, it can't have been easy growing up as the only girl with six brothers now."

"And things aren't so bad for you?"

He shrugged again and chomped on a biscuit. "I'm just a weakling and they all harbor a secret suspicion that I'm gay. Which is stupid because I'm pretty sure that not having big muscles doesn't make you gay. Not that it'd be a problem if I were, just..."

"Just you're not?"

"Don't think so," Donte said, almost as if he wished he were. "It'd be nice to find someone though. Which is hard around here, especially when I'm competing against five of my own brothers."

"You could get away for a while," Piper said. "University maybe. Or just a year abroad volunteering or something. Something to give you perspective."

"Huh," said Donte. "Yeah, maybe. I'm not the uni type, but volunteering doesn't sound bad. I might look into that."

Piper pulled a face. "Please don't tell your parents or Cam that I told you to leave the village."

Donte laughed. "I won't, don't worry." He finished his tea and stood up. "And I won't let you down with this power of attorney. Thanks for trusting me, Piper. It means a lot and I'm trying to do good here, I swear."

Piper watched him drive away and hoped that what he said was true. She had a niggling feeling that something else was going on, but she didn't know what. She couldn't help but trust Donte though, if only as a tribute to his sister.

"I'VE BEEN LOOKING after this dog since before you were born," Arthur grumbled. "I think I know what I'm doing."

"That's so not true," said Piper. "Billy can't be more than a few years old."

"Maybe," sniffed Arthur. "But I still know what I'm doing. Me and Billy go back a way. We're good together him and I."

"I really don't know how to thank you," said Piper. Outside she could hear the rumble of the taxi engine.

"It's me that should be thanking you. I could use the company," Arthur said. "I'll be glad of someone around the house with me, believe it or not."

"I'll miss you," Piper blurted out.

To her astonishment, Arthur blushed. "Well," he said. "I'll miss having someone next door as well. I was getting quite used to having someone there. And your tea isn't bad either, for a yank, that is."

"I'd, uh, better..." But she didn't move.

Arthur moved in closer. "You know, life's full of problems. If it isn't losing your job then it's fixing the kitchen sink. If it isn't one of your kids then it's a flat tire. If you look at it the right way, life's just a series of things going wrong."

"Cheerful, Arthur, thank you."

"Hold your horses there. I said 'if you look at it the right way.' But look at it another way and it's just a series of challenges so you can prove yourself, that's all." His eyes were cloudy and blue. "There's a lot to be said for admitting your mistakes. Mind you, there's a lot to be said for denying everything as well. Just depends on who you're talking to."

The cab outside beeped its horn.

"You're a good woman, any fool can see that," Arthur went on. "So whatever happens next, wherever you go or return to or come back from or anything in between, it'll be for the right. It'll have to be for the right, because you're the one doing it, if you see what I mean."

"I'm not so sure I do," Piper said faintly.

"I mean that you'll come right in the end. Now run off out of here. I've got a dog to feed and my programs are coming on."

Piper felt the package in her hands sticky with sweat. "One more thing. If you see Cam. I mean, when you see Cam. Could you give her this?"

"What is it?" Arthur asked suspiciously, taking the package.

"Just some old letters of Lucy's," Piper said.

"S'pose I can then. Now close the door behind you as you go," said Arthur, shuffling back off down the hallway.

It wasn't until she was in the back seat of the cab, pulling away from the village green and the pub and the bookshop and Cam and Billy and Arthur, that Piper's eyes started to fill with tears.

She held herself together until the car passed the village limits, then she sniffed and shook her shoulders. "This is exciting," she whispered ferociously.

"What's that, love?" asked the driver.

"Nothing," said Piper. "Nothing at all."

CHAPTER THIRTY ONE

If she tried exceptionally hard, Cam didn't have to look at Lucy's house. Considering she was dragging Billy back to Arthur's, right next door, this was something of an achievement. Not to mention the fact that she'd have to start work on the place again the next day.

But it hurt to look at.

It hurt to know that it was empty.

And in the same way that she'd ignored the taunts of the guys in her apprenticeship classes, the teasing of her brothers, the strange feelings she got when she saw pretty women, she figured if she could ignore everything, it might just go away.

"Come on, Billy," she said, pulling him through Arthur's gate.

He finally relented and she knocked on the door and then went in without waiting for an answer.

"I've got your shopping in," she shouted. "I'll just put it on the kitchen table."

"There's no need to shout, I'm not deaf," grumbled Arthur as he shuffled into the kitchen. "And I hope you got the good bacon this time, that last pack was like eating shoe leather."

Cam unhooked Billy's leash and let him go to his water bowl, dumped the bags on the kitchen table, and then saw a small, square package. "What's this?" she asked, picking it up.

"Oh, that Piper said to give you those," Arthur said, nosy-ing around in the shopping bags. "Said they're Lucy's letters and you should have them."

A tiny pang of something shook through Cam. She'd adored Lucy. Having something so personal of hers meant something special. Having Piper leave her a gift was even more special.

Then she remembered that Arthur hadn't told Piper anything she'd wanted to know.

"These are what Piper wanted to talk to you about," she said.

"I know that," said Arthur, pulling bananas out of a bag. "I told her I wouldn't tell her. Doesn't do to tell outsiders too much. Besides, wasn't sure it was any of her business. She didn't even know Luce."

"I did," pointed out Cam.

"You did," said Arthur with a sniff. "But you ain't asked me."

Cam took a breath and stopped herself rolling her eyes. "Consider this me asking then," she said. "What's all this mystery over Lucy? Who was this Twinkle Toes? Did she really have a… a boyfriend? Lover? Something?"

"You youngsters always make it sound like you invented sex. You know Lucy and I were at it long before you were born," Arthur said, pulling out a kitchen chair and sitting in it. "Not together, mind. Not that I'd have minded. Lucy was quite the looker in her day. All big blue eyes and blond curls. You'd not have thought it, but she was a real heartbreaker."

"So?" Cam said, pulling out a chair of her own. "What happened then? These letters seem pretty, well, passionate, I suppose. They were obviously in love. Deeply in love. But then the letters just stopped."

"Sounds about right," said Arthur. "I wasn't in the middle of it though, not personally. But I saw enough of what went on to make my own guesses. Then later, decades later, Luce told me some of it."

"Some of what?" asked Cam, exasperated. "Who was this man?"

Arthur sighed. "He was an outsider. Not from the village.

This was in the late forties, mind, things were different back then. You know there used to be a big army barracks up where the Short Farm is now? Right up until D-Day we had folks tearing through the village in those Jeeps. Then after there were some stationed there, well, well into the fifties from what I remember."

"Okay," Cam said, she'd had no idea about all this.

"It's a tale as old as time," said Arthur. "No mystery to it at all really. Lucy met one of the soldiers, fell in love. Not that they made an announcement about it or anything. But it was clear if you cared to look. She might go to the dances with her girlfriends, but she ended up dancing with him more often than not."

"So what?" asked Cam, impatient and not seeing the story. "They fell in love. Did he get moved on? Posted somewhere else? Killed in some kind of accident?"

"No, no," Arthur. "Well, eventually he got posted elsewhere. Eventually he went home. But Lucy had called things off by then. Or they mutually had. I don't really know exactly how it happened."

"But why?" pushed Cam.

Arthur sighed. "Things were different then, I told you. This bloke, he wasn't just a soldier, he was a foreigner."

"An American?"

"No, though in some eyes that might have been bad enough." Arthur put his hands on the table. "He was Indian. Came with a bunch of Commonwealth troops that were posted here."

"Oh," said Cam. And then, "Oh," again as she started to understand.

"I'm not going to make excuses, girl. I hope we all know different now, though I'm sure some of us still don't. But a mixed race relationship back then, well, it was something that just didn't happen. And, of course, he'd have wanted to go back to India, I suppose. I don't know."

"That's heartbreaking."

"I'll tell you something that I do know," Arthur said, looking at her with his rheumy eyes. "Lucy was a character. She was fun and full of life. She lived her life to the absolute fullest. But there was nothing she regretted more than letting this fella walk away. Nothing. Right up until she died, she'd have told you herself. Get a sherry in her and she'd have told the queen."

Cam took a breath. "She could have... I don't know, found him, tracked him down."

Arthur shook his head. "Things worked different before this whole internet thing. You know that. And I think it hurt her too much anyway. I think she felt like she didn't deserve him, not anymore, not after letting him go. You know what I mean."

Cam nodded, a lump in her throat so big that it was hard to swallow.

"She told me once that if she could have her whole life to do over again, that's the only thing she'd do different. Said she'd let other people make a decision for her, a decision that was hers alone. That she'd put aside what she wanted just to please others, and it wasn't something she'd ever do again," said Arthur. He eyed her again. "It's not nice to have those regrets. Not when you're too old to do anything about them." He made a noisy attempt to clear his throat. "You catching my meaning there?"

She was. All too clearly. "Arthur..."

"It's none of my business," said Arthur getting up and picking up more shopping. "Not in the slightest. And maybe you done what you did for the best of everyone involved. I'm just saying that you shouldn't regret things." He turned an eye back to her. "That and that Piper is a good-looking woman. If I were fifty years younger..."

"She still wouldn't be interested in you," Cam said.

Arthur knew. He knew and somehow, she didn't really care.

"You'd better be going or Isabella will have your head," he said, piling tins in a cupboard. "It's about dinner time for you."

Cam tucked Lucy's letters into her pocket and left Arthur and Billy to their dinner.

LORENZO WAS SITTING in his chair by the window, pipe on the sill, when Cam found him.

"Mum says that the vet called and he'll be in at nine, not eight. Some emergency he has to deal with first," she said.

"Ah, of course," Lorenzo said, tamping some tobacco into his pipe.

Cam was about to leave, was already turning, when she changed her mind. "Dad?"

"Yes?"

"Was it hard to move here? I mean hard to be an outsider, hard to be a foreigner?"

Lorenzo's dark eyes flashed. "Somebody been speaking out of turn?"

"No, not really. I was just curious. You never talk about it. I know you love living here. I know you wanted to live here. But it can't all have been sweetness and light."

"Of course it wasn't. It was a long time ago. And this is a small village. Of course there were some small-minded people who called me names." He pulled out a matchbox. "The village shop wouldn't serve me the first time I went inside."

"And yet you stayed," Cam said.

Her father shrugged. "I loved it here. I don't know why. Something spoke to me here. I came from the seaside, I'd never been to a farm, I'd never been to England. But the second I set foot on this land I knew that I'd come home. I can't explain it, that's just how it was."

"And mum…"

He laughed. "Your mother was foolish enough and in love enough to trust a crazy young man with her future."

"I can't imagine what it was like, leaving everything like that," said Cam, leaning against the door-frame.

"Camilla, if you learn nothing else from me, then please, I want you to remember this, because it's very, very important."

"More important than how to milk the cows or when to turn

the fields over?"

He shook his head. "You are joking because you are uncomfortable. This is serious. I mean this, Camilla."

She bit her lip. "Sorry, dad."

"When you love something, really love something, when it is the only thing you want, the only thing you can think of, then you should do anything to get this thing. Anything. Any sacrifice is worth it, any pain or unpleasantness will be repaid in time, any effort or sadness will be erased. We have one life, Camilla, and we cannot spend it not loving. Because in the end, that is all your life is, a sum total of all the things you've loved."

Cam blinked away mistiness from her eyes.

"I am not saying things were easy," Lorenzo said. "But I am saying that I would never, ever do anything differently. Because everything I did led me here, to this, to having this conversation with my only daughter. Do you see what I mean?"

She nodded.

"I see you, Camilla, I know your soul. I see all that you do for others. I see that you're struggling. But I am just a silly old farmer, maybe I cannot help you, even if I would like to. So that is all my wisdom for you. Do what you love, be what you love, have what you love, chase what you love. Nothing else will matter."

He paused, lit his pipe, and puffed a few times until sweet smoke laced the air.

"But what if that thing that you love belongs to someone else?" she said, not able to look at him.

"Well, that depends. If it is a *thing* that you love you can make every effort to make it yours, but you cannot take it, that would be stealing."

"Right," she said, trying to hold the tears in.

There was only the hint of a pause before he went on. "If, on the other hand, it is, say, a *person* that you love. Well, a person belongs to no one but themselves. A person should make his or her own decision. And to make such a decision for them, on their behalf, well, that would be arrogance, would it not?"

She could barely breathe.

"It is the one thing the English do not do well," he said. "Love. It is the one thing I missed about Italy. Which is why I had to bring your mother here. But maybe you're different than me. And that's okay."

The shadows were growing longer.

"Go on, tell your mother you delivered her message and that I will be with her shortly, once I'm done with my pipe."

Cam slipped out of the room, making it down to the kitchen but pausing before she went inside.

And for the first time she knew that she'd made a horrible, terrible mistake in letting Piper go.

She knew that her father was right, she knew that love had to win because if it didn't then how could the world be a good place in the end? Because if it didn't, how could she live with the regret that Lucy had carried for all those years?

Love had to win.

And whatever else she didn't know, she knew that she loved Piper. Loved her more than she'd loved anyone in her whole life.

She'd made a terrible mistake. And she didn't know how to fix it.

CHAPTER THIRTY TWO

They strolled along the river bank and Piper could smell the ocean in the air.

"It's just for the next four weeks," Lex was saying. "But if this is what you want, I could make it a permanent thing. I mean, a permanent summer thing. I'm pretty sure the university likes me."

"Every summer in London?" Piper said. "I'm not sure how I'd swing that with work."

There was quiet for a second, then Lex asked the inevitable question. "What about work? Have you given it any thought?"

Piper blew out a breath. "Honestly? Not really. I took all this as a chance to get away from everything, a chance to clear my head. But I need to get back to real life, I guess."

"It'll be easier when you get back to the city. Call some contacts, make some connections, you'll be working again before you know it." Lex paused for a moment. "Or not."

"What's that supposed to mean?"

"Just…" Lex sighed. "Just, well, I make enough to support us for a while. If you need some time, then you should take some time, that's all."

"I don't think that's a good idea." She didn't want to not work. No, she didn't want to be dependent on Lex. Which was weird, because she'd always leaned on her before.

"There are a lot of options. You could go back to school, for example."

"I could," Piper said, trying to remain open-minded.

"Or not," Lex said. "You could find another editing job."

"Mmm."

Lex stopped so Piper stopped too. "What do you want?" she asked. She was smiling, the question wasn't meant badly. "I mean, if you could do anything, what would that thing be?"

Piper had a vision of herself curled up in an armchair in front of a fire. Her laptop was on her knee and she was typing happily away. And Cam was there, stretched out on the couch next to her, eyes half-closed.

"I don't know," Piper said, and she started walking again.

"Okay, okay. There's no big rush," said Lex, hurrying along to catch her up. "But I'm here to support you, Pipes, I hope you know that."

Which somehow made it all worse. Piper found that she was blinking furiously, that tears were threatening, and she really didn't know why. She sniffed.

"So what's next?" Lex said. "I've got the whole rest of the day off. Big Ben? Buckingham Palace? A walk through Kensington Gardens? Take your pick. The world is your oyster."

"I hate oysters," mumbled Piper.

Lex laughed and hooked an arm through hers. "Then the world is your lobster, is that better?"

Reluctantly, Piper laughed. "Better taste-wise. Not so sure about linguistically, but I'll take it. How about a walk through the gardens, that sounds nice."

"Your wish is my command," Lex said with a grin.

THE PROBLEM WAS that Lex wasn't trying.

No, that was unfair.

The problem was that Lex didn't really have to try. She'd always been charming and pretty and everything else. She'd always known exactly what to say and how to say it. And Piper had always loved her for that, for the ease with which she lived her life.

So Lex was just being Lex.

"After you," Lex said, sweeping Piper through the park gates.

The sun was shining and people were everywhere and it felt like a holiday. It felt like there was expectation in the air, the promise of happiness and fulfillment.

Lex took her arm again and Piper let it happen because it was supposed to happen, because she had to get over this hiccup and get back to her life. Because even if Lex didn't have to try, she did. And she was going to.

"Do you want to talk?" Lex said.

"About?"

"Us."

She shook her head. Because what was the point? There was nothing to be said, nothing that would change what had happened. The past was the past, Piper told herself firmly. If she could persuade herself to forget it, or get over it at least, then she could start to re-build her life.

Except any mention of the word build just brought Cam to mind.

"I thought we could maybe grab an ice cream, then later I've got dinner reservations," Lex said, trying to fill the air with chatter. "You're going to love this place, a colleague recommended it and…"

Piper filtered the rest out.

Why, she asked herself, was it so right to re-build this relationship and so wrong to build one with Cam?

But then Cam had been the one that wanted her to try again with Lex. Cam had even suggested it.

"Are you listening?" Lex asked.

Piper pulled herself back into the conversation. "I'm listening," she said. "Sorry. I'm a bit out of it."

"We could blame jet-lag," said Lex. "But you've been here for weeks. Need a nap?"

There was an old twinkle in her eyes and Piper knew what she meant and knew she should agree, but instead she pointed over Lex's shoulder. "There's ice cream over there," she said.

Lex grinned and took her hand. "Ice cream it is then."

PIPER SLIPPED AS she stepped off the curb and Lex's hand caught her under the elbow.

"You haven't changed," Lex said, helping her back up onto the sidewalk. "Are you okay?"

Piper nodded but Lex didn't remove her hand and Piper wanted to want this. She truly did.

Lex had been her everything. They'd built a life together. Lex was what she should want. And now Lex was pulling her in and wrapping her arms around her and…

And just holding her for what felt like a long, long time. Long enough that Piper settled into the hug. Long enough that she blinked in the light when Lex finally let her go.

"It isn't working, is it?" Lex said.

The very tip of her nose was pink, a sure sign that she was upset. Piper shook her head. "It's not," she said quietly. "I wish it were, but it's not."

Lex hooked an arm through Piper's and propelled her slowly along the street. "It's alright, you know."

"Is it really?"

Lex laughed. "Of course it is. It's alright for a relationship to run its course. It's alright for needs to change, priorities to change. And if I'm honest, I shouldn't have come to you, it was unfair. I guess I was feeling nostalgic, guilty definitely. I guess I thought that maybe we could turn back the clock."

"Time travel has never really been my thing."

"Yeah, mine neither." They turned a corner. "I'm sorry, Piper. Sorry about everything. Sorry for screwing up what we had, sorry for asking for another chance, sorry for… for doing what I did. But I'm not sorry about everything that came before. I'm not sorry about what we had."

"It was good, wasn't it?" said Piper, smiling a little.

"We were very good together," agreed Lex. "You do know that I'm going to be a hard act to follow, right?"

"I don't doubt it."

Lex stopped again and turned to look at her. "You're certainly going to be a tough act to follow, Piper Garland. Whatever else may have happened or may happen, you are brilliant and beautiful and deserving of the happiest of lives."

Piper bowed her head. "Thank you," she said. "I'm not sure I ever really properly said thank you to you before. Thank you for saving me, for helping me build a life. Thank you for being there when I thought I had no one. Most people would have met a depressed adult orphan and run a mile. You stuck around."

"I had no choice," said Lex. "I was in love with you from the second I saw you. Even now I'm still a little in love with you. I'm not sure that ever goes away. I'm not sure I ever want it to."

"I'm sorry," Piper said, squeezing Lex's hand. "I'm sorry things changed. I'm sorry we changed. I'm sorry that I can't make everything better again."

"It's not your job to make things better again," Lex said stoutly. "And it shouldn't be." She cleared her throat. "Do you think we can still be friends?"

"I certainly hope so," said Piper. "I mean, you do know pretty much everything embarrassing about me, it would seem dangerous not to be friends with you."

"Oh, I don't know, you know a fair few things about me too," Lex said airily.

They started to walk again.

"If you don't mind me asking, and you really don't have to answer, is there, um, is there someone else?" Lex asked after a while.

Piper sighed. "No," she said. "I mean, there was, but not now. No, there's no one."

"You sure about that?" asked Lex.

"Sure."

Lex took her hand. "You know I wouldn't undo all this for the world. I mean, falling in love with you in the first place. It was the most terrifying, wonderfully horrific, humiliating, beautiful experience I've ever had. I truly wish I can experience it again in my lifetime. But if I can't, well, at least I had it once."

"Your point?"

"I know you, Pipes. Don't avoid something because it's frightening. Or complicated. Or different. Those are exactly the times when you should be jumping in with both feet, those are exactly the experiences that are going to change you, shape you, teach you. Those are the situations where you need to push yourself."

"That's ridiculous," Piper said. "Doing things just because you're scared of them is not an intelligent way to make decisions."

"Please yourself," Lex said. "But I'm right."

"I thought you were going to feed me?"

"I am, my dear, as long as you can still find it in your heart to sit at a table with me."

Piper groaned. "Is this what it's going to be like being exes? You full of dubious wisdom and bad jokes?"

"It might be," Lex said. "We've never really been exes before, so I suspect we'll have to figure things out as we go along. And I'll buy you dinner if you tell me about your mysterious woman. Deal?"

"I'll think about it," Piper said.

"You can have two desserts."

"Deal."

CHAPTER THIRTY THREE

Cam went to the dinner table because that was what happened at dinner time. She wasn't particularly hungry. Nor did she especially feel like being around other people. But not going would create even more trouble and questions, so in the end, she slid quietly into the kitchen.

"How was work?" Isabella asked immediately, because as quietly as Cam had entered, nothing got past her mother's eagle eye.

"Fine," said Cam, collecting a plate.

Work had been distinctly not fine. The house was echoingly empty and she kept expecting to see Piper around every corner. Working in the empty house had done nothing but give her time to think about all the mistakes she'd made.

She should have told her family. At least that way she'd have support.

She should never have told Piper to go. She should have stood up for what she wanted, made her side of the story known. She should have asked her to stay, even if the answer had been no, at least she would have tried.

And now it was all too late. She couldn't turn the clock back and had no idea how to get back to the place she wanted to be in. Piper was with Lex and there was no way she was going to break up a relationship.

Which left her alone and sad and wondering just what the hell she was doing with her life.

The doorbell rang.

"Carmel," said Isabella.

Carmel groaned but he was definitely sitting closest to the door. Besides, he'd yet to receive his plate and there was every chance that Isabella would hold the spaghetti hostage until he did as he was told.

He was back a moment later with someone else in tow. A paunchy man with pallid skin and a loud tie. Donte's chair scraped back as he stood up.

"So sorry to intrude," said the man.

Donte cleared his throat. "Mum, dad, this is David Chancellor, my boss. Mr. Chancellor, this is..." He gestured. "Everybody."

Chancellor painted on a smile that was too wide to be real and nodded around the table. "I'm sure I've met some of you in passing," he said. Then he caught Cam's eye. "And you must be Camilla, am I right?"

Reluctantly, she nodded.

"I didn't expect to run into you, and you'll get an email from me tomorrow, but since I'm here, I might as well tell you that your offer on the cottage has been accepted. Congratulations."

There was a buzz of chatter around the table and Isabella blew her daughter a kiss. Cam wondered why she didn't feel happy, why she couldn't summon up a smile at the thought of getting what she'd wanted for so long. All she could do was see that picture of Piper sitting by the fire again.

"I actually just popped in to steal Donte for a moment, if I may?" Chancellor said.

"Of course," said Donte, starting to move.

"No, no," Isabella said. "Sit, eat, you're a guest in our house now."

"Oh, I don't need but a minute," said Chancellor. "Donte holds power of attorney for an American woman whose house we're selling. I just need him to sign the final sale contract and then we're golden."

Donte turned bright red.

"I won't hear of it," grumbled Isabella. "You're in my house, in my kitchen, it's dinner time, so now you sit. Carlos, get the man a chair."

"No, I can't possibly—"

"Sit, eat," Lorenzo interrupted.

Chancellor took one look at Lorenzo's face and then sat in the chair that had been hastily provided for him. As soon as he sat, the normal chatter started to fill the air.

Cam picked at her food. A cottage of her own. She supposed it was better than living in the van. But still. The thought of renovating, building, decorating, furnishing, filled her with a heavy dread. The energy all that would take, and she couldn't even raise a fork to her mouth.

"Cam's not eating," Cosmo said loudly.

Cam sighed as all eyes at the table turned to her.

"I'll have hers," said Christophoro immediately.

"Oh no you won't," said Lorenzo.

"Why aren't you eating?" Carlos asked suspiciously.

"Nothing, it's fine, I'm just not that hungry, that's all," Cam stammered.

"The only thing that makes a girl lose her appetite like that is being in love," Isabella teased.

Carlos wolf-whistled and Cosmo balled up his fists and scowled in fake anger. "Tell me who he is and I'll beat him to a pulp," he growled.

Something in Cam crumbled and began to flake away.

"Leave your sister alone," Isabella said. "She'll tell us about him when she's ready."

Cam's whole body started to tremble. But this was the right thing to do. This is what she should have done from the very beginning. She had to do this, even if everything was broken and over, she couldn't bear the weight of this secret any more.

"Actually," she said. "It's not a he."

There was a sudden, stunned silence, as everyone looked at

her. Then Donte's face spread into a smile. "I knew it," he said. "Piper."

It took every ounce of courage that Cam had to nod, but she did.

"Right, that's it," Carmel said, standing up. "Let's get her."

Cam's heart started to thud. "No, please, Carmel."

But it was too late, all six of her brothers were getting to their feet. She was shaking now, not knowing how to stop what she'd started, not believing this was happening. The thought of what they would do to Piper if they found her, when they found her, she could barely breathe.

"Stop!" she shouted.

In an instant there was complete quiet.

"Stop?" Carmel asked. "But I thought this was what you wanted?"

"You and the rest of these neanderthals beating up a woman for being gay?" Cam said, hardly believing she had to say the words.

Carmel frowned. "What on earth are you talking about?"

"You going to get Piper."

"Yes," he said, slowly. "Us going to get Piper. As in get her. Get her and bring her here. Get her and make you smile again and let you two get things sorted out." He paused for a second. "Did you really think that we'd do something like that? That we'd hurt her? Or you?"

Cam swallowed and felt blood rising in her cheeks. She'd overreacted, acted without thinking. These were her brothers. She looked down at the table.

Carmel put his hand on her shoulder. "I really don't care if you're gay or whatever you choose to be," he said quietly.

"Me neither," piped up Cosmo.

"Couldn't give a monkey's," Casmiro put in.

Cam looked up at her mother and father.

"We care that you're happy, *Vita Mia*," Isabella said.

Lorenzo smiled. "*L'anima di una donna vive in amore.*"

Everyone turned to him.

"Papa," said Carmel.

"What?" Lorenzo said, frowning comically. "I speak English every day perfectly. But there are some things that we need Italian for. Love is one of those things." He grinned at Cam. "I told you, the English are terrible at love."

Cam laughed and felt her heart lightening. "What are you going to do?" she asked Carmel.

"We're going to find Piper," he said seriously.

"Not if I find her first," Cosmo put in.

"I'm driving," said Donte.

"Oh no," Carlos said. "You drive like an Italian, I'm driving."

"We'll have to take Cam's van," said Christophoro. "We won't all fit in anything else."

"But... how?" Cam said.

"We'll figure it out along the way," said Carmel. He scratched his nose. "Might be better if you come with us, actually. She might not take well to being kidnapped by six swarthy Italians."

"Wait a moment, please." David Chancellor pulled a sheaf of papers from his jacket pocket. "Donte, if I could just get you to sign these before you leave."

Donte looked at Chancellor, then looked at his brothers, then took a deep breath. "No."

"No?" Chancellor said, eyebrows rising.

"You're selling to a developer and hiding it under a fake name," Donte said. "It's illegal, and more to the point, it's specifically what the client, Piper, told you she didn't want to do. And I won't be a part of it."

Chancellor's mouth opened then closed.

Donte grinned and picked up Cam's van keys from the bowl by the door. "And you can screw your job," he said as he walked out. "You boys with me or not?"

One by one, all five of the Fabbri boys walked out of the kitchen, leaving Chancellor staring after them.

"Best leave the table, dear," Isabella said to Chancellor.

Without a word, he stood up and a moment later they heard the front door slam.

"Go on," said Isabella to Cam. "You'll want to go with them. You can't trust the six of them alone, especially driving to London. They'll need your clear head."

"But how are we even going to find her?" Cam asked.

"Trust in fate," Isabella said. "Alternatively, Mary at the shop said that Piper was friendly with a woman teaching at a university in London. You might want to follow up that lead. I'm sure universities keep track of their teachers."

Cam got up, legs still shaking.

"Oh, and I'd better give the boys snacks for the journey," Isabella said, picking up tupperware and hurrying out of the kitchen.

"This is crazy," Cam said.

"It is crazy," said Lorenzo. "But perhaps necessary. *L'amore è nel vostro cuore, non di rimanere, ma per essere condivisa*. If you love her, then you must go, there is no other choice. You must tell her."

Cam looked at her father. "Papa, you know I'm English, right?"

Lorenzo nodded.

"But you keep telling me the English are terrible at love."

"Perhaps I need to hold on to a little of my Italian pride," he said. "And perhaps I need my daughter to prove me wrong."

"It really doesn't matter?" Cam asked. "All this, me, Piper, her being a woman, this whole mess?"

Lorenzo smiled. "It matters that you're happy. That is all any man can ever wish for his children. If this is your chance at happiness, then you must chase it, my love."

"Like you did," said Cam.

"Like I did," agreed Lorenzo. "My father never spoke to me again after I moved here, did I ever tell you that?"

Cam shook her head. "Do you regret it?"

"Breaking my relationship with my father?" Lorenzo asked. "Of course I do. I named my youngest son after him, didn't I?" Which explained once and for all why Donte didn't have a name beginning with C. Her father smiled. "But I would have regretted not coming here more, I think."

Outside the horn of the van beeped loudly.

"Go, child," Lorenzo said. "Go find her."

CHAPTER THIRTY FOUR

The suitcase was heavier than she'd remembered. Piper dragged it off the train and toward the airport.

It was time to face reality, she'd decided. No more playing around. Lex had helped her re-book her ticket and she was leaving. She'd go home and start putting out feelers for a new job, and maybe even buy that couch she'd been lacking for so long.

Before long, Lucy's house would sell and she'd have a little money in the bank and then she was going to find an amazing job and then... and then, maybe, one day, she'd find someone amazing to share this life with.

At least that was the plan.

She tugged at the handle of the case, forcing it to follow her into the airport itself. The whole place smelled of suntan lotion and coffee, hoards of people lining up to check in. Piper dragged her case to the displays and found the check-in desk she needed.

Then she pulled at the case again and set off to find the right number.

She would be happy one day.

She just didn't know exactly when that day would be.

Making up with Lex had been a good thing, a healthy thing. Letting the anger go, realizing they'd both changed, that they weren't the same people that they had been when they met, was important. Realizing that they'd both helped each other grow into these new people was tough to accept, but in the end necessary.

So now she could focus on the future.

She pulled the case onto an escalator and held tight to the handrail. It was one of those ridiculously short escalators, so almost immediately she was forced to get off again.

She yanked at the case and it didn't follow. And then, somehow, she was falling, rolling her ankle off the edge of a step, the case finally coming free and crashing down beside her.

"Oh Lord, are you alright, dear?" asked an older woman coming down the escalator behind her.

Piper shuffled out of the way, burning red with embarrassment. "I'm fine, really, just a silly accident."

She pulled herself upright and then winced as she put weight on her ankle.

"You don't look very fine," the woman said. She caught Piper's elbow. "Here, there's a bench over there, let's get you off your feet. Do you think you can walk that far?"

Piper nodded dumbly, and the two set off.

❋ ❋ ❋

"It's a university, how can it be hard to find?" Carlos grumbled.

Cam rolled her eyes. "Be patient," she said.

It had been a long night. Driving down had taken longer than they all thought and at some point, they'd had to stop for a couple of hours so that everyone could grab a nap. Even now, Carlos in particular was cranky and sleep deprived.

"What's that?" Cosmo said, pointing out of the window toward a large gray building.

"Post office, you idiot," said Christophoro. He had his phone in his hand and was trying to follow the route on Google Maps.

Maybe it was best if she left them to it, Cam thought. She still wasn't exactly sure how or why she'd been dragged on this trip. It wasn't as if she couldn't have done this alone, or called Piper, or handled things in some other way. But the boys were certain that she needed to chase the woman and she was too tired and too disheartened to disobey.

So here she was.

"It's going to be alright," Donte said, patting her knee. "Just you wait and see."

"Yeah, right up until she thinks I'm a crazy stalker lady and calls the police."

"She won't do that," said Donte. "Besides, I know you've messaged her, she must know that you're coming."

"She hasn't answered," Cam said, which was part of the problem and a growing worry. She sighed. "And what about you? Just up and quitting your job like that, what were you thinking?"

"I was thinking that David Chancellor is an arsehole," Donte said firmly.

"Don!"

"It's true. He was going to screw Piper over. I've spent the last two weeks trying to find a different buyer for the house so that I could keep my job and keep our promise to Piper not to sell the house to a developer. And this was the last straw. He's dodgy and I won't have a part in it."

"Even if that means having to work on the farm?"

Donte shrugged. "I'll think of something, don't worry. I just want to feel good about myself, that's all."

"Yeah," Cam said, looking out of the window at the city passing by. "Yeah, I get that."

"Piper makes you feel good about yourself?" Donte guessed.

"Piper makes me feel good just in general," admitted Cam. "But I'm not sure she sees that. I'm not sure I let her see that. I... I kind of sent her packing. Sent her off to patch things up with her ex."

Donte's eyes sparkled. "So we could be crashing a reunion here?"

"Um, maybe?"

He laughed. "Well, best you get things off your chest in any case. At least this way she'll know how you feel, right?"

"This is it," Carlos shouted from the front seat. "Let me just pull into a parking space and then Carmel, you and Cam run in and try and track down this Lex person."

Cam's stomach did a somersault. Was this really what she wanted?

But the sun was shining and people were living their lives and she suddenly didn't want another morning without Piper. She didn't want Piper not to know. She didn't want Piper to think that she didn't want her. So she unbuckled her seatbelt and prepared to jump out.

❋ ❋ ❋

"It looks badly twisted," said the woman, gazing down at Piper's ankle doubtfully.

"Because Cam wasn't there to catch me," Piper said quietly.

"What's that dear?"

"Nothing."

"Are you sure you don't want me to call someone? There must be a doctor here, or some sort of ambulance service. I could get someone to help you."

Piper shook her head. "It'll be fine," she said. "No fuss. My flight isn't for a while yet, I've got plenty of time."

"I don't like leaving you," the woman said. She had kindly gray eyes and a nice smile.

Piper held up her phone. "I can call if I need some help," she said, not mentioning the fact that her phone was already switched off. There was no reason to have it on and she wanted to avoid the temptation of calling Lex or, god forbid, even Cam, in a moment of weakness before leaving the country.

The woman sighed and looked at her watch. "Well, if you're really sure, my dear. I'm afraid I do have to go. My flight will be boarding soon."

"Of course," said Piper. "Thank you for helping. And I'll be fine, really."

She watched the woman walk away and then slumped back onto the bench.

All this for a twisted ankle and a sudden, painful realization.

Cam had been catching her for the last month. She'd come to rely on the fact that there'd be someone there to stop her falling.

Except this time there'd been nobody.

Because she was stubborn and foolish and she hadn't been honest, not with herself and certainly not with Cam.

In that moment when she fell, the tiny millisecond between losing control and hitting the ground, she'd known with a full certainty that she'd made a dreadful mistake. Had known that the only person she wanted, the only eyes she wanted to look into, the only hands she wanted to catch her, were Cam's.

And here she was getting ready to leave and she hadn't even told her.

She'd been so caught up in the logistics of things, so wrapped up in the idea of having to return to her old life, of protecting Cam, of giving Cam what she wanted and needed, that she hadn't taken a heartbeat to think about what she wanted herself.

And now that she did, the answer was a very simple one.

She wanted Cam.

It was too late. She could see that now. It wouldn't be fair just to show up again. Maybe she could call. One day. Not today. Maybe when there was a little distance she could call and tell the truth and let the chips fall where they may.

She sighed and steeled herself.

If she hadn't been so stupid, so stubborn, so sure that she knew what was right, then it would never have come to this. If only she'd told Cam that her feelings were deeper, that she wanted to have this be more than just fun.

But she hadn't. And the truth was that now she had a flight to catch and an increasingly small amount of time to catch it in.

She managed to get up and gingerly put her foot on the ground. She tested her weight on it, hissing air through her teeth at the initial sharp pain.

Once she got used to it though, she found that she could just about hobble her way down the corridor. Once she'd checked in and no longer had the suitcase, then things would be easier.

She started to make her way slowly, slowly toward her check-in desk.

But her head was filled with 'if onlys'.

It was getting harder and harder to walk.

She could see the long lines of people snaking through the airport. She could see the numbers lit up over the check-in desks. She could see suitcases and trolleys and holidaymakers.

Each step was slower than the last. The pain was growing now, swelling and burning up her leg. But that wasn't all. Her chest was hurting, her heart pounding, her pulse racing as she blinked away tear after furious tear.

How could she not have seen this before? How could she not have known that she was falling in love? How could she have thought that she would ever just get over Cam?

She managed to drag herself into the departure hall and identify the desk she needed. It wasn't far. She cleared her throat and made one last effort.

But she didn't see the child's folded pushchair that was sticking out of the hand of the man in front of her. It hit her just below the knee on her bad leg and she felt the muscle give and the weightlessness of falling.

Then someone caught her elbow and she never hit the ground.

CHAPTER THIRTY FIVE

"I don't want to keep a wedding dress in the attic." Cam slammed her mouth closed. She hadn't meant to say that, the words had just leaked out somehow. They'd simply emerged the second she laid a hand on Piper.

"You... what?" Piper asked.

"What happened to you?"

Piper blushed. "Fell down an escalator."

"You can't blame me for this one," Cam said, looking at Piper's swollen ankle. "I wasn't here to blind you."

"You weren't," Piper agreed. "But you were in my head."

"So it's still my fault?"

Piper nodded solemnly. "And I'd feel bad about that except you've apparently decided that we do live in a romantic comedy, despite the fact that you assured me we didn't."

"Meaning?"

"Meaning you're doing the grand romantic gesture, the showing up at the airport thing."

"In my defense, I didn't actually know you were going to be at the airport," said Cam. "This wasn't exactly planned."

"Yet here you are."

"Here I am."

"Mumbling something about keeping wedding dresses in

attics."

Cam shrugged. "I talked to Arthur about Lucy. I found out who Twinkle Toes was."

"Are you going to enlighten me?"

"He was an Indian soldier stationed near the village. They were madly in love, but it was the forties and relationships like that didn't work out. So she let him go. Or he let her go. One or the other."

"Doomed love," said Piper.

Cam scratched her nose. "Which got me thinking that maybe we're not so doomed after all."

Piper swallowed hard. "Uh, do you think we could sit down somewhere? My ankle does kind of hurt."

Quickly, Cam put Piper's arm over her shoulder and helped her walk toward the nearest bench.

"So how did you get here? If you didn't know I was at the airport? I mean—"

Cam held up a hand to interrupt her. "Lex was involved. It's a long story, and just for now maybe we need to forget about logistics. Just for a few minutes. Just for the next, say, quarter of an hour, can we pretend that life is a movie? That things do work out in the end? Just because you want them to?"

"Okay," Piper said. "In that case, there's something I need to say."

"No, I came all the way here, I tracked you down, I get to go first," Cam said firmly. "You're going to need to listen."

Piper covered up a smile and tried to look serious. "Okay then."

Cam rubbed her face. "Here's the thing... There are a million reasons why something between us can't work, a million reasons why we shouldn't try, a million reasons why we should be sensible and you should get on your plane and I should just go on home. And there's only one reason that we should be together."

"Just one?"

"Just one," Cam said. "You see, I don't want to regret things.

I spend my life helping other people and never putting myself first and, honestly, that's not a bad thing. I don't want to be selfish. I don't want to think only of myself. But sometimes, just sometimes, we have to do that."

"I don't think you're selfish."

"I'm not," Cam said, looking down at her hands. "But I'm about to be. People are always telling me that I need to learn to put myself first. I'm not sure that's the problem though, learning, I mean. I know how to. I've just never been in a situation when it was really the best thing to do."

Piper folded her hands neatly together. "But you are now?"

"I am now," Cam said quietly. "See, that one reason, the only, sole reason that we should be together is because I love you."

A shiver ran across Piper's skin and suddenly the world seemed a little brighter, a little softer, a little better. "You do?"

"I do," Cam said. "And I know that you don't necessarily want this, I know what you said about Lex. That she saved you, that you built something together, that you don't know if you can ever have that again with anyone. And I understand that. Just... just I think we should try. That's all."

"I didn't mean..." Piper sighed. "I didn't mean that I'd never fall in love again, I didn't mean I couldn't have another relationship, I think I just meant that I wasn't ready yet. Is all that why you sent me off back to Lex?"

Cam nodded. "It was the best thing for you."

"It was," said Piper. "It was the best thing because it gave me closure, because it made me realize something, something very important. Actually, several things, unlike you I can't just distill my revelations down to one reason."

Cam rolled her eyes. "Go on then, it's your turn to spill your heart."

Piper took a deep breath. "I realized that I can't rely on other people to save me all the time. I realized that I need to save myself, that waiting for someone to catch me when I fall is stupid, I need to try not to fall in the first place."

"We all fall sometimes," Cam put in.

"We do. But I should try harder to be less clumsy," said Piper. "And... and that Lex was good for me and I was good for her, but we've outgrown each other and that's okay. And it's okay to want to start over, it's okay to start building a new foundation. We don't have to live in the same house forever."

"That would be pretty bad for business," said Cam.

"But most importantly, I realized that... that I love you. I never wanted to. I never wanted to change your life in such a huge way. But I just can't help it. Walking away from you was the stupidest thing I ever did and I haven't been able to forget your face since."

"You walked away because I made you," Cam said. "And that was on me."

Piper reached out and took Cam's hand. "What happens when our fifteen minutes of pretending to live in a movie are over?" she asked.

Cam laughed. "We could start another fifteen minutes?" she said. "Or, alternatively, we could be adults about this and find a way to make all this work. Together. But our fifteen minutes isn't up yet."

A tinny voice announced a flight number and Piper stiffened. "That's mine."

"Doesn't matter," said Cam. "We're still inside our movie." She squeezed Piper's hand tight. "This is up to you. I've said what I needed to say. I want you to stay, Piper. But if you choose not to, if this is all too much, then I'll let you go."

"You won't kidnap me and prevent me leaving the country. Good to know." And Piper was already starting to stand up.

"Where are you going?"

"Where are *we* going," Piper said tugging at Cam's hand.

Cam let herself be pulled up and then automatically took Piper's case in one hand as Piper started limping toward the doors of the airport.

"Come on," Piper said, turning back. "You'd better hurry before reality intrudes again. We've got to get out of here before our fifteen minutes are up."

Cam hurried to catch up with her as Piper stepped outside the automatic doors into the bright morning sun.

Piper stopped still. "What the hell...?"

Cam looked to see four brothers standing sheepishly in front of the illegally parked van whilst Carmel talked with a serious looking policeman. "Oh, shit."

But Piper was already limp-marching over to the police. "This is all my fault," she said. "I didn't understand your English parking signs. I'm so sorry, but you can't give us a ticket."

"And why would that be, madam?" the police officer asked.

"Because this van belongs to the love of my life and we truly, desperately need it so that we can run away together," Piper said airily. "So if you could just let us be on our way..."

Cam stepped up, ready to apologize, but the policeman stopped her dead with a raised eyebrow.

"This the love of your life, is it?" he asked.

For the rest of her life, Cam would never forget the look on Piper's face as she turned around. The pureness, the honesty of it, the relief that she felt as she knew, suddenly, that whatever happened, it was all going to be okay.

And then Piper was taking her in her arms and pulling her in and they were kissing. Distantly, Cam could hear the policeman clearing his throat in embarrassment, could hear her brothers cheering and whooping and clapping.

But all she could feel, all she could taste, all she could think of, was Piper.

Piper pulled back a scant centimeter. "You know, your fifteen minutes are up," she whispered.

"Then we're going to need fifteen minutes more," said Cam.

"Best I can do is a whole lifetime. Take it or leave it."

And Cam's heart swelled. "*Lo accetto*," she said, because maybe her father was right and maybe, sometimes, love needed Italian passion.

Piper's eyebrow raised. "That better mean that you take it," she said. "Otherwise I'm going right back into that airport."

But Cam was already leaning back in to kiss her.

Car horns beeped, suitcase wheels clattered, planes screamed into the sky, but Cam heard none of it as Piper held her tight.

EPILOGUE

"Carlos, put that tray down there," Cam shouted.

"Why are you still here?" asked Piper, coming out of the bedroom.

"I'm going, I'm going," Cam said.

"You'd better. Joey's train comes in at twelve exactly. You can't be late for her." Piper looked at her watch. "Why don't I go?"

Cam shook her head. "No. I said I'd do it, and I want to. I'm dying to meet Joey. Besides, if you go the two of you are likely to spend the rest of the afternoon catching up and you'll never be back in time."

"Go on then," Piper said, dropping a kiss on Cam's cheek.

"Nobody panic, I'm here to save the day," announced Beth, bursting into the little cottage. "Now what needs doing?"

"Nothing," Piper and Cam chorused.

"Actually, sis," said Cosmo. "My tux is at the dry cleaner, can you pick it up on your way back?"

"Sure," Cam said absently, picking up her van keys from the side table. "And I'm out of here. I'll be back by one with Joey in tow and with Cosmo's suit. Anything else?"

"I could use some icing sugar," Isabella called from the kitchen.

"Forget it," Piper said, a threatening gleam in her eye. "We'll get some from Mary at the shop. Now leave before you have a list as long as your arm."

Cam rolled her eyes but slipped out of the cottage into the summer sunlight. Her heart filled a little as she saw flowers bobbing their heads in the flowerbeds outside the door. It was hard to believe the cottage was really finished.

Two years of work, on and off, and they'd only moved in last week. Which really was just in time and... Time. Right. She jogged to the van and hoisted herself up into the driver's seat, slamming the door shut an instant before the scream rang out from the open kitchen window.

Oblivious, Cam backed out of the drive and was on her way. She couldn't be late. After all, it was her wedding day.

❋ ❋ ❋

"*Madonna santa,*" Isabella said, looking at the red water in the kitchen sink.

"Jesus Christ," echoed Beth, who'd run in to see what the scream was about.

"I was watching Cam drive away," wailed Piper, clutching a tea towel around her hand. "I wasn't paying attention."

"It can't be that bad," Beth said.

"I don't know, there's lots of blood," said Isabella. Outside the boys were shouting and laughing as they set up chairs for the wedding.

"Let me look," said Beth, prying the towel away from Piper's hand. She paled visibly. "Yeah, okay, we're going to need stitches. Isabella, you got things under control here?"

"I can't go to the hospital," Piper said. "I'm getting married, remember? I need to be here, there's a million things to do."

"All of which I will do," Isabella said.

"We'll go to casualty now, it's not even lunch time, we'll be in and out, don't you worry. We'll be back in plenty of time and besides, you've lost enough blood here that you'll be fainting down the aisle if we don't get you stitched up."

Piper pulled the towel tighter around her hand and looked at

Isabella. "The flowers are coming and then—"

"It's nothing, I've got this. You go and get yourself better," Isabella said. She turned back to the cake she was finishing decorating. "Tell those doctors that you need a plain white bandage and if they don't hurry up they'll have an angry Italian woman chasing them."

Piper managed a laugh as Beth escorted her out of the kitchen and into the sunlit garden.

"I can't believe I did this. There must have been a knife in the washing up bowl or something," Piper said as she got into Beth's van.

"Because the English have this weird aversion to using their dishwashers," Beth said. "Tell me about it. But you don't need to worry. We've got loads of time."

"I hope so," Piper said, looking out of the window as Beth backed out of the drive. "We can't be late."

※ ※ ※

"How can it be late?" Cam practically screeched.

"Madam, I don't control the trains, I just do what I'm told," said the young man behind the counter. "All I can tell you is that the noon train is delayed."

"Well, when will it be here?"

The man shrugged. "It'll come when it comes. It's a train, it can't get lost. Just sit tight and have a cup of tea."

Cam gritted her teeth and walked away before she said something she might regret.

※ ※ ※

"How can there be so many people here?" Piper said, looking around.

The uncomfortable plastic seats were filled with families and Beth shrugged. "Not a clue. Come on, we need to check you in."

"What's going on?" Piper asked the receptionist behind the desk.

"Ugh, it's a Saturday morning. These would be the normal football and rugby injuries," she said, shaking her head. "Most of them are kids, but a fair few are idiot dads who've forgotten how old they are."

Piper sighed. "Look, I know that I shouldn't ask for special treatment, and normally I really wouldn't, I swear. Trust me, I'm American, I love your healthcare system and I'd never abuse it—"

"The thing is," broke in Beth. "She's getting married this afternoon. Is there any way you could maybe hurry things along a little bit?"

The woman eyed both of them, obviously trying to decide whether to believe them or not. Then she smiled. "I'll see what I can do," she said. "In the meantime, try and find a seat if you can."

Piper groaned as Beth led her away.

* * *

The train chugged into the station a mere fifty-five minutes late and the doors slid open. The second there was room, a tall figure squeezed out and jumped down to the platform, yanking a huge backpack after her.

Cam grinned. She might have known that Joey was going to be the first one off the train. But she didn't move. Suddenly, she was shy. The two of them had met over Zoom, but not actually in person, and now Cam slightly regretted offering to pick the woman up.

After all, Joey was Piper's friend, not hers.

She needn't have worried, however, since Joey loomed over her laughing and then swept her up into a tight hug.

"You've no idea how happy I am to finally meet you in person," Joey said. Her dark hair was cropped close to her scalp and Cam could see tattoos snaking out from under the collar of her t-shirt. "I thought I'd never get here."

"Well, you're just in time," Cam said. "We should make it in time as long as we get our skates on. Nice trip?"

"Long trip," Joey said. "But never fear, I'm getting my second wind now and I'm ready to party the night away. Where's Pipes?"

"Safe at home supervising the catering," Cam grinned. "So let's get you to the van. We've just got to make one stop on the way and then we'll go straight home."

✽ ✽ ✽

If anything, the hospital was filling up. Piper sniffed, smelling disinfectant, and settled back into the chair that they'd finally been able to claim. "There's no way we're going to make it in time," she wailed.

Beth winked at her and slid her phone back into her pocket. "Trust me," she said. "Just trust me. It's all in hand. And you shouldn't be so miserable. Aren't you happy? Today's the day. You've been waiting two whole years for this."

"I am happy," Piper said. She felt her stomach settle slightly and a smile inch across her face. "So happy. I don't think you can understand just how happy I am."

Beth snorted. "Thanks for the reminder of my single status. But good to know that this isn't just a green card marriage."

"Hey, I've got my own visa, thank you very much. My Start-Up visa isn't linked to marrying Cam at all. Though I suppose we should look into a spouse visa now that we're finally getting hitched."

"Finally? Two years isn't exactly that long."

"It is when I proposed to Cam twenty-one months ago to the day today," Piper said, pulling an embarrassed face. "I just didn't want her to escape."

"After three months? Impressive. And also impressively restrained of Cam to put you off until now," laughed Beth.

"Well, she wanted to get the cottage finished first, and that made sense, so..."

"Huh, Cam being logical, that makes a change. And if I'm not mistaken, here comes our savior."

Piper turned to see Isabella bustling into the crowded waiting room, two dress bags in her hands.

"Do not panic," Isabella said immediately. "We have everything under control. Well, except the vicar was already threatening to leave, but Carmel said to leave that up to him and the boys, so I suppose that I will have to trust in them to do something right for a change." She turned a beaming smile onto Piper.

"What are you doing here?" Piper asked.

"She's brought everything we need to get ready," Beth said. "So we can go straight from here to the ceremony."

"Yes, yes, it'll all be fine," Isabella said. She handed one bag to Beth. "You go and get changed. I will help Piper with her hair and makeup. It is probably best if she doesn't change into white until she has her stitches in."

"Good plan," Piper said, unable to stop herself grinning. "And it's nice to be taken care of for once."

"Everything is going to be fine," Beth said, picking up her dress and heading to the bathroom.

"And you, everything will be fine for you too," said Isabella.

"Is Cam back yet with Joey?"

"No, no," Isabella said airily. "But she will come soon, do not worry. Now, let me have a look at your hair. It is nice for it to be natural, no?"

"Everything should be natural," Piper said firmly. "No slathering on makeup or hairspray. I just want to look pretty."

"You always do," Isabella said, brushing out her hair and ignoring the strange looks from the other patients.

"Flattery will get you everywhere," Piper smiled.

Isabella cleared her throat. "I would like to say something, and maybe it is not my place to say. But I would like to say anyway. You make my Camilla very happy. And I am very happy knowing that she is happy."

Piper blushed.

"You know, I always wanted a daughter. Do not get me wrong, I love my boys, but a little girl is all I ever wanted," Isabella said.

"You lucked out with Cam then," grinned Piper.

"I am beginning to think that I am more lucky than I ever realized," Isabella said quietly, brush still gliding through Piper's short hair. "Because perhaps now I have two daughters. That is, if you will accept me as a poor substitute for what you have lost."

Suddenly, the waiting room was looking blurry and Piper was sniffing and blinking and then Isabella was hugging her tight.

"I think I'd like that, Isabella."

"No, no, *tesoro*, I think now you can call me Mama, no?"

And the only reason Piper didn't dissolve into a puddle of tears was because a nurse began calling her name.

❊ ❊ ❊

"What is this website then?" Joey asked, settling comfortably into the passenger seat of the van as Cam drove.

"It's brilliant," Cam said. "Well, I think so. It's called Crossing the Pond and it started out as a blog. But then it kind of grew. And now there's everything that an American or Canadian could need to know about living in the UK. Visa rules, language differences, there's even a job board. Piper has really found her calling. And after the wedding, she's planning on making a reverse site for people from the UK that want to work or study in the US."

"Huh, that does sound useful," Joey said. "I didn't think she'd be an entrepreneur. I'm glad she's found something she's good at."

"Oh, she has," Cam said fervently, pulling into a parking space outside of a small dry cleaner. "Just sit tight for a second, I need to pick up my brother's suit and then we'll have to rush to get home."

Joey watched as Cam went into the store and then stomped

out again, empty-handed, a few minutes later. She pulled out her phone and began to talk to someone, obviously angry and Joey frowned.

Something was going on here and she didn't quite know what. She pulled out her own phone and keyed in Piper's number.

She'd just finished her call when Cam stormed back into the car.

"I don't believe this," Cam said. "Piper's in the hospital."

"Yes," Joey began, but before she could get further, Cam spoke again.

"And my stupid brother didn't leave his tux at this dry cleaners, but at one on the complete other side of the village and now there's no way that anything can happen and we're going to end up canceling the wedding and..." She trailed off into sobs.

Joey pursed her lips then took matters into her own hands. She got out of the van, marched over to the driver's side and opened the door. "Slide over," she said.

"But, but..." stammered Cam.

"Slide over, we don't have time for this."

Cam did as she was told and Joey got into the driver's seat and started the engine.

"Alright, which road back to your place?"

"This one," Cam said. "The one we're on. But I have to go to the hospital, I—"

"Calm down," Joey said, screeching out of the parking space and back onto the road before really putting her foot down. "Piper's fine, I just talked to her and she's in the middle of getting stitched up. Everything is in hand."

"Yes, but—"

"But nothing," Joey said. "I'm dropping you off at home so you can get changed, I'll pick up your brother and take him to get his suit and by the time I'm back, Piper should be back too. I told you, it's all under control. Beth and your mother are with Piper and your brothers are taking care of the vicar."

"Oh God," Cam said. "What are they doing to him?"

"Just sit back and enjoy the ride," Joey said as she sped up so much that the van started to rattle. "You're going to make it."

※ ※ ※

Piper pulled on the white suit she'd chosen, hanging her regular clothes in the dress bag that was hanging on the back of the toilet door.

Not exactly how she'd imagined she'd be preparing for her wedding. But at this point she supposed she was lucky there was going to be a wedding at all. Her left hand was bandaged, but not too thickly, and at least the bandage was white, at Isabella's insistence.

She let herself out of the cubicle and looked in the mirror. She looked... fine, she guessed. And for a second there was a little spike of pain. Her mother would have loved this. Her father would have been so proud to walk her down the aisle.

She blinked away tears. She couldn't afford more time to re-do her makeup.

"Are you ready?" Beth said, sticking her head around the door and then freezing. "Wow, you look amazing. Really. But we have to run."

Collecting all her things together, Piper jogged out of the bathroom, following Beth who she trusted to know her way back to the car.

She was half-way through the waiting room before she realized that the noise she was hearing wasn't the normal chatter.

People were clapping, cheering, and whistling and Piper's cheeks blushed red and she slowed her steps.

"Come on," Beth said, grabbing her elbow.

"Go on, love," shouted a man with an icepack over his eye.

"Good luck," cried someone else.

"Congratulations," said a woman by the door.

And Piper laughed as Beth practically dragged her to the van.

* * *

Cam was shaking, actually visibly trembling. She felt sick and afraid and she couldn't see straight. This was a nightmare, she thought, as she looked through the french windows into the garden to see everyone she knew seated on chairs in front of a temporary altar.

"She's here." Lorenzo rushed into the living room. "She's here, the van is drawing up and I saw your van right behind it. Everyone's here."

Cam let out a breath and just as suddenly as it had started, the trembling stopped. "It's actually going to happen."

"You should not doubt us so much, my little doubting Thomas," Lorenzo smiled. "We will all always take care of you and handle your troubles. You just have to allow us the space to do so."

He straightened his tie and opened up the large french doors. Then he took his daughter's arm.

"Thank you, dad," Cam said. "For everything. For accepting Piper. For the wedding. For being the best dad I could ever hope for. And for deciding not to live in the sun by the sea, but to move to where it's rainy ninety percent of the time."

Lorenzo patted her arm. "I love you," he said simply. "I am proud of you. There is much more that I could say, but those two things are what you need to know now. And we must be going."

She could hear his voice thickening and knew that he couldn't say more because he would break down. So she took one last look at the aisle in front of her and nodded.

Slowly, Lorenzo helped her start her walk toward the flower-decked altar.

* * *

"Good boy," Piper said, patting Billy's enormous head. She

watched Cam's back as she disappeared down the aisle and had a lump in her throat.

Originally, Cam had wanted to make that walk together. But knowing how much it meant to Lorenzo to walk his daughter down the aisle, Piper had said no. She'd known that she'd miss her father, she'd known that it would be hard. But she needed to do this for Cam and for Lorenzo.

Besides, she had Billy, already pulling at his leash, a bow-tie around his neck, to escort her.

She waited until Cam turned, until she could see that beautiful face, finally see the dress that she'd chosen. White lace framed her breastbone and Piper's breath caught in her throat.

Cam grinned at her and Piper laughed.

This should be overwhelming, and yet it wasn't. It felt natural and perfect and just right.

She was so busy grinning like a maniac at her soon-to-be-wife that she didn't notice Lorenzo marching straight back up the aisle toward her.

She didn't notice until he took her arm gently in his own. "Come," he said.

Piper stopped. "But…"

He looked at her with big, brown eyes. "But what?" he said. "You are my daughter now. It is my job to walk you down the aisle."

And Piper's vision blurred once again as Lorenzo and Billy escorted her all the way down to Cam.

"I told him not to," Cam hissed as she approached. "I told him it would make you cry."

"He's an angel," Piper whispered back, before kissing Lorenzo firmly on the cheek and letting go of his arm.

Lorenzo beamed proudly.

The vicar cleared his throat. "We are gathathered here…" he began, then dissolved into a fit of coughing.

"Crap," Cam said. She turned around to glare at Carmel, who was hiding a grin in the front row.

"What?" Piper asked.

"The boys needed to stop the vicar leaving since we were running late. I think they got him drunk," Cam whispered. "It's Donte with that horrific rum he brought back from Brazil. We should have told him to stay there and finish his teaching assignment instead of getting him back for the wedding."

Piper snorted with laughter. "This should be fun then."

"We are gathered here today," the vicar said, having apparently found his focus again.

And Piper took Cam's hands in her own and let the words flow over her as the sun shone down and the birds sang and everyone they loved watched.

※ ※ ※

Twilight was falling and in the garden, fairy lights were twinkling in the trees. Music was playing and people were starting to dance, food was weighing heavy on tables, and there was laughter in the air.

Cam was taking a break when she felt a pair of arms snake around her from behind. Piper nuzzled into her neck, kissing her in a way that made her heart beat faster and gave her goosebumps.

"Do you think we can sneak away for twenty minutes?" Piper asked. "There's something I think we should do."

Cam turned around and raised an eyebrow. "You know we have the whole rest of our lives to do that, right?"

Piper laughed. "That wasn't what I was talking about. But I like the way you think. Come on, come with me. And bring your bouquet."

Quietly, they left the house and walked in the warmth of the evening arm in arm down the lane into the village. "I don't know what you think you're going to find down here," Cam said. "Everyone we know is back at the house."

"Not quite everyone," said Piper.

Cam didn't understand until they were right outside the

church gates and Piper was letting them both in. Then she smiled gently and let Piper guide her toward the fresh, gray stones on the right side of the churchyard beneath the wall.

Piper stooped and laid her bouquet on Lucy's grave. "I like to think she'd have been happy for us," she said. "But I didn't know her."

"Happy? She'd have been ecstatic," Cam said. "There was nothing Lucy loved more than a wedding. Mind you, she would have attempted flamenco dancing after a glass or two of wine, she always did."

Piper laughed. "I think I'd have liked her."

"You would," said Cam. She was quiet for a moment, then she said: "It reminds me how lucky we are, to find each other, to have each other. To live in a time and place and with family and friends that accept us for what we are. Remembering that Lucy never had all this, that she had to let it all go."

Piper nodded. "We are lucky. So lucky."

"Well, at least she'll have company in the afterlife," said Cam. She took a step over to the next stone and laid her own bouquet down. "Here you go, Arthur, I'm sure you and Lucy are getting up to no good."

"It's a shame he missed the wedding," Piper said.

"He was almost a hundred, he was ready to go and said so himself," said Cam. "Besides, there's no better way to go than falling asleep in your bed after a long life well lived."

Piper took her hand. "You are my world," she said. "My everything. I couldn't imagine waking up without you, I couldn't imagine being without you."

"Fortunately, you don't have to," Cam said, holding out her hand to admire her sparkling new ring. "You're stuck with me."

They let themselves out of the churchyard, closing the gates behind them, and Piper took Cam's arm. "I can't think of anyone else I'd rather be stuck with," she said.

"Even if that means being constantly blinded by my presence and spending half your life in casualty?" asked Cam.

"It's a small price to pay," Piper laughed.

And together they walked back up the lane. Toward the lights of their little cottage garden, toward their friends and family, toward home.

THANKS FOR READING!

If you liked this book, why not leave a review? Reviews are so important to independent authors, they help new readers discover us, and give us valuable feedback. Every review is very much appreciated.

And if you want to stay up to date with the latest Sienna Waters news and new releases, then check me out at:

www.siennawaters.com

Keep reading for a sneak peek of my next book!

BOOKS FROM SIENNA WATERS

The Oakview Series:

Coffee For Two
Saving the World
Rescue My Heart
Dance With Me
Learn to Love
Away from Home
Picture Me Perfect

The Monday's Child Series:

Fair of Face
Full of Grace
Full of Woe

The Hawkin Island Series:

More than Me

Standalone Books:

The Opposite of You
French Press
The Wrong Date
Everything We Never Wanted
Fair Trade
One For The Road
The Real Story
A Big Straight Wedding

A Perfect Mess

Love By Numbers

Ready, Set, Bake

Tea Leaves & Tourniquets

The Best Time

A Quiet Life

Watching Henry

Count On You

The Life Coach
Crossing the Pond
Not Only One Bed

TURN THE PAGE TO GET A SNEAK PREVIEW OF NOT ONLY ONE BED

NOT ONLY ONE BED

Chapter One

Trix put down her knife and fork though she'd barely eaten anything. Her stomach rumbled with what she was pretty sure was excitement rather than hunger, but she picked up her wine glass and drained it anyway to quell the sound.

"Not so hungry, eh?" said Anne-Marie.

"I, uh, had a big breakfast?" ventured Trix.

Anne-Marie fluttered a hand at her as though she didn't believe a word of it and spooned the last of her risotto into her mouth. She chewed approximately three hundred times, which should have been impossible. Who could chew risotto for that long?

Be patient, Trix schooled herself. You know it's coming, just be patient. She took a look around her. Half of London was in the room. Or half of the kind of London that was important, anyway. This was exactly the kind of place she'd known that Anne-Marie would choose for lunch. Hip, fashionable, but classy at the same time.

Trix calmed herself with a deep breath and turned her attention back to her boss.

Anne-Marie swallowed and took a sip of her own wine and swallowed again until Trix was about ready to scream again.

Another sip of wine and she was seriously considering reaching over the table and grabbing her boss by the throat and shaking her. She sat on her hands.

"So," Anne-Marie said finally.

"So."

"I think I'm supposed to start off with 'I suppose you're wondering why I've asked you here.'" A grin. Anne-Marie tucked a lock of deep chestnut hair behind her ear and Trix wondered if she dyed it. She must dye it. The woman was well over fifty with little crinkles of wrinkles around her dark eyes. Not unattractive.

"Mmm," Trix said, anxious to get on with matters.

"But you've been with Levoisier and Partners long enough to know what these little lunches are all about," continued Anne-Marie.

Trix crossed her legs and wondered if she had time to go and pee. No. She really didn't. If she did, there was every chance that Anne-Marie would order dessert and then she'd have to wait another half an hour.

"You're aware that there have been a couple of retirements, some re-shuffling amongst us."

Trix nodded with what she hoped was just the right amount of enthusiasm.

"And that, of course, you have shown such taste, such… discernment in your choices up to now."

Trix swallowed. Being a literary agent meant that having taste, having discernment, wasn't just a question of showing class or of having the right furniture or knowing the right people. Having taste was part of her job, the one talent that she needed to choose the right books, the right authors, the right everything.

"And so, we, well, I," Anne-Marie gave a coy little smile. "*I* have decided that the time is ripe and that you, my dear, should be propelled into the upper echelons of our little company."

Little company. A company that currently represented four out of the ten authors on *The Times* bestseller list. Trix swallowed again. She was so close. Everything she'd ever wanted was just about to be handed to her. Her stomach clenched and rumbled again.

"It is my absolute pleasure, *chérie*, to offer you the position of head of romance acquisitions."

Trix's mouth was already open, the words of gratitude were already starting to spill out, she couldn't help herself. "Thank you, of…" Her mouth slammed shut as her ears caught her brain up with what had just happened. There was a long second of silence. "Romance?" she finally managed to croak.

Anne-Marie beamed and nodded. "Just so."

"But…" She tried and couldn't form the words.

Anne-Marie settled back into her chair. "But you were expecting something else. Literary fiction, perhaps?"

Trix bit her tongue and nodded.

Anne-Marie shrugged. "You are a fool then."

"A fool?" A niggle of indignation was enough to unfreeze her thoughts. "A fool? I've been molded for that position, promised it by not just you but your deputy and my boss. It's been the reason I've stayed with the company and the reason I've worked so hard and—"

"And do not think I do not know this," interrupted Anne-Marie. "But what I am offering you is a far juicier cherry." She frowned and leaned forward again. "Literary fiction is all very well, but who reads those books now? Romance is, by far, the largest chunk of the literary market. It's booming more than ever, its readers are voracious, its authors are the wealthiest, and you, my dear, are just the person to take over the department."

Suddenly, Trix was desperate for a drink. She picked up her glass only to find it empty. Anne-Marie picked up the wine bottle and emptied the last inch into Trix's glass.

"Ah," she said. "Just look. The last of the bottle. In France, we say that this means that you will be the next one married."

Trix eyed the deep red in her glass and found she'd suddenly lost her taste for it. She pushed the glass away. "Anne-Marie," she said, attempting to sound reasonable.

"No, no," said the dark-haired woman. "You need to think this through carefully, Trix. I don't offer you this job lightly. It's a big deal, bigger than I think you perhaps realize." Her eyes narrowed. "And I do hope that you're not going to be one of those snobby women who look down on romance novels?"

Trix took a breath and shook her head. "No, no, of course not."

"Good." Anne-Marie smiled again. "Romance novels sell dreams, *chérie*, don't you ever forget that." She checked her watch and gave a sharp nod. "And I shall be leaving you, I have a meeting this afternoon."

Trix just about stopped herself from snorting at this. A meeting. Anne-Marie had drunk ninety percent of the wine herself and she had a feeling that any meetings involved the rendez-vous of pillow and head.

"Ah, yes," said Anne-Marie. "I have not forgotten about your little sabbatical, do not worry. You will not be expected to start until your return. In fact, by the time you come back, we will have moved you into one of the corner offices. Just do not forget to have your assistant send you some manuscripts so you can get ahead of what we're looking for this season."

She paused and eyed Trix carefully.

"This is a big opportunity. Do not let me down. Do not let yourself down. It would behoove you to learn more about romance before you leap to judgment." She smiled, more sympathetically this time. "You have worked long and hard, Trix. Perhaps you have let the more personal things slide by. Perhaps it would do you good to indulge in a little… romance during your sabbatical. Remind yourself of why love is important."

It was the alcohol talking. It had to be. If it wasn't then Trix was pretty sure that her boss had just told her to get a date.

Anne-Marie stood up from the table and stalked away across the restaurant on heels so high that Trix wondered if her brain ever got oxygen-starved. Maybe she'd been uncharitable about the alcohol. Maybe it was a cultural thing. Anne-Marie didn't seem to be out of control. Not that that should be a surprise.

The woman had a reputation for being the sharpest knife in the drawer, someone that knew her stuff, that could handle anything.

Too bad that this time she'd made a mistake.

CHASTITY SNORTED WITH laughter and then hiccuped as she tried to silence herself. "Sorry, sorry," she managed to say.

"You'd better be," said Trix, settling down behind her desk.

"It's just that..." Chastity dissolved into giggles again and collapsed into the visitor's chair, blue-tipped hair swinging and jewelry clattering as she wiped at her eyes. "It's just that... you..."

"Me what?" Trix said.

Generally, she liked Chastity. Blue hair and eyebrow rings aside, the woman had sense and was a bulldog on the phone, keeping Trix's time free to do her actual job rather than pamper sensitive authors. Currently though she was considering sending Chastity back to whatever Youth Training Scheme had sent her.

Chastity took a couple of deep breaths and gained a modicum of control. "You..." And lost it again. "Romance," she choked out.

Trix tapped her fingers on her desk. "I don't see what's so funny."

With a great effort of will Chastity restrained herself. "It's just that, well, you're not exactly a romantic, are you? You dumped the last woman you were seeing because she sent flowers to the office."

"It was unprofessional."

"Right," said Chastity. "And she was the only date I've known you to go on, and I've been here for five years now. You're not a romantic, face it, Trix."

Trix blew out a breath. There was no point denying it. "It's all nonsense and I don't have time for it."

"See?" said Chastity. Then she took pity on her boss. "But AM's right about one thing, romance is by far the biggest slice of the pie. This is quite the coup from a career point of view."

"I wanted literary fiction," Trix said. The news hadn't quite sunk in yet.

"You wanted to be surrounded by old white men smoking pipes? You've got the chance to do so much more with romance."

Trix wasn't going to say it, she refused to say it. But deep inside she knew she felt it. Romance was sad. It was small. It was for bored housewives and horny teenagers. Anyone who was anyone read literature, not thick paperbacks with suspiciously muscled half-naked men on the covers and sticky pages.

But she knew well enough not to criticize anyone else's reading tastes out loud. Particularly when she was about to head up the department. The last thing she needed was word getting out that she thought the entire section should be locked up in a mental hospital for hysterical women.

"Look, I'll send you some 'scripts," Chastity was saying. "I'll pick through them and send you some good ones and maybe you'll change your mind. Maybe romance isn't what you think it is."

"Right," said Trix without much hope.

"And, um, it's not my place to say anything, but it wouldn't do you any harm to get a little… personal experience as well."

Trix raised an eyebrow.

"You know, date a little more? Get some on the ground experience, learn what your writers are writing about."

Trix pursed her lips but said nothing. Chastity sighed.

"Fine. I'll send you some manuscripts while you're away. And if that's all you've got for me, I'm out of here. Enjoy your holiday."

"It's not a holiday."

"Your sabbatical."

"Visiting a father I haven't seen for longer than I can remember?"

Chastity shrugged. "You decided to go, no one forced you."

Which wasn't exactly true. Trix had drunkenly agreed to a Zoom call and then half-nodded off and woken up to find herself somewhat agreeing to visit the States. She'd assumed her mother would get her off the hook, but had been surprised to find that her mother had actually suggested the idea. She'd had no idea that her parents even spoke to each other anymore.

"And then there's your sister's wedding," Chastity added.

"Half-sister," corrected Trix.

"Still, something to look forward to. And a chance to learn a bit more about romance." She chuckled again as she got up. "You and romance," she said, shaking her head.

"I don't know what you're laughing at," said Trix. "Has the humor of someone called Chastity working in romance acquisitions been lost on you?"

Chastity's eyes and mouth turned into perfectly round circles as the news dawned on her and even Trix had to laugh.

"You don't laugh at me, I won't laugh at you," she said, finally.

"Deal," said Chastity. She looked up at the clock on the wall. "But if you don't get out of here now you're going to miss that flight of yours."

Trix sighed. As if that would be a bad thing.

CHAPTER TWO

Kel gave her trademarked half-grin. The one that melted hearts, the one that made her dimples stand out and her green eyes sparkle.

"I guess I could think about it," the blonde on the other side of the counter said, a little too doubtfully for Kel's taste.

"Just a drink, no pressure," Kel said. "You're here for summer school, right?"

The blonde nodded and Kel handed over her change then picked up a frequent drinker card. She carefully stamped one little coffee cup and then scrawled her number at the top.

"Here, you buy nine coffees and you get the barista for free," she said, with a wink.

The blonde laughed. "You're cute, but to be honest, I just got out of a relationship and—"

"Woah, hold on there. You're cool, I'm cool, I'm just suggesting a drink, not that we get married or anything." Kel paused, looking up thoughtfully. "Though, I suppose if the evening ended that way…"

And the blonde laughed again. "Okay, okay, you're right. A drink never hurt anyone." She leaned on the counter and arched an eyebrow. "Or maybe a little more than a drink?"

"Sex is good for the soul," said Kel, earnestly.

The blonde was still laughing as she picked up her coffee and walked toward the door.

"Call me," Kel said after her.

"Oh, she will," said Joey, coming in from the back room.

"What makes you so sure?"

"Don't they all?" Joey said.

Kel liked her new boss. Joey was butch, had a shaved head and plenty of tattoos, and was also straight. A fact that Kel had found out the hard way by trying to tempt her into bed. A night that made her cringe a little and made Joey laugh like hell.

"Most of them do," Kel muttered darkly.

Joey rolled her eyes. "Don't be so touchy. One girl turns you down and suddenly your playboy reputation is ruined?"

"No."

"Then cheer up. I don't want you sulking, it drives customers away. You and me both need this job, so let's at least make an attempt to keep the clientele happy."

"Business is always slow in the summer," Kel said, leaning back against the counter with her arms folded. "It picks up again in September when real classes start. So don't worry about takings being down for a couple of months."

Joey raised an eyebrow. "Should that not have been on the list of things to tell me before I bought this place?"

"All's fair in love and war, or in love and business, I guess," laughed Kel. "But seriously, don't worry. This place is a good little earner. I've worked here for three years now, trust me."

"I do. That's why you're still here, despite the fact that you talk your way into the beds of half our female customers."

"Can't help the fact that women love me," Kel grinned.

Joey propped herself up next to one of the refrigerated cake displays. "Three years is a long time, don't you get tired of it?"

"Tired of what? Hitting on women and having fun?"

"Sitting around in a small college town," Joey said. "Isn't there more that you want?"

"Jesus, Joe. Don't pull any punches, will you? Besides, didn't you literally just move from the city to this small college town? That would rather imply that there's something desirable about living here."

"There is," said Joey. "Because I've hit forty, because I burnt out of working in finance and had money to spare. Because my best friend found the love of her life and left the country."

"Leaving you behind to count your heartbreaks?" Kel said. "I've already offered to keep you company but you firmly play for the other team."

"I needed the change," Joey said. "But that's me. You've been in Mount Cline your whole life, right? Don't you think about escaping?"

Kel rubbed at her eyes, her grin deserting her. This conversation wasn't headed where she wanted it to head.

"Okay, okay," Joey said. "I'll come clean." She flushed and bit her lip. "Um, you left the laptop in the back room open."

"I definitely don't look at porn at work," Kel smirked, trying to get control of the conversation again.

"Yeah, but you do look at expensive art colleges in London," said Joey.

Kel slumped and then shrugged. "What of it? It's not like I'm going to end up there or anything."

"Why not?"

Jesus. For a morning that had started off cheerful and sunny, things were getting serious fast. Not the way Kel preferred to live life. She shrugged again. "Do I look like I can afford an expensive art college to you?"

"You're talented."

"What would you know about it?" But her heart swelled a little because she was, she knew, talented. Unfortunately, talent didn't pay the bills. At least not in Kel's world.

"Well, there's probably a scholarship or something, isn't there?"

"There is."

"So…"

Joey trailed off and Kel really, really didn't want to be having this conversation.

"So it's not enough."

"How do you know? Why don't you at least look? Apply? Get

the information?" Joey pressed.

Kel squeezed her eyes tight shut in the hopes that Joey would disappear, or that the earth would crumble beneath her feet, or, at the very least, a customer would walk in. But nothing happened for a long minute. She sighed.

"Already have."

"You applied?"

Kel nodded.

"Then why are you such a Debbie Downer about it?" Joey asked. She took a step forward, leaning down so that she was looking into Kel's eyes. "Ah. Right. Don't want to hope, right?"

"Maybe," Kel said, looking away.

Joey laughed. "That's crazy. What's life without hope?"

"I am hoping," said Kel. "I'm just hoping privately, that's all."

Joey shook her head. "You're weird, you know that? You're quite happy to share your bed with any attractive woman that comes along." She held up a hand to stop Kel interrupting. "I'm not judging, I've got no problem with that. But you share your body so easily and yet your hopes, your dreams, they're just for you."

"Doesn't do any good talking about things that haven't happened yet."

"Bullshit."

Kel sighed. "Look, I applied, I haven't even got in yet. And even if I do get in, I can't afford to go. It's just a pipe dream. Something I tried to see if I could."

"But you want it?"

"I've wanted it since as long as I can remember," admitted Kel, not entirely sure why she was admitting it.

"So why now?" pressed Joey. "I mean, don't get me wrong, but you're twenty eight, Kel, not exactly freshman age."

"You kidding? You think that kids from families like mine go to college?"

"Families like yours?" asked Joey, confused.

Sometimes Kel forgot that Joey hadn't grown up in town, that she didn't know everything and everyone. Maybe because she'd felt so comfortable around her since the moment she'd walked through the doors.

"A deadbeat dad and a drunk for a mom don't exactly equal a ginormous college fund," said Kel. "Besides, I wasn't ready. I needed to find myself, find what I wanted. If you'd have handed me a bunch of cash when I was eighteen I'd have blown it on, I don't know, trips to Burning Man and paintbrushes, probably. Artists grow into themselves."

"And now you know that this is what you want."

Kel sighed. "Look, can we stop this conversation?"

"If you tell me that this is what you want."

"Fine. Yes. This is what I want. I'm dying to get in and I have no idea what I'll do if I do get in but I'll try and work things out and in the meantime I'd really rather not jinx things by talking about them. Fair?"

"Fair," Joey said. Then she grinned. "But you're gonna get in."

"How do you know?"

"Sixth sense," said Joey, mysteriously.

Kel treated her to a spectacular eye roll.

"Dismiss it all you like, but I've got a sense for these things."

"Then I'd better find a sugar mommy, 'cos that's the only way I'm going to be able to pay for a place like this."

Joey grinned at her. "Just as long as you're not counting on me, I spent everything I have buying this place. A place that you've currently informed me won't start turning a profit until September."

"Maybe we'll both be needing a sugar mommy."

Joey sighed. "Yeah, even I might switch teams for someone rich enough."

Kel pulled the handle of the coffee machine, eliciting a hiss of steam. "Might as well have a little caffeine whilst we wait for Bill or Billess Gates to walk through the door."

Joey's eye lit up and she turned to pull a plate out of the refrigerated cabinet. "And I've perfected carrot cake," she said proudly, offering the plate up to Kel.

Kel forced herself to keep a straight face and forced herself to take a piece, the smallest she could find which was tough given that Joey had cut the cake into doorstop sized pieces. "Mmm," she said. "Look delicious." Which, to be fair, it did. Unfortunately, she was pretty sure that she could smell... cayenne pepper?

She took a bite and her eyes started to water unprompted. She tried desperately to swallow but ended up coughing and grabbing for a napkin to spit the cake into.

"Ah," said Joey. "Not my finest creation?"

Secretly, Kel was beginning to wonder just what had made Joey buy a cake and coffee shop when, as she'd admitted on her first day, she'd never baked a cake in her life. "Um, it could use a little work."

Joey's face fell and Kel sighed.

"Come on, there's no one coming in this afternoon. Put the closed sign up and I'll walk you through the carrot cake recipe," Kel said, aware of the fact that she was talking herself out of an afternoon's worth of tips on the off chance that someone did come in.

Joey brightened up. "I'll let you take half the cake home."

"Which cake?" asked Kel suspiciously. "Because I'm sending the one that you've just given me to Poison Control as evidence."

"The good cake," Joey promised. "Come on. I'll need to bake a good cake to impress my potential sugar mommy or daddy."

If only that was all it took, Kel thought, as she followed Joey into the kitchen.

Get Your Copy of Not Only One Bed Now!

Printed in Great Britain
by Amazon